THE MADRONE TREE

DAVID DUNCAN

THE MADRONE TREE

♥ ♥ ♥ THE MACMILLAN COMPANY

NEW YORK: 1949

For E. M. S.

THE MADRONE TREE

CHAPTER ONE

❦ ❦ ❦ FROM A DISHWATER SKY THE INCESSANT FEBRUARY RAIN drizzled on Jonesville. The mill had been closed for a month and the town hibernated in primeval silence, waiting for the scream of the bandsaw to awaken it. The sounds which intruded were natural ones—the slap of the high surf breaking on the Black Angels a mile away, the rolling wail of the redwoods when a persistent gust from the sea drew their branches taut, the drip of water from sloping eaves. The rain itself was silent. With drops too fine to break a ringlet on the dark roadway pools, it saturated the air and passed like a wet mop over the landscape.

Through the afternoon dusk the Reverend Manley Foxx drove along Blinder Road to where it intersected the highway. He stopped well back from the crossing to avoid the muddy water which was certain to spatter from the wheels of the daily bus, now gathering speed from its stop at the general store three blocks down the street. The bus passed with a whine of wet tires, and Foxx geared his car forward, slowing again as the figure of a man crossed in front of him. In spite of the pulled down hat and upturned collar, Foxx recognized the pedestrian as Edward Spence and tapped his horn lightly to attract attention. Spence replied with a turn of his head and a curt two-fingered salute before proceeding on toward the store. Foxx smiled thinly, crossed the highway, and drove the quarter of a mile which took him to the eastward limit of town and the home of Ivor Jones.

Ivor Jones, mill owner and boss of Jonesville, lived in a low but massive log house set among a few forest giants which he had preserved from the saw for his personal enjoyment. Despite the size of the house, its interior was given over principally to a rustic living room where on infrequent occasions Jones entertained lumber customers and where on one day of the Christmas season each year he held open house for the entire population. Aside from the living room, the house contained one bedroom, a small kitchen, and a bath. Ivor Jones was a bachelor, employed no servants, and had no relatives of whom anyone had ever heard.

Manley Foxx slid from behind the wheel and strode up the flagstone path toward the entrance. He paused midway to examine a rose bush which carried a single pink bud, its outer petals just beginning to unfurl. He stood tall and unbending for several seconds, looking at it before he proceeded to the entrance, where he pushed through the doorway without knocking and walked into the hallway. At the entrance to the living room he stopped to pull off his gloves while his eyes searched the unlit interior for its occupant. He saw him finally, the bushy grayed head silhouetted against a window at the far end of the room. Foxx coughed lightly and stepped forward.

"That you, Manley?" a deep voice called. "Sit down. I'll turn on a lamp."

"Not on my account, Mr. Jones. I enjoy the darkness too." Foxx sat down on the lounge and crossed his long legs.

Jones grunted and heaved himself to his feet. "When I have a guest, I like to see him." He snapped on a table lamp, and a cone of yellow light settled over the burnished wood and rich fabric of the sofa. By contrast, the outer corners of the room were thrown into even darker gloom.

"That's better," said Jones, subsiding into a deep armchair.

"You sent for me," said Foxx.

"So I did. So I did." Jones strained forward to reach a snuff box on the low table before him. After depositing a large pinch inside his lower lip, he leaned back and folded his arms across his chest. "Care for a fire?"

"As you wish. I hadn't intended to stay long."

"You don't have to. Still, a fire—" He restlessly pushed himself upward again. "A man gets cold without knowing it. This dampness comes right into the house."

The fire was already laid. Jones touched a match to the paper under the pile of logs and returned to his chair. He sat in silence for a moment, watching the mounting flames.

"You sent for me," Foxx repeated a little impatiently.

Jones turned his head slowly to look at his visitor. "Yes, I sent for you. I get nervous when the mill is down." He used a cuspidor beside his chair. "Everyone gets nervous."

Foxx waited without comment. He thought that Jones looked strikingly childlike in spite of his heavy body and grayed hair. Or perhaps because of them. They were like a disguise which emphasized rather than hid what was beneath. With most adults it was difficult to imagine what they were like as children, but with Jones the transition from childhood to the border of senility was all in evidence. The slightly pouting lips, the heavy jaw, the bulldog position of the head were characteristics of a child who never had been quite sure of himself.

"It's when the mill is down that some of the men begin getting ideas," continued Jones. "Maybe some of the women, too."

"Such as?"

Jones shrugged. "Things that do them no good. You know what I mean. Work is what keeps people happy. When they're idle, they get disgruntled and have to blame it on some one. They blame it on me because I own the mill. As though I can control the weather."

Foxx stroked the side of his thin face reflectively. "Of whom, in particular, are you speaking?"

"Who? Hadn't really given the matter much thought. It's general. Dodge, down at the store, mentioned that some of the women were complaining because their bills were getting so big. I make it possible for them to get credit while there's no work, and then they complain. That's the way things go." He shifted in his chair to face Foxx. "And then I noticed an empty seat in church last Sunday."

Foxx sniffed. "I thought so. You're referring to the absence of Mars Venderstone." Jones answered with a slow affirmative nod. Foxx continued. "One Sunday isn't much. Why does that worry you? Perhaps he was ill."

"He wasn't ill. You know that as well as I do. And it's been two Sundays."

Foxx's expression took no notice of the correction. "All right, then. I know where he was. He's a young man."

"He's also a popular man with the rest of my employees. Someday he'll be head sawyer in Oban Kildonan's place. I don't want another like Oban Kildonan."

"Then you shouldn't have put Ailsa Kildonan to work in your mill." Foxx arose abruptly and paced back and forth in front of the fire. "Ailsa Kildonan is like her father. You shouldn't have put her to work!"

"In Jonesville," Ivor Jones emphasized softly, "I put to work whom I please. Ailsa Kildonan's less of a threat when she's working than when she isn't. That's why I called you. I want to see Mars Venderstone back in church next sunday."

Foxx shot a glance of anger at his host. "You place a great deal of importance on his behavior during the Sabbath. There are six other days in the week."

Jones's lips twisted into a crooked smile. "When a man sees a girl evenings, it's for reasons I can understand. When he sees a girl on Sundays, it might be serious. I don't want it to get serious."

Foxx twined his fingers together behind his back and looked down at the older man. With an almost visible effort he forced his voice to sound reasonable instead of contemptuous.

"Perhaps it's the evenings with which I am most concerned," he said. "They are the more dangerous. But I'd like to remind you that for many years I've told you the solution to the problem.

4

You've paid no attention. The girl has grown into a woman."

"A damned pretty one," mused Jones. "Reminds me of her mother."

"Mr. Jones!" Foxx's tone was sharp. "Are you condoning the girl's behavior?"

Jones scowled upward from beneath shaggy brows. "Don't be a fool, Manley. And don't expect me to follow your advice where the Kildonans are concerned. You want me to make them leave Jonesville. I won't do it. Oban Kildonan may not be a churchman, but he's a damned good head sawyer."

"In fact," cut in Foxx with malice, "without him you'd lose a considerable proportion of your production. A mill succeeds or fails according to the ability of the head sawyer."

"Sure," agreed Jones. "He knows his job."

"Then don't suggest that you've kept him here out of kindness or because the other men respect him. You've kept him here because he makes money for you, and that's the whole reason." He paused. "I'm not stirred by such motivation. I would cast him out as I would a wolf from a flock of sheep. You've harbored a serpent and permitted his young to mature, so that now I'll have to rid you of the problem whether you ask me to or not. Mars Venderstone will not only stop seeing Ailsa Kildonan on Sundays; he shall stop seeing her altogether. No one shall see her. No one. They shall all go—the father, the wife, and the daughter!" A resonant oratorical quality had entered Foxx's voice. He sounded faintly exultant. Ivor Jones rose slowly to his feet and his voice vibrated with sudden anger.

"Let's not forget, Manley, that this town is still known as Jonesville—not Foxxburg. I brought you here to work with the people who live here, not to chase out the ones who disagree with you. I want to see Mars Venderstone back in church Sunday. I think that's all." He spat into the fire.

Manley Foxx drew on his gloves slowly. "The definition of my duties comes from a higher authority than yours, Mr. Jones. If I've served you during the time I've been here, I'm content. But such service should be considered as coincidence. My intention has been to serve only my church. Good day." For a moment Foxx was a tall shadow in the hallway. Then he drew the outer door shut behind him and started back along the flagstones toward his car.

The rosebush caught his attention and again brought him to a halt. He looked at the opening bud silently. Then his gloved hand went out to it and his fingers tore the stem free. He shook the beads of water from the outer petals and walked slowly on toward the car, holding the bud beneath his nose and breathing in its fragrance. After opening his car door, he paused, the bud in his hand, as though undecided as to where to put it while he drove.

"The girl must be isolated," he whispered. Then he shuddered and with a quick gesture flung the rosebud from him. It landed in a pool of muddy water and lay there as he drove away.

To be an educator and not be educated; to be a pedant but not a scholar; to be continually thinking and arrive at no conclusions; to be schoolteacher and principal of the grammar school in Jonesville. Reverend Foxx, tapping on his horn at the intersection, startled Edward Spence. He turned back and looked at the black sedan. The reflection of the water on the car windows made the driver invisible, but Edward knew the automobile and waved. Then he jammed his hands back in his pockets and slopped on toward the post office. To love knowledge and have so little; to want freedom, yet remain in Jonesville; to profess a range of interests and have only one. A disease, he told himself. A disease, and you don't want to be cured.

Mrs. Parker came out of the darkness ahead of him and said good evening. He repeated her words back at her and walked on, hearing his reply and seeing the empty sidewalk ahead. He turned and looked back to make sure he had really passed her. Mrs. Parker had a daughter who was thirteen and in the eighth grade. She had reached adolescence early and the school board was considering removing her from school. She had been seen in parked cars after sundown a few times, or so some of the towns-folk said. Mrs. Parker felt the disgrace.

The town was full of false fronts. The garage was made of two gabled sheds which had been squared off in front. The moving-picture house had a front of white stucco. The general store and post office had a clapboard front two stories high. To see things as they were, you had to get off the highway and look at the town sidewise. Only the church was solid.

Mr. Dodge was at the post-office window and shook his head when Edward asked for mail.

"Are you sure?"

"Yes," said Mr. Dodge. "I'm sorry." His voice was as flat as his answer.

Edward walked away. Receiving no mail closed off another avenue of escape. Lately he had become a prolific correspondent, posting letters to friends of a decade back. They didn't answer. They must have families by now and a multitude of local interests. They would wonder briefly why Edward Spence had written them after so long a time, and then put the letter aside.

He found himself standing in front of the magazine stand. He had the seventh- and eighth-grade English papers to correct, but that would take up only a portion of the evening. He would need something to read. The lurid covers of the pulp section kept pulling his attention. He stood before the conservative maga-zines, turning his eyes but not his head toward the pictures of half-clad girls being choked, burned, shot or otherwise mauled by villains or mechanical monsters. The contorted faces of the victims showed an agony which was only half sincere. He wanted to buy one. The contents might fall far short of the promise on the cover, but he wanted to have one to look at. It would be a change. He couldn't though; it would never do.

"I saw Mr. Spence reading *Wicked Love*," someone would snigger. "Fine thing for a teacher!" No, of course he couldn't.

Ula Westerly would find it in his room and tell Stella Graw, who would tell Manley Foxx. Foxx would make it the subject of

7

a sermon, sparing nothing, not even his name. He could fairly hear it. And he could see the congregation sitting with moist lips and liquid eyes, absorbing with vicarious perversity the sin suggested to them. With a sigh he picked up a conservative woman's magazine in which he was certain to find a number of lingerie advertisements. He paid for it and thrust it under his coat for protection from the rain, holding it against his body with his elbow.

Outside again he started back the way he had come, his head down, watching his toes swing out in front of him as he stepped along. In front of Larry's Bar he ran into a man. His head struck the other's shoulder and he jumped back instinctively.

"I beg your pardon!" said Edward.

"Thinking too hard, Mr. Spence?" said a low, pleasant voice.

Edward looked into the brown smiling face of Mars Venderstone. The blue eyes regarded him steadily. Then he looked at Venderstone's companion and felt weak. There was the pale oval face with its frame of black hair, the wide expressionless eyes, the smile that was not a smile, the attitude of casual indifference. Behind the face was the dusk of evening and the swirl of mist through the distant trees. That was the way he saw her in his dreams.

"I'm very sorry," he said.

Venderstone laughed. "Care to join us in a glass of beer?"

Edward flushed. "Thanks. But I don't think I can. Thanks anyway." He kept staring at Ailsa Kildonan until he realized he was blocking the way. He stepped aside quickly, and the magazine slid from under his coat and sprawled on the wet sidewalk with the comely matron on the cover smiling up at him.

"Stupid," he said, bending to recover it. The other two laughed and walked past him into the bar. The indignity of his position made him associate the laughter with himself. It wasn't so, of course. It was just another one of those things.

The vines over Ula Westerly's gate showered water on him as he pushed through. He went around to the side of the house and

8 🐾

up the outside stairway to his room on the second floor. The stairway was his. He'd had it built five years before.

"To give you greater privacy," he had told Miss Westerly, though it was his own privacy he was thinking of. It didn't help any, though. It made the dreams more plausible, but no one ever came up the staircase except himself. Now the boards were weathered and the balustrade was loose.

In his room he took off his coat and put the magazine on his desk. Then he found a note under the door that led down into the house. It was the usual Saturday evening note from his landlady asking him down for dinner, mentioning that Stella Graw would be there too. He tore up the note. He saw Stella Graw five days a week at school and didn't want to see her on Saturday evening. He didn't want to see anyone. But even so, the shredded note was only a gesture. He would go down as always and perform that wonderful feat of talking and acting as though he were completely absorbed.

He took off his wool knit tie and white shirt. While the water ran in his corner washbasin, he searched his temples in the mirror for signs of gray hair. He couldn't find any. Then he squeezed soap on his brush and started to shave.

High in the organ loft Stella Graw's white fingers slid over the keys of the console with power and sureness. Above and behind her the music poured into the void of the empty church. A light glowed over the keyboard and another burned in the church vestibule. Between them dusk hovered above the rows of silent pews and climbed toward darkness up the giant redwood trunks which formed the walls and vaulted ceiling of the nave.

She finished her number and leaned back, listening intently to catch the lingering echo of the final chord. The echo emphasized the sense of being alone and unwatched. On Sunday, with a congregation below her, there would be no echo. She was always a little afraid when she came to the church at night to rehearse her music, but the fear wasn't quite strong enough to make her flood the interior with light. She fancied quite often that some-one was below, listening to her recital, and light would only dis-pel the illusion. Sometimes she even went so far as to leave the outer vestibule door unlocked after she had entered.

She had done that tonight and also had worn the dress she would wear at church the following morning. It was of dove-gray silk, discreetly covering her arms and shoulders, and with a long full skirt which hid her legs without impeding their movement over the pedals. Thus correctly attired, it was easy to imagine herself viewed by the entire congregation or by a solitary and devoted listener.

She studied the next number carefully for several minutes, her hands folded in her lap, then turned her head toward the choir loft as she would do the next morning to get her signal from the choirmaster. The signal came and she returned her attention to the keyboard. This number was an accompaniment for the choir and was played entirely from the orchestral clavier, with the emphasis on reeds and strings. It sounded thin without the voices of the choir. She played with a certain stiff delicacy, frequently glancing toward the spot which would be occupied by the choir-master. The number finished, she felt relieved and rubbed her hands together to flex her fingers. She was alone again.

She arranged her music in proper order for tomorrow's serv-ice, and then—after a searching glance toward the dim interior of the church—bent down and pulled off her shoes. Her hands trembled a little as she pulled the bombarde stops for the pedals and brought in the swell oboes and the diapason greats. She breathed deeply and commenced playing Bach's *Magnificat*. For a few measures the music followed its normal course. Then, as she opened rank after rank of pipes, the tonal qualities began to fight and the tempo increased. Her feet danced across the pedals. She built up an avalanche of pure sound with the heavy bass rolling and groaning like some great beast of the chase tortured by the piercing notes of the flutes and strings. It became terrify-ingly loud, as loud as she could make it. Then, before she had completed even the first part, she stopped. For an instant the echo of the final notes vibrated through the empty church. In the silence that followed she looked about her fearfully, reached for her shoes, and quickly replaced them on her feet.

She stood up, breathing rapidly, and switched off the light over the console, then felt her way down the steep stairway from the loft to the choir railing. Here she picked up her coat and descended the rest of the way to the floor of the nave. Her footsteps made no sound on the heavy oiled planks as she walked swiftly down the long aisle to the vestibule. She snapped off the vestibule light and stepped outside, pausing to close and lock the great doors behind her.

The wet breeze made her hug her coat about her as she walked toward the solitary car in the parking area. Halfway there she paused to look back at the Bull Woods rising like a dark wall against the sky behind the church. She gnawed her lips nervously, then turned and proceeded to the car.

The black sedan belonged to Manley Foxx, but she borrowed it on evenings when she practiced at the organ. The church was a quarter of a mile from the parsonage, with no houses in between.

She drove in his driveway, closed the car door silently, and slipped up the steps of the house to drop car keys and church keys into the mailbox. Then she went out to the road and scurried along the remaining fifty yards to her own house. It was a tiny house, immaculate, prim, and smelling faintly of rose water. She locked herself in and pulled all the blinds before going to her bedroom to change clothes. She hung the dove-gray dress carefully in the closet and selected a suit of navy blue and a white blouse to wear beneath her jacket. The only ornamentation was an opal brooch set in silver, which she fastened at her throat. She sat before her mirror, combing her blond hair into neat wings above her temples and regarding her reflection carefully in the glass.

Her breathing had returned to normal, but she thought she

11

could still detect an unnatural flush in her cheeks and a hard brilliance about her eyes which wouldn't blink away. Would Edward Spence notice it? Probably not. The breeze would redden her cheeks still more by the time she'd walked to Ula Westerly's. She slid into her coat, tucked her purse under her arm, and departed.

After his bus left Jonesville, the driver relaxed in his seat and lit a cigarette. About a half mile north of town the road tunneled abruptly into a redwood forest, and evening just as suddenly became night. Fog was rolling in from the sea, with the mistlike rain falling through it. The headlights beat against the murk, cutting a white path for the bus to follow.

The passenger load was light. An old man and woman sat in the rear, conversing in low tones. Three girls made a party in the center of the bus. Two of them sat together and a third just across the aisle. A sailor kept tossing remarks at the isolated one until he had all three giggling. There was a man on the right, four seats back, who sat with his long nose touching the window while he stared out into the night. He had been sitting that way for a long time.

A few minutes after they entered the forest, the driver caught a movement in the rear-view mirror and glanced up. His long-nosed passenger, wearing hat and raincoat, was standing just behind him. The driver felt the tap of a finger on his shoulder.

"What's wrong?" he asked.

The passenger bent close to his ear.

"If you don't mind, I should like to get off." The voice was mild. "I've missed my stop."

The driver peered to left and right ahead of him. All he could see were the giant tree trunks, their shadows falling in swift succession as the headlights passed them.

"Your ticket reads Eureka."

"I know," murmured the passenger. "It was made out that way back East. But I want off here."

12 🐦

"What do you want off here for? There's nothing but trees."

"So I've observed. I like trees."

The driver took his foot off the gas. "You sure you know where you're going? It's two miles back to Jonesville."

"And if you don't stop, it will soon be three. This coach has brakes, I suppose?" The tone was still mild. The driver eased the bus over to the shoulder and brought it to a stop. With the motor idling, the windshield wipers became audible as they rhythmically polished the glass.

"I guess you know what you're doing." He opened the door.

"I'm sure of it. I have a suitcase in the rear." He hopped down to the roadway and waited for the driver to follow. The driver grudgingly squirmed from his seat and went around to the side of the bus, where he unlocked the storage compartment. His flashlight played over the collection of bags.

"You'll have to tell me which is yours."

"Of course. That one. The tan leather."

The light found the gold lettering on the bag indicated.

"Twist," said the driver. "Bleeker Twist. That you?"

"It is, indeed. That's all I have."

The driver hauled the suitcase out and set it on the asphalt. "This isn't a regular stop, you know."

"It's one of the advantages the motor coach has over the train."

"You'll ruin that bag getting it wet."

"I think not. The leather has been well cared for. Let me offer you this for your trouble." Mr. Twist thrust a bill into the driver's hand.

"We're not supposed to take tips. This is part of my job."

"But you just explained that it wasn't part of your job. Thank you. I'll take the suitcase and you can be on your way."

The driver squirted his flashlight on the bill before putting it in his pocket.

"It's just a dollar," said Mr. Twist.

The driver turned his flashlight on his passenger. "That's

13

fine. Thanks," he said. Then he stopped and stared. Quite unmistakably there was something moving under Mr. Twist's coat which was not a part of Mr. Twist. He watched, fascinated, as the black-and-tan face of a Siamese cat pushed into view through the unbuttoned throat of the overcoat.

"A cat!"

Mr. Twist chuckled. "Against the rules to carry animals, I understand."

"Yes," said the driver. "Good thing I didn't know." The cat flowed upward until its whole body reposed on its owner's shoulder. The sapphire eyes blinked angrily at the flashlight.

"Sorry to deceive you." Mr. Twist picked up his suitcase. "Come, Andramalech," he said, and with the cat still perched on his shoulder, he started back down the road toward Jonesville. The driver watched until a trickle of water down the back of his neck recalled him to the weather and his duties. He shook his head, locked the storage compartment, got back into the bus, and started north again.

In Larry's Bar, Mars Venderstone finished his second glass of beer and looked questioningly at the girl on the opposite side of the booth. She frowned slightly.

"No, I have to go home. You know how Father is."

"You're old enough that your father shouldn't have anything to say about it."

She smiled fleetingly. "It isn't that. He worries, and I don't want him to worry."

"Well, maybe," said Mars grudgingly. "I suppose it's natural you should care what he thinks. One of these days, though, I hope it's me you think about."

Ailsa Kildonan smiled again and said nothing. She slid from her seat and stood up, waiting for Mars to join her. Together they walked down the sidewalk to Venderstone's car.

"I suppose it's no use asking if you'll go some place with me later this evening? After dinner?"

"No," she said. They got in the car and drove slowly through town and out along the highway.

"I suppose you know I'm taking chances, being seen with you," he said, half jokingly.

Ailsa didn't return his smile. "I told you that a week ago."

"It could mean my job."

"Or mine."

"A job means more to a man than a woman. I got a chance of being head sawyer some day."

"I know. When Father is gone."

"He doesn't have to go anywhere. Sooner or later he'll quit. He isn't getting any younger."

"He won't quit for a long time yet—unless he has to." She turned her head to look at him. "Maybe that's why you're being so brave about being seen with me."

He scowled. "I don't get you."

"Maybe you think a little trouble might help you get the job sooner."

"You're crazy," he said.

"It's not pleasant," she said evenly, "to have you act as though you're doing me a favor by taking me out."

"I didn't mean it that way. It was just my way of saying I liked you well enough to take you out, even though people would talk about it."

"You remember it all the time, don't you?"

"Remember what?"

"Oh, let's skip it."

"Well, you don't have to act so high and mighty about it. Facts are facts. People think there's something queer goes on in the Bull Woods and they think you Kildonans have a hand in it."

"I suppose that's what you think too."

"I don't either, but you've got to admit that your father's the kind of man who could make trouble at the mill."

"You're getting things a little confused aren't you? What

15

people think about the Bull Woods and what they think of my father at the mill are two different things. And besides, there's been no trouble at the mill."

"A long time ago there was."

"A long time ago is right. About twelve years ago. Maybe if a few people had listened to my father then, there wouldn't be so many now who can't afford a decent meal."

"I'm doing all right."

"Sure. You haven't got a wife and children."

"I don't know why you should worry about it. Your father gets paid twice what anyone else does."

She laughed shortly. "Maybe that makes the trouble twelve years ago worth while."

"I don't want to talk about it."

"You brought it up."

"I didn't bring it up. I just mentioned about how people might talk, and you started giving me a lecture. I don't like being lectured by a woman, especially by one who can't hold her head up when she walks down the street."

"You'd better take me home," she said quietly.

"That's right where we're going." He drove in silence for several moments, his dark brows contracted. "Look," he said. "I'm sorry I said that."

"Just forget about it."

"But I'm really sorry. It's just that you make a man so mad the way you rattle on as though there's nothing unusual about—"

"Can't you drop it?" she cut in, anger entering her voice for the first time. "There's nothing unusual about me at all."

"Maybe that's what you think," he said, his conciliatory mood vanishing. "Anytime a girl as pretty as you keeps living with her parents out in the Bull Woods, something is up. It's not all just talk."

"A lot of it's just big ears."

"You could go away if you wanted to."

"I will go away. When mother gets better. But it won't be because of what people say. You'd better slow down; there's the road to our house."

"I'll just stop instead." He brought the car to a halt at the side of the highway.

"I can walk the rest of the way."

"Not for a minute, you can't. There're still a few things I've got to say. I've been seeing you for about a month now. Maybe you don't think it's a favor, but you don't need to act like you've been doing me one. I've tried to show you what a decent sort of man I am."

"I didn't say you weren't."

"But maybe I've been too nice to you. I ought to treat you the way I treat other women."

"I think the other women would enjoy it more. There are other men, too."

"Not while you're seeing me, there isn't." He looked at her keenly in the darkness. "Or is that why you're always so cool? They'd better be careful. I can break any man in this town."

"You sound rather foolish, Mars."

"I do, eh? Maybe it's that schoolteacher. I saw the way he looked at you tonight."

"Mr. Spence? He doesn't know I'm alive."

"I could twist him in two."

"I'm sure he wouldn't know why you were doing it."

"Him or anybody else in this town."

"Maybe you'd like to start on Manley Foxx," she said with a touch of malice.

"Foxx? He's a preacher. What's he got to do with it?"

She suddenly laughed. "So there's one man you're afraid of!"

"I'm not a damned bit afraid of him!"

"What did he come to see you about yesterday?"

"I already told you he wanted to know why I wasn't in church. I told him I was sick."

"Because you were afraid to tell him where you really were?"

"I just didn't want any trouble. Besides, it was none of his business what I was doing. Foxx hasn't had anything to do with you."

"You sound pretty sure of that."

"I guess I've heard what's been said about you on Sundays."

"And believed most of it, too. Mr. Foxx doesn't have to worry about you. You'd better go back to church."

"I'll go back to church when I'm ready and not before. I'll show you who's afraid of Manley Foxx." He suddenly seized her shoulders and pulled her against him, his powerful hands forcing her face upward toward his. She offered no resistance when he kissed her and released her again. "I'll show you." He started the motor angrily and turned on the headlights.

"Now who the hell is that?" he exclaimed.

The car lights picked up the figure of an approaching man. He carried a heavy suitcase in his hand and had a cat perched on his shoulder. Venderstone let his motor idle. The stranger walked up to the side of the car and set his suitcase on the asphalt pavement. He smiled at Mars and Ailsa and thrust his head close against the window.

"Good evening," he said. "Can you tell me where I am?"

"What's wrong? You lost?" said Venderstone suspiciously.

"I'm a little uncertain of my whereabouts. There should be a town in this vicinity."

"Down the road a ways. It's not far."

"Fine. I'll proceed then."

"Your car broke down?"

"I have no car."

"You traveling by foot?"

"As you see." He bent to recover his suitcase.

"I like your cat," exclaimed Ailsa.

The stranger straightened and lifted a hand to stroke the cat's fur. "Poor fellow. He doesn't care for the wet. His name is Andramalech." Then he nodded politely and continued on down the highway.

"What do you know about that?" said Venderstone, putting the car in gear. "Where do you suppose he came from?"

"I don't know," said Ailsa, "but he had an awfully nice voice."

"You'd think so. Sounded like some movie actor to me." He turned the car off the highway onto a dirt road filled with gleaming pools of water. He followed its winding course among the trees for about two hundred yards and stopped before the wide front of a log house.

"I'll just let you off and go on back," he said. "Your family doesn't want to see me." He hesitated. "We didn't do so well tonight. You think we'd do any better tomorrow?"

Ailsa opened the car door and stepped to the ground outside. "Honestly, Mars, I don't think we would. You'd better go back to church."

He looked at her a moment, then shrugged and pulled the car door shut. She watched him drive away without visible emotion. She was still a little angry at some of the things he'd said, but she knew he'd said them because of wounded vanity as much as anything else. He probably wouldn't be back, and that was a good thing. Nothing that came out of Jonesville would ever do her much good. It would be a relief some day to go to a new place where she wouldn't be considered a witch. She looked about her at the towering trees of the Bull Woods, then turned and started for the house.

CHAPTER TWO

✿ ✿ ✿ EDWARD SPENCE DRAINED HIS COFFEE CUP AND SET IT BACK
on his saucer. He pushed his plate a few inches forward on the
table and wiped his lips with his napkin. His face ached from
smiling. He longed to scowl just to reverse the tension on his
facial muscles. He had paid verbal tribute to the food, to Ula
Westerly, and Stella. Now he had to sit out a conventional after-
dinner hour before he could escape to his room and crawl into
bed with his magazine.

Was it like this with everyone? Smiling because they were supposed to smile, uttering pat phrases which came automatically to
the lips and left the mind free to think about other things?

"We always have such gay times at Ula's house!" Stella said.
Edward looked at her closely, forgetting for a moment to smile
because he was interested in discovering whether her smile was
real or not. Did she really think they were having a gay time?
She didn't look gay; she looked tired. There were faint shadows
under her eyes which lent to her expression a tinge of melan-
choly. He had noticed the expression before. Sometimes at school,
where she was the other teacher, he surprised her in a moment
of repose and caught a fleeting impression of bitterness which
always vanished upon his approach. He'd never attempted to
discover whether or not his observation had any real basis—
there was reason enough for some bitterness in every person's
life—but he had noticed that the expression gave her face a

warmth and character which temporarily triumphed over the crisp and characterless clothing she habitually wore. At such times—had he not known her so well—he might have found her pretty. As it was, he always found her rather stiff and formal, attentive to her manners and the banalities of small talk. He associated her, for some reason, with corsets, although when he analyzed this association he had to admit that her figure was in no need of artificial molding.

When she noticed his intent stare, she flushed, and Edward quickly shifted his attention to Miss Westerly. Miss Westerly was getting old. Her figure was stringy and her hair was always frowzy by the time dinner was over.

.They left the table and moved into the parlor. Never a big room, the parlor gave the impression of being overstuffed like the furniture that was in it. Miss Westerly collected glass and porcelain figures and displayed them on high narrow shelves along the walls and on whatnots in the corners. She liked furniture. Every chair had its table and every table its lamp. In the center of the room was a large oval coffee table which effectively prevented leg-stretching by anyone seated in the room. Edward edged past it into the blue armchair. He was careful about the lamp beside it. Once he had knocked it over and fractured the shade. Fortunately, he didn't smoke, and so it was possible for him to sit quite still once he reached his seat. He felt cramped, but the cramping wasn't all due to Miss Westerly's parlor. The parlor was only a part of the general factor of crampedness which surrounded him daily. For his own purposes he referred to it as the G of Crampedness as he'd learned in college to talk about the G of Intelligence or the G of Artistic Ability. Actually Miss Westerly's parlor was no worse than many others. In another mood he might have considered it cozy.

"I think it's so nice being inside on a rainy night," said Ula Westerly. "So safe and cozy."

"I was just thinking the same thing," said Edward.

21

"Great minds run in the same channel," said Stella. Everyone chuckled.

"More likely it's telepathy," said Ula. "Things like that happen too often for coincidence."

"But I hadn't actually said anything," Edward said.

"You were thinking it, and as far as telepathy is concerned, that's the same thing. You were thinking how cozy and comfortable this room was, and that's what made me say what I did."

"I guess so," said Edward, shifting his foot so that the leg of the coffee table didn't press quite so hard against his ankle. His foot inadvertently touched Stella's and she withdrew hers quickly. "Excuse me," he said.

"Of course," she said.

Ula Westerly beamed. "Are you two playing footie?" Stella blushed scarlet. Hell, thought Edward. Corsets.

Stella had done better than he in adjusting to Jonesville. In addition to teaching school, she played the organ at church each Sunday and met with the girls' club each Friday evening. That, no doubt, explained why she stayed in Jonesville. She'd won recognition. His own reasons for remaining were less subject to scrutiny. He'd only recently begun to be aware of them himself. Coming face to face with Ailsa Kildonan in front of Larry's Bar had been a shock. There she'd been, looking at him as though she knew all about him. He couldn't remember whether she'd spoken or not; it seemed as though she had, although he had no memory of anything she might have said. And where was she now? Getting drunk with Mars Venderstone? Or were they in a parked car somewhere doing God knows what? Even in a parked car, Ailsa Kildonan wouldn't be cramped. She always seemed to have lots and lots of space about her. The solitude of the Bull Woods clung to her even when she came into town, although, as with Miss Westerly's parlor, the Bull Woods were merely a manifestation of another general factor to which he hadn't put a name. It was the opposite of the G of Crampedness. He grew uneasy thinking about it. At the moment he disliked

Mars Venderstone intensely, but he experienced a queasy delight in picturing Mars and Ailsa together. Ula Westerly brought in a plate of dried figs.

"Why don't you play the piano for us, Stella?" she said.

"I really couldn't," said Stella. "I've just been practicing the organ, and if I tried the piano now, I'd be terrible."

"Of course you wouldn't. You play beautifully. Please do!"

"Honestly, Ula."

"Come on now."

"Well, if you two will sing," she suggested hopefully.

"You know I can't sing," said Ula. "But Edward will sing. He has a lovely voice. Come on, Edward."

"I won't sing unless you do," said Edward. Oh, God, he thought, why can't we get this period over by sitting quietly in our chairs until it's time to leave? Why make the situation worse by being noisy about it? Courtesy forced him to the piano, where he moved the end of the sofa to enable Stella to pull the piano bench from under the keyboard. She sat down and arched her wrists above the keys.

"What shall we sing?"

"What do you want to sing, Edward?"

"Let's sing 'Juanita.' " They sang "Juanita." Ula was correct about her inability to sing, but she bravely continued her efforts while they ran through "Juanita," "Listen to the Mocking Bird" and "Flow Gently Sweet Afton." After Mary's dream was thoroughly disturbed, Edward crammed two dried figs into his mouth and sat down again.

"You're not giving up already, are you?" asked Ula.

"I thought we were through," he mumbled. He could feel the perspiration crawling across his stomach, and he had difficulty swallowing the figs. Stella turned her back on the piano but remained seated on the bench. She was stiff and straight the way she sat at her desk in school. Her feet were flat on the floor, close together, and her hands were folded in her lap. Until Miss Westerly had started telling him that Stella was the most eligible girl in Jonesville, he'd never thought much about her. Since then the distaste aroused by Ula's suggestions had compelled him to look at Stella more closely, and he was in constant terror lest this perverse attention be misinterpreted. At first he told himself this was unfair to Stella, who never showed by glance, gesture or word that she was the slightest bit interested in him other than as an acquaintance. Indeed, with further observation he discovered that whatever tokens of recognition she made toward his presence could be more easily interpreted as indicating just the opposite of interest. Her behavior was a study in withdrawals both mental and physical, and like all withdrawals, made him wonder what there was to conceal. He became conscious of her body for the first time only because it was always so well hidden.

"I suppose we could play hearts or three-handed bridge," said Ula.

"Three-handed bridge would be fun," said Stella.

Here it comes again, thought Edward. He picked frantically for an alternative.

"Have you had any visions or seen any more ghosts lately, Miss Westerly?" By the way his landlady brightened he could tell that the three-handed bridge was temporarily averted.

"Why, yes," she said in a newsy manner, sitting on the edge of her chair. "I have. Someone is going to die."

"Die?" said Edward. This was better than cards anyhow. Miss Westerly had a habit of seeing things.

"Last night there was something in my room. A man."

"A man?" said Stella.

"The vision of a man."

"Goodness!" said Edward.

"There was this dark figure. I've been trying all day to think of who it might be because always before when I've seen someone like that, the person has died."

"Was it like the others?" asked Edward.

"It came the same way. I was in bed. There was a little light in the room from the arc light on Blinder Road. He seemed to come from the doorway, although the door was closed, of course."

"My," said Edward. That seemed sufficient. The piano playing and the singing were a long way off. Miss Westerly said someone was going to die, and that was worth talking about whether it was true or not. Someone was going to die, certainly. Someone was always dying. She was safe as long as she didn't attempt identification. He tried a fig. When he was younger, the idea of persons manifesting themselves to others through hallucinations had been fascinating. But somehow he had lost faith in such manifestations along with faith in other spiritual matters. The external world was always firm to the touch no matter how much one longed for the nebulous and mystical. It was only by looking inward that you found cause to tremble. And how much worse that could be, really. If he should see a ghost, would it be the less terrifying because he knew it to be a product of his own imagination? From an external world he could flee; from himself flight was impossible. Where would I turn, he thought, should my eyes produce a monster?

"Mrs. Whipple saw it," said Miss Westerly. The conversation had somehow changed again. "It was near the edge of the Bull Woods. She had been picking wild raspberries."

"That was last fall," said Stella. "I heard about it."

"I've wondered about that picking wild raspberries. Mrs. Whipple lives on the other side of town. Raspberries grow all around her."

"Well," said Stella, "I'm sure I don't know. She had her boy along."

"He was the one who saw it first. He called his mother and asked her what it was. Then they both saw it moving among the trees at the edge of the woods. It was sort of pale."

"It might just have been someone out for a walk," said Stella.

"It might have been," said Ula, "but it couldn't be someone out for a walk every time. Sometimes it might be someone walking and sometimes it might be pure imagination, like the time Mr. Hibbley claims it chased him home and sat in a tree all night watching his house. But that doesn't take care of it all the time. Of course, the Kildonans have strange ways. They've a hand in it, I'll bet anything. Look at the way young Venderstone has gone."

"I don't like to think about it," said Stella.

Edward realized that she was looking at him, and he reached for another fig. Was it self-consciousness on his part that made him think the glance had significance? And right after mention of Venderstone, too. He chewed the fig and looked out the front window. All he could see was the reflection of the room with the two women sitting in it. They were both looking at him and waiting for him to say something.

"It's rubbish," he said. That was what a man should say. It indicated the proper male cynicism.

"You say that about everything which can't be explained," said Ula. "You have to believe in the supernatural sometimes."

"I don't think so," said Edward.

"How about Floyd Hooks? Can you explain how he finds water?"

"You are committing a common error," said Edward. "You're assuming that because the supernatural can't be explained, anything which can't be explained is, therefore, supernatural." He felt content with this reply but Ula Westerly was unimpressed. She sniffed.

"And you think that nothing is supernatural no matter what. Floyd Hooks finds water and nobody else does. It certainly isn't natural."

"But neither is it uncommon. Dowsers have been locating well sites for thousands of years."

"You can't say he does it by using his brains. He hasn't got any."

"I'm sure I don't know how he does it," said Edward. The admission annoyed him, but the abilities of the water witch were demonstrable and couldn't be denied. Floyd Hooks was always trotted out as an example whenever anyone in Jonesville indicated doubt as to the existence of supernatural powers. His unexplained talent was proof of whatever the imagination might want to pose as a possibility. If Hooks could dowse, then Mrs. Whipple could see ghosts. "Indeed," he continued, pursuing his own thought rather than the conversation, "it may have been Floyd whom Mrs. Whipple saw. Floyd's mental peculiarities give him certain privileges denied the rest of us." His attempt at sarcasm was lost.

"Anyone would recognize Floyd Hooks by the way he walks," said Ula. "You mark my words, the Kildonans are behind it."

"That's what I meant when I said 'rubbish,' " said Edward.

"And that's how things go too far," said Ula Westerly. "But the Kildonans won't get far with Mars Venderstone. The Reverend Foxx won't stand for it. If Venderstone strays, too many others might follow."

Well, that shouldn't bother anyone where Edward was concerned. No one would follow him. There was something wrong with the reflection of the room. Something was moving through it that had no counterpart in the room itself.

"I think someone's at the door," he said.

He was right. There was a soft but insistent knock.

"Who in the world?" said Ula, and she crossed the room to open the door.

A man stood in the wet entry. He was thinnish, with a long nose and a receding chin. Water dripped from every crease in his coat. When he took off his hat and bowed, the water ran from his hat brim and dripped on Miss Westerly's carpet. Then he straightened and peered with beady eyes into the interior.

"Good evening," he said. "Miss Westerly?"

"Speaking," she said suspiciously.

"How fortunate to find you so easily! The directions given me at your local saloon were a trifle obscure."

Miss Westerly stiffened. "If it's all the same, I'd rather my name wasn't bandied about in the saloon. What do you want?"

The stranger grinned. "It wasn't bandied—simply mentioned.

I am looking for a place to spend the night. They told me you might offer such accommodation."

"Whoever said that must have been drunk," said Ula Westerly. "I've got one extra apartment and it's rented regular. Everybody knows that." She glared at the dripping stranger.

"Not everyone," he said. "I didn't know it."

"Well, you do now. Good heavens! Where did that cat come from?"

Unperturbed by Miss Westerly's exclamation, the Siamese cat slithered into the room and leaped to the sofa where it began kneading the cushions with wet paws.

"I must claim ownership," said the stranger.

"Then get it out of here! My mohair will be ruined!"

"Quite so." The cat's owner followed the cat into the room, leaving a trail of mud and water across the floor. He lifted the cat to his shoulder and retraced his steps. At the door he paused.

"Extremely sorry. Andramalech is not accustomed to the rain. Since you have no vacancy, could you tell me where I might find one?"

"No, I couldn't," said Ula crossly. "There's no hotel in Jonesville. All the single men live at the mill barracks on the south edge of town. Maybe you can find a bed there."

"Sounds a bit public but on such a night one cannot be too selective. My thanks." He doffed his hat again and stepped back into the night. Miss Westerly closed the door and looked at her carpet.

"The idea!" she said. "Imagine those men in the saloon sending him here. Even if I had a room, I wouldn't rent it to such a queer-looking person. Did you hear what he called that cat? One of the fallen angels. Reverend Foxx has mentioned the name dozens of times. Now what are you up to, Edward?"

Edward wasn't sure whether he was prompted by generosity or a desire to escape from his present company, but he was going out the door and the rain felt good on his face. There had been something in the stranger's voice—the pedantic accent—which called to him as something from the past. He ran across the front yard to the gate.

"I say, sir!" he called.

The man with the cat was already a dark blur on the roadway, but he stopped at Edward's call.

"Yes?" he said.

"The upstairs apartment of which Miss Westerly spoke—it's mine. I'd be happy to share it with you. I'm pretty sure you'll find nothing else in Jonesville tonight."

The figure walked back toward him. "How very kind of you. But I wouldn't put you at odds with your landlady."

"That won't matter a bit. I've had the room eight years."

"In that case you must feel secure." The stranger arrived at the gate and set his suitcase down in the mud. "My name is Bleeker Twist."

"And I am Edward Spence." As they shook hands, Bleeker Twist leaned forward and peered intently into Edward's face.

"Edward Spence," he repeated.

Edward led him around to the side of the house. "You see, I have a private entrance, so you'll inconvenience no one."

"No one but yourself. This is certainly decent of you."

"Go right on up. I'll join you as soon as I pay my respects to my hostess."

"Why not let me make out alone for awhile? Unless you were ready to leave. . . ."

"I leave them with the greatest of pleasure," said Edward, and wondered immediately why he should make such a confession to a stranger. Bleeker Twist looked down at him from halfway up the stairs and smiled.

"Of all the idiotic things to do, Edward Spence," said Ula Westerly. "It's one thing to be kind to the stranger at your gates, but it's another to invite him into your bed. A man wandering around at night is up to no good. He may be a criminal of some kind."

"Well, I've already done it," said Edward.

"I never knew you to do anything so impulsive."

29

"It was the cat," he said. "I couldn't bear to think of the cat out in the rain."

"Such nonsense!"

"I suppose I'd better go up and see what I can do for him. The dinner was wonderful. I'm sorry to run off this way. Good night, Miss Graw."

"Good night, Mr. Spence," said Stella. Her voice was level but her lips drooped at the corners. Curiously, it made her appear relaxed for the first time that evening. Edward went back to the front door.

"Well, you needn't go out in the rain again," said Miss Westerly. "You can use my stairway."

He laughed nervously. "So I can. I always forget about it." He walked through the house to the hallway and up the stairs to his room. His door was locked on the inside and he had to knock for admittance.

Bleeker Twist had already made himself at home. His cat lay curled up on the bed; his wet overcoat and hat hung from the wardrobe door; his muddy shoes lay beside his muddy suitcase on a newspaper he had spread out on the floor. Dressed in a crumpled gray suit, he walked restlessly around the room in his stocking feet.

"I see you're getting dried out," said Edward. "That's fine. How about a cup of coffee?"

"Thank you, I'd like one."

Edward went into his kitchenette and turned on the electric plate. "How do you happen to be stranded in Jonesville?"

"I'm not stranded," said Twist, padding after Edward and examining the contents of the shelves.

"Oh, you mean you're here on purpose?"

"Why not?"

"Well," Edward hesitated, "no reason why not, I suppose. I just thought you must be stranded."

Twist padded back into the other room. "That would seem

30 ⚘

most logical. As a matter of fact, I think I am here because of you."

"Me?" Edward stood in the kitchenette door with the coffeepot in his hand. "I'm sure you must be mistaken."

"I think not. You're the Jonesville principal, are you not?"

Edward sighed. "I see," he said. "You're a book salesman." He put the coffeepot on the electric plate.

"Certainly not. I am interested in the forest giants which dwarf the soul and make a man stay little."

Edward started nervously. His guest had uttered words which had often crossed his own mind. In fact, they were his own words. He stepped slowly from the kitchenette. Twist was seated in an armchair smiling mysteriously.

"But if you came here to see me, why didn't you ask for me?"

"I didn't come to see you," said Twist easily. "I said I came because of you. That is different."

Edward edged his way over to the bed and sat down. He reached out a hand and stroked the cat.

"This is rather strange," he said.

"Not at all." Twist took a large black pipe from his coat pocket and searched other pockets until he found a tobacco pouch. "Doesn't your landlady claim to have psychic powers?"

"Yes, she does," said Edward, "though I don't know how you'd know that. You didn't seem to have met her."

"Never saw her before." Twist's grin was broader. "She doesn't have a monopoly, however."

Edward shifted uneasily. "She just claims to have such powers."

"That's what I said." Twist put a match to his pipe and sucked the flame into the bowl. "Has your roof leaked any this winter?"

Edward stopped stroking the cat and stood up. "Look here, what is this? You seem to know a great deal!"

"Baffling, isn't it? I also know that you went to school at Southern California and that you had a professor named Kavanaugh whom you didn't like."

Edward examined the face across from him closely, the long

nose and slanting forehead, the small dark eyes, the short sandy hair. It was wholly unfamiliar.

"Maybe you were there too," he said.

"No, I've never been west of the Mississippi before." Twist puffed solemnly.

"Then maybe you'll explain things."

"You don't believe I'm psychic?"

"Certainly not."

Twist laughed easily. "Well, well. This is a poor way to repay hospitality, but the temptation was too great. The explanation is very simple."

"I still don't get it," said Edward.

"I hate to tell you," said Twist. "A mystery is so enjoyable and the solution must always be so prosaic by contrast. To put your mind at rest, all I have to do is mention Hubert Sisel." He looked at Edward meditatively.

"Oh," said Edward, "of course. You know him?"

"I do. You wrote him a letter a few months ago."

"Yes. He's in the department of philosophy at Ohio State."

"He was," said Twist. "That was four years ago. Your letter was forwarded. He is now in the department of psychology at Medina University."

"Oh," said Edward again. "Psychology, you say?"

"Yes. That's where I met him."

"You're a teacher then?"

"Not at the moment. I'm on a research fellowship."

"I see." Edward was uncomfortable again. "In psychology?"

"Yes."

"Oh." Edward licked his lips. "You worked with Sisel?"

"He is one of the instructors in my department."

"Your department?"

"I am on leave at present. Sisel is acting head until I return."

"Oh." Edward put his hands in his pockets and walked over to the window. "And Sisel showed you my letter?"

Twist nodded. "I couldn't recall much of it or I would have spun the mystery out a little longer."

"How is Hubert now?"

"Very busy trying to support a wife and three children on a professor's salary."

"He didn't answer the letter."

"No?"

"I suppose he doesn't remember me very well." Edward turned back from the window to face his guest. Twist looked at him curiously.

"Yes, he remembered you."

"Why was he showing my letter around in the psychology department? Was something wrong with it?"

"Not at all," said Twist quickly. "He wasn't showing it around."

"He showed it to you."

"Yes, I was in his office one day discussing places to spend my leave. I wanted a quiet location. Sisel pulled your letter out of his file basket and said, 'Here, read this if you want to know about a quiet place.' That's all there was to it."

"Oh." Edward sat down on the bed again. He rubbed the cat's thick fur. "That's how you happened to read it?"

"Yes, what did you think?"

"It's nothing—nothing at all. Did you read all of it?"

"Just the first four pages. The part about the forest giants which dwarf the soul."

Edward smiled. "And is that why you came here?"

"I have never seen the big trees. My ticket was to Eureka, but right after the bus left Jonesville, I remembered it was where your letter came from and decided to stop here instead. I planned to search you out after I found a place to live."

"I'm certainly glad I hauled you in from the rain."

"And I too. Your coffee is percolating too fast."

Edward brought in two cups, some sugar, and a can of milk. Then he poured the coffee. When he gave Twist his cup, he found his guest smiling at him.

33

"You require the conventional gesture for security, do you not, Mr. Spence? It gives a substance to that which is wholly vaporous. Ah, what fears are hidden behind the cream in one's coffee. And I shall take sugar too, if you please. Thus do we stave off our demons."

"So you intend to stay here, then?"

"For a time," said Twist. He got up and walked around the room with his coffee cup. "I have certain studies to make and certain experiments to attempt. I don't want them conducted under the glare of publicity." He sipped loudly from his cup. "The project I have in mind is somewhat world-shaking." He looked at Edward over the bridge of his nose. "I intend to dethrone every leader of every organization throughout the world."

"Well," said Edward.

Twist smiled. "What a kind fellow you are! You do not laugh; you do not order me out of the room; you do not attempt to call for help. Should I have uttered such a statement among my learned colleagues, one of the three alternatives would certainly have been utilized. You see why I seek out the small town? You sit there undetermined in your attitude. You are willing to hear more before making a decision. Then by all means let me disarm you. Not in my time will I see the accomplishment of my ends. I merely start the pebble rolling which will someday become a landslide. Kings, emperors, and dictators shall eventually cease to exist. Yes, and presidents and congressmen, labor secretaries and bishops. They shall all go. But not a hand will be raised against them. They will vanish because there will be no one seeking their leadership. The individual will no longer need it." He gulped down the rest of his coffee and set the cup on the bureau. "Do I bore you?"

"No," said Edward, "certainly not. You startle me a little."

"It's a startling idea." Twist paced rapidly back and forth. "The mind of man was never properly put together by nature. Because of the original defect, no man is complete by himself. He can grow only in the company of others. This has beneficial results, but just as certainly it is the root of every misfortune which comes to one man from the hands of another. I intend to remedy the original error by making men complete in themselves." He stopped pacing. "Well, well. This is no time to launch into such a lengthy discussion. I am simply repaying your kindness by satisfying your curiosity regarding myself." He dropped into his chair again. "As you can see, my most pressing need is a place to work—a room, a house, a cabin. Is there nothing available?"

Edward shook his head. "If Miss Westerly could think of nothing, I don't know who could."

"Pah! Miss Westerly views me with suspicion. Andramalech made tracks on her sofa and I made tracks on her rug. Such an attitude would inhibit thought. Surely in such a region as this there would be vacation cabins empty at this time of year."

"You should have stopped farther south. Jonesville has no summer visitors." Edward arose and carried the coffee cups back to the kitchen. He returned and looked at Twist thoughtfully. "As a matter of fact, there is an empty cabin."

"There, you see? So simple."

"Not quite so simple. It's in the Bull Woods."

"Well? And where are the Bull Woods?"

"It's a strip of timber owned by Oban Kildonan. He built the cabin there eight or nine years ago for the very purpose you mention—to rent to summer visitors. But it has never been rented."

"Then it should be in excellent condition. Better and better."

"I'm not so sure. Even if Oban Kildonan agrees to rent it, you may not want it. No one around here ever goes into the Bull Woods except the Kildonans."

"Ah, now." Bleeker Twist lifted his head. "I smell something. What is wrong with the Kildonans, and what is wrong with the Bull Woods?"

"I don't know that anything is wrong with either of them," said Edward uneasily.

"Come, come. You mentioned the cabin in the first place, so don't be reticent now. What is it?"

Edward shrugged. "Simply local superstition. Naturally, I don't subscribe to it, but since I'm a public servant, I can't defy it openly. Certain influential citizens wouldn't like it. If you're going to be here any length of time, you won't want to incur their hostility either."

Twist raised his eyebrows. "My, my! You tell me of a cabin because I need one. You tell me it will make certain people dislike me if I take it. I must interpret that as meaning either that you want me to be disliked or you want to displease the influential citizens you mentioned."

Edward flushed. "I was thinking only of your welfare."

"Indeed you were not," said Twist amiably. "You were thinking of everything except my welfare. Nevertheless, I am interested in the cabin. Now suppose you tell me what is wrong with the Bull Woods."

"They're supposed to be haunted," said Edward.

"So? I see by your face that you expect me to laugh. I think you would be relieved if I did. What haunts the woods?"

"There is a legend," said Edward. "Not exactly a legend, because the original story is true enough. About seventy-five years ago an itinerant missionary was gored to death in the Bull Woods. The circumstances indicated a bull, hence the name."

"You mean no one actually saw the bull?"

"That's right. He left tracks, however. I think myself that the owner must have recovered the beast and gotten him quietly out of the locality. This area was hardly populated in those days. That's about all that's known. The incident was published as an obituary in a church paper which is still on file at the state library. No mention is made of anyone who saw a bull."

"I see," said Twist, "that in spite of your skepticism, you went to the trouble of tracking down the documents."

"I did that when I first came here," said Edward. "I thought then that part of an educator's job was to eradicate superstition."

"And you were unsuccessful, as your previous remarks indicate. Hmm, that follows. A superstition is a symptom, not a disease.

Even had you succeeded in washing it out, another would have taken its place. What is the story now? Does the bull appear on dark nights and devastate the countryside?"

Edward shook his head. "We have a church in Jonesville. The bull has become its symbol of evil. Naturally, the symbolism has spread to things associated with the original bull—the woods and the family which lives there."

"The Kildonans?"

Edward nodded. He had never talked about the subject in just this way before. In Jonesville it couldn't be viewed objectively. "Some people take the allegory literally."

"Wait, now," said Twist, lifting a finger. "Is your present church a descendant of the one represented by the missionary?"

"No. Jonesville had no church until about twelve years ago. That's when Manley Foxx arrived. There had been some labor trouble at the mill."

Twist grinned appreciatively. "I see that Jonesville too has its social and political upheavals. Manley Foxx is a clergyman?"

"In Jonesville he would be considered something more than that," said Edward. "It was after he came that the legend of the bull was revived. No one lives here now who remembers the original circumstances. People stay out of the Bull Woods."

"Hmm," said Twist. "A story doesn't become a legend without reason. You cannot haunt the landscape with a man who died seventy-five years ago or with the bull who killed him—unless there are recurrences. What keeps the story alive?"

"There are manifestations," said Edward.

"Now we have it. What sort of manifestations?"

"There is a madrone tree," said Edward.

"How casually you say that, Mr. Spence. I'm not familiar with your Western flora. What is a madrone tree?"

"They are common enough in the mountains farther east."

"But I am not in the mountains. I am in your apartment."

"I was just trying to think of how to describe one," said Edward a little impatiently. "The tree grows to a good size, perhaps sixty or seventy feet, which still makes it only a shrub compared to the redwoods. It has small light-green leaves in clusters on wide-spreading branches. The outer bark is reddish pink, but this scales off to leave an undercoat which is satin-smooth and tan—like skin."

"You've felt it, I see," said Twist.

Edward flushed and lowered his hand which had been giving its own kinesthetic description of the tree.

"Please continue," said Twist, "and forgive my observation."

Edward folded his hands over his knee. "Maybe that gives you a picture of it. The madrone tree in the Bull Woods stands by itself in a little clearing, supposedly the same spot where the missionary was killed, although there's no way of knowing. On frequent occasions—and I have seen it myself—there have appeared marks on the bark as though some beast had been using the trunk to sharpen its horns."

"And wouldn't that be possible?"

"Certainly. But there's no reason why it has to be a bull."

"It is tangible evidence at any rate. I shall have to see your madrone tree. And what other manifestations have there been?"

"The other is less tangible but easier to explain. Certain people claim to have seen a figure in white at various times moving among the trees where the Bull Woods approach closest to the town. I've never see it myself, and even if I did, I shouldn't think it remarkable."

"Why not?"

"Why, because there's no reason why it shouldn't be a real person."

Twist laughed again and shook his head. "You puzzle me. You assume that because the figure might turn out to be a real person, the matter is disposed of. My friend, belief in ghosts, goblins, and devils does not spring entirely from man's inability to understand his environment. Quite frequently the belief is a protection. If you can fix the responsibility for some ghastly deed upon supernatural powers, then you don't have to face the awful fact that the deed was committed by a human being like yourself. What a blessing it would be if Satan could return to earth and take personal credit for the monstrous acts committed by men these last ten years! What a cleansing it would give us! So don't tell me that everything is satisfactorily explained because the figure in the Bull Woods is probably human. That is the least satisfactory explanation you could give. You told me earlier that no one went into the Bull Woods except the Kildonans."

"Yes. There are three of them. If they choose to walk through their own woods, it's their business."

"That's better. And in that case, there is no reason for superstition." Bleeker Twist stood up. "Is there some way we can telephone Mr. Kildonan? I'd like to inquire about that cabin."

"He has no telephone," said Edward. "And let me advise you to think this thing over. Remember that by going there and living in the Bull Woods unharmed, you are discrediting one of the dogmas of local religion. Manley Foxx won't appreciate it."

"It seems the Kildonans should have discredited the belief long ago."

"But they are evil themselves, and so are immune."

"Is that the story?"

"You'll have ample opportunity to hear it. I think Oban Kildonan was a Wobbly years ago—lots of the older lumbermen were—but now he's only a nonconformist. He refuses to go to church or to allow his wife or daughter to go."

"Do his wife and daughter want to go?"

"I don't think so."

"Do you go?"

"Yes, I go."

"Such is the lot of the schoolteacher," said Twist. He recovered his muddy shoes and started putting them on. "How far is it to the Kildonans'?"

"Good heavens, man! There's no use going out there tonight. Get a good rest and go in the morning."

Twist looked at his watch. "This early darkness confuses you.

39

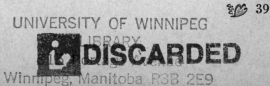

It is only a little past eight o'clock. If I can make my arrangements tonight, I shall not have to waste tomorrow."

"But it's still raining."

"And I have no guarantee that it will not be raining tomorrow. Rain is no wetter at night."

"But puddles are harder to see. If I had a car, I'd be glad to take you."

"No, no. I am already in your debt. However, I shall need directions." Twist finished tying his shoes and went after his raincoat.

"I think I'd better go with you. You'll never find the place alone. "

"But that is far too much for you to do!"

"I'll come along anyhow. As you point out, it's quite early. Besides, you'll need help with the suitcase. We can swing it between us on a stick."

"Andramalech is not half so eager as you," said Twist, picking up his hat.

Edward looked at him sharply, but Twist was engaged in buttoning the cat inside the raincoat. He got his own coat from the closet and settled his hat firmly on top of his head. Then they went out the door and softly descended the stairway. It occurred to Edward that for the first time since it had been built, he was using the stairway for its original purpose—to go secretly some night on a visit to Ailsa Kildonan. He looked back through the window as they went out the gate. Ula Westerly was sitting by herself reading a magazine. Stella Graw had gone home.

CHAPTER THREE

❧ ❧ ❧ THE TWO MEN STRODE ALONG THE BLACK ASPHALT WITH the suitcase swinging on a stick between them. On either side the giant trees of the Bull Woods soared upward into the mist.

"Ah, the power of superstition!" murmured Twist. "Twice before today I have been along this highway, once by bus and once by foot, and on both occasions my only feeling was one of awe for the grandeur of these trees. But now on this third passage I carry new knowledge with me. I listen and look for sounds and visions which are not of the trees themselves."

"Here is where we turn," said Edward. A dirt road led off to their left. It was narrow and crooked, giving ground to every tree that barred its progress. Several times they lost it completely and only found it again by walking around until they struck a puddle. Water wouldn't stand on the forest floor itself.

"Oban Kildonan has never let an ax touch this strip of timber," Edward explained in a whisper. "These are the original big trees."

"Could stand a bit of thinning," said Twist as he stumbled over a root and dropped his end of the stick. He picked it up again and they went on until they caught a gleam of light through the trees.

"That should be the house," said Edward.

The light reflected on the pools of water and made their progress easier. They came to a clearing presently, and the log house loomed ahead of them. Edward's footsteps dragged as they crossed

❧ 41

the yard, but he had to hang on to his end of the stick. Bleeker Twist pulled him across the clearing and up to the house. Perhaps Ailsa wasn't home anyhow. He had seen her earlier with Mars Venderstone.

It was Bleeker Twist who rapped on the door. It opened and there was Ailsa herself. She looked at them with surprise and stood several seconds waiting for one of them to speak.

"Good evening," said Twist at last.

Ailsa looked at him closely. "Why it's the man with the cat! And Mr. Spence." She hesitated. "Won't you come in out of the rain?"

"Well, now," said Twist easily as he stepped across the threshold. "How unfortunate that one cannot see even an hour ahead. I could have come here when I first met you and saved myself a long wet walk."

Edward looked about the living room curiously, almost fearfully. He'd often imagined himself where he now was, but he'd always pictured the interior of the house as similar to that of other millworker houses he'd seen. Most of them were company-built structures based on a standard minimum design occasionally altered by the addition of a porch or extra bedroom. The Kildonan house was not one of them. Oban had built it himself on his own land many years before, and it reflected both his superior financial position and superior skill. The big room was paneled in redwood darkened by age, while beams of the same material supported a wide low-pitched ceiling. From the thick log walls to the huge stone fireplace, the impression was one of mass.

Edward was even more surprised at the size of the library shelved against one wall. Some of the titles he knew from college days; others were books he'd always promised himself to read but had so far managed to avoid. There was little fiction except for a number of the classics. Most of the titles proclaimed contents of philosophical or sociological nature. It shocked him to realize that Ailsa Kildonan might be more familiar with the economics of Adam Smith than he was. It gave the volumes a sinister quality, so that Spencer's *First Principles* which he had never read, struck him as inevitably containing some secret formula for the subversion of mankind. He was still wondering why this error should impress him so forcibly when he saw that Ailsa was gesturing toward the sofa.

"Won't you sit down?" she said.

"We came to see your father," blurted Edward.

"Oh," she said, and he couldn't tell whether she was disappointed, surprised, or merely curious. "He's with Mother." She paused as she was about to leave the room. "Who shall I say wants to see him?"

"Tell him it's Bleeker Twist," said Twist.

"Oh," she said again, and disappeared.

"Well," said Twist. "I feel much relieved. I'm glad to find that it was not solely on my account that you undertook this journey through the rain. A pretty girl." He grinned and unbuttoned his coat, letting Andramalech slide to the floor. The cat walked around his legs, rubbing himself.

"It's hard for me to come here without a valid reason," said Edward, and wondered again why he should make such confessions to a stranger. Except that Twist wasn't a stranger anymore.

"She is a valid reason," Twist replied. "But I forget, you are a public servant and she is among the evil ones." He laughed shortly. Edward felt lonely and unprotected. Oban Kildonan's entrance was a relief, even though the old man looked at them with suspicion.

"Good evening," he said in subterranean tones. He was a squat, powerful figure with a shock of black hair lobbing across his forehead. The hand he extended to Edward had only three fingers on it. Edward managed an introduction.

"Mr. Kildonan, Mr. Twist."

"How do you do," rumbled Kildonan. He waved at the lounge. "Sit you down." His invitation held a note of command. The two men obeyed. "I have not seen you here before, Mr. Spence."

"That's right," said Edward.

"You're out of your territory, young man. What brings you here of a damp evening?" To Edward's relief, Twist answered the question.

"All on my account, Mr. Kildonan. I have a desire for privacy, and Mr. Spence tells me you have that commodity in abundance."

Kildonan looked amused. "That I have. I'm intending to keep it. What's in your mind?" He stood before them with his thumbs hooked at his belt and his head down, looking at them from under shaggy brows.

"I understand you have a vacant cabin."

"And so I do. It's been vacant these many years."

"Yes," murmured Twist. "The cabin is what I have in mind. I need such a place to pursue certain studies. I want to rent it." He took out his pipe. Oban Kildonan looked at him warily a moment, then crossed the room and jabbed at the fire with the poker.

"You're not from these parts, I take it?"

"No," said Twist.

"Then you can't know what you're asking."

"I have some notion," said Twist. "Mr. Spence has given me an idea of the difficulties I may expect."

"Mr. Spence has, has he? And what would Mr. Spence be telling you?" Kildonan strode back across the room to plant himself in front of them again. Bleeker Twist smiled.

"He has told me that your family is held in considerable disrepute and that if I take the cabin, I shall come in for my share of it."

Oban stared at him a moment, then threw back his head and roared with laughter. "You do not mince words. I am surprised to see Mr. Spence. He'll end up in trouble from being here." He stopped laughing and contracted his brows. "Now tell me this. Are you sent by someone to make mischief in the Bull Woods?"

"Good heavens, no," said Twist casually.

"Some like to have it that the woods are an evil place. Aye, damn them! They fear the truth I have to speak and have tried

44

to bottle me up with monsters!" Kildonan clasped his hands behind his back and stomped about the room. "I'll not have more stories added."

"The result might be just the opposite," Twist pointed out.

"It might be at that. What sort of studies do you follow? I'll not have my woods burned by explosions or my sleep troubled by noises in the nighttime."

"My only equipment is my brain," said Twist quietly. "My brain and a few books. You will not know I'm there."

"Look you, man," Kildonan seemed to be reaching a decision. "There's things in my own woods which even I don't understand. I think I have a glimmer of the truth, and when I know for sure it will go hard on those behind it. No one has been harmed in my time and maybe no one will be, but I give you fair warning. Tell me now, are you a churchman?"

"I must confess," said Twist, "that I have not been in a church since I was expelled from Sunday school at the age of ten. It had to do with the disappearance of a few bottles of sacramental wine."

"You are an atheist then?"

Twist shrugged. "It has always amazed me that there should be such a cult as atheism. I cannot understand why one should belabor a God in whom one professes not to believe. No, sir, I am not an atheist nor a member of any other sect. Your Reverend Foxx will not care for me."

"So you know of Foxx?"

"Mr. Spence has mentioned him to me."

"Mr. Spence seems to have given you rather complete information."

"A bit here and there. I have put things together. And now, Mr. Kildonan, since you have given me my warning, do I get the cabin?"

For reply Kildonan strode to the hall doorway. "Ailsa," he called. He came back to the fireplace and waited until she appeared.

"Yes, Father."

"Ailsa, this gentleman," he pointed at Twist, "is renting the cabin. I am going with him to show him the way. It has a stove and a few pots in it, but he will be needing some blankets." Kildonan looked at Twist. "What more he needs, he can get for himself."

"Yes, Father. I'll get the blankets and a lantern." Ailsa spoke softly and disappeared again.

"Couldn't we find it?" asked Twist. "There's no need of your getting wet."

"It's no matter. Have you nothing of your own?"

"My suitcase is outside."

Ailsa returned to the room with an armload of blankets which she deposited on the end of the lounge. She crossed the room to the fireplace and got a lantern from the mantel.

"I can show them the way," she said quietly.

"You stay with your mother," replied Oban.

The girl adjusted the wick and set a match to it. "You were complaining of your rheumatism today."

Her father frowned. "A little walk will make it no worse."

"And besides, Mother is asking for you."

"What is it she wants?"

"I think she wants you to read the rest of the story you started. She says my voice is too light for the exciting parts."

Oban scowled and glanced at the men. "I'll see."

Twist stood up. "Before you go, could we settle on the amount?"

Kildonan pushed his hair back from his eyes. "Take the place. If you can stay there, you'll owe me nothing." He strode from the room.

Ailsa followed her father as far as the hall where she got a wool jacket and a pair of overshoes from the closet. She put them on quickly and returned to the living room. Andramalech had leaped up on the blankets. She picked him up and buried her nose in his fur.

"I can carry the cat," she said, "and the lantern." She got it from the mantel and stepped out into the night.

"Are you responsible for this?" whispered Twist to Edward as they watched her leave the room.

"I'm sure I can't be."

Twist had his suitcase, so Edward picked up the blankets and followed. They went around the side of the house and struck the dirt road again. It took them a little farther into the timber before it narrowed down to a footpath. They walked in single file with Ailsa leading the way. Edward could hear her overshoes flapping against each other. High above them the wind was soughing in the treetops, and water came down in sporadic showers when sudden gusts shook the branches.

"It isn't far," said Ailsa.

Edward's heart was pounding harder than his exertions warranted. There is no reason for it, he told himself. This is a very ordinary thing. But the swinging lantern ahead and the circling shadows were not ordinary. Nothing had ever happened like this before. It came about so easily, so logically. Ailsa paused with the light held high to allow the men to clamber over a particularly difficult tangle of roots. Edward passed so close to her that he could feel the heat of the lantern and see the beads of mist sparkling in her hair. They waited while she preceded them again. In a short while he would return by this same path, just himself and Ailsa. That was the way he had seen it many times—the night, the trees, and the girl. The whole scene was completely familiar. But the people in it were strange. He was not acting as he acted in his dreams. His heart was pounding. And Ailsa—Ailsa was simply leading the way to the cabin. There was a wall which needed tearing down, but there was no way to destroy it unless she sensed its presence too.

They came to an opening in the trees and saw ahead of them the square outlines of a cabin. Ailsa pushed open the door and went in. While Edward and Bleeker Twist were putting down their burdens, she found another lantern and lighted it.

"This is it," she said. "It should be a quiet place to work." Bleeker Twist smiled. "I see you listen in hallways, Miss Kildonan." He looked around him appreciatively. The cabin was one large room with a double bunk along one wall and a small coal range on the other side. It had two square windows for ventilation. There was a rough table and a couple of cast-off chairs in the center of the room. "It will do nicely," he said.

"There is a spring a little farther down the path. You can find it in the morning unless you want me to show you now."

"Not tonight!" said Twist. "I have had enough water for one evening. What do you think of my quarters, Mr. Spence?"

"Not overfurnished, but adequate," said Edward mechanically. Ailsa was slowly stroking the cat. She lifted him from her shoulder and dropped him on the floor. Andramalech walked stiff-legged to the open door and stared out into the trees.

"I see my larder contains half a can of coffee," said Twist. "I thought the cabin was unused."

"It's probably stale," said Ailsa. "Sometimes I've come here in the afternoons to read."

"Well, I might offer a cup anyway."

"No," said Ailsa. "I have to go back." She hesitated. "Is there anything else you need?"

"No, thank you," said Twist.

Ailsa stepped outside. "Are you coming, Mr. Spence?"

"Yes," said Edward, "I'm coming. Maybe I'll drop around in a couple of days and see if you need anything."

"Do not think you have to offer material aid at every encounter. Your company will be sufficient reward. Good night." Twist took Edward's elbow and led him to the door. Ailsa was standing outside waiting. "Good night," Twist repeated. Then he closed the cabin door.

Edward didn't move for several seconds. Ailsa had the lantern and he expected her to walk ahead. She smiled at him.

"The path isn't so narrow that we have to walk single file, Mr. Spence."

"Of course not," he said, jerking himself forward. He took the lantern from her hand and started vigorously back along the path. She kept pace with him easily.

"Who is Mr. Twist?" she asked.

"I don't know," he said. "I really don't know much about him."

"Didn't he tell you anything?"

"Well, he talked a lot. He knows an old college friend of mine."

"How did he know about the cabin?"

"I told him."

"How did you know?"

"I've seen it sometimes." He stopped talking abruptly. How could he have seen it without being there? Would Ailsa notice? "What I mean is, I've heard you had one."

"Oh," she said. They walked awhile in silence. He listened to the even slapping of her unbuckled galoshes and glanced at her furtively. Her face was smooth and untroubled. With her head uncovered and her hair tumbled around the open throat of her jacket, she looked amazingly at ease. Too much so, somehow. She was like the books in her father's library. Volumes which he would have considered dull elsewhere had become mysterious by appearing in the Kildonan house; Ailsa's informality, which he might have praised in another, acquired the nature of a disguise. She was dissembling. Behind the informality lay another personality—something primitive, something completely unmoral. She caught him looking at her and gave him a quick smile.

"What is it?"

"Nothing," he said. The word repeated itself in his mind. Nothing. They were getting closer and closer to the place where he must tell Ailsa good night. After eight years he was walking alone with her. Not eight years, actually. She'd been little more than a child when he first came. It was only the last four or five years that he'd begun to notice. Soon he would tell her good night and go about his business. Nothing.

"There's something I've wanted to talk to you about for a long time," said Ailsa.

"Yes?" he said. Her statement sent a surge of blood to his head.

"I haven't wanted to call on you in town. It isn't . . . well, why mention the reasons? You know Jonesville as well as I do."

"Yes," he repeated. Jonesville would have whispered. And yet, she had wanted to call on him. He felt curiously weak, almost frightened. He had always imagined himself bold but he was completely unprepared for her casual confidence in herself. "What is it?" His voice was barely audible.

"Father wants me to go away to school," she said. "I guess he's right. If I don't go soon, I'll begin to feel I'm too old. I thought some time I might talk to you about the best place to go and about what courses to take."

"Oh," he said. This was incredible. In the dark night with the rain sifting through the giant trees, she had suddenly started talking about education. It was part of the disguise. She was lifting the veil of the prosaic to hide the exotic which lay behind. Or perhaps she was merely providing an excuse for them to meet somewhere. A clever excuse adapted to his own profession.

"I didn't know you wanted to go to school," he said carefully.

"I don't know how you could know. But, really, there isn't much in Jonesville, is there? I hate to leave until Mother is on her feet again, but Father thinks he can manage." She made it sound so sincere, so conversational.

"I thought perhaps you were getting married," he said.

"Married?"

"To Mars Venderstone." The name slid almost shyly from his lips. It was a dagger with which he was going to cut the veil of pretense away. She was Ailsa Kildonan who lived in the Bull Woods. She looked at him curiously and laughed.

"I should say not! Don't tell me people are saying such things in town?"

"Not exactly," he said hesitantly. His dagger had slipped and gone into his own body. Nobody had mentioned marriage where Ailsa and Mars were concerned. They'd said much worse.

"I should hope not," she said. "Mars is . . . well, he's a frightfully jealous person. He needs some girl who will love him because he's big and handsome, and who doesn't want to talk much. He thinks it's gallant to fight other men who look at his girl." She laughed again. "That's a frightful way to talk about someone, isn't it?"

"I don't know," said Edward. He was struck with uneasy fears. Even in his dreams he'd never contemplated the reaction of Mars Venderstone. He knew now he could never face Venderstone again without inward cringing. He walked on, feeling like a fool. He could hear her breathing beside him but was afraid to look at her again. Drops of water from the trees sizzled on the roof of the swinging lantern. At the edge of the clearing they stopped and looked across at the house. From this side the windows were dark. They stood in silence a few moments, and then Ailsa reached out a hand for the lantern.

"I guess you can make your way all right from here," she said. Her voice was faintly crisp, and he realized that she'd been waiting for him to say something. He hadn't told her he'd be glad to talk to her about choosing a school. He hadn't entered into the plot at all. Such things were beyond his experience. The moment was passing.

"Wait," he said, and putting the lantern on the ground, he suddenly seized her arm. He felt the soft contours beneath his fingers and tightened his grip until he knew it was giving her pain. She swung toward him, her hands against his chest, and he seized the other arm.

"I'm coming back to see you!" he choked. "I'm coming again!" He tried to pull her to him but she held herself away.

"Please don't!" she whispered. "Please, please don't!"

51

He released her abruptly and she swung down to pick up the lantern. For a second she stared at him, her lips half open in astonishment. Then she turned and ran quickly across the yard to the house. He stood in the darkness until he heard the door slam. Then in utter misery he started along the muddy lane leading to the highway. So great was his dejection that he had progressed over half the distance before he realized he was being followed.

The discovery struck him with terror. He had a vision of Mars Venderstone's huge figure stalking out of the trees to assault him. He stood with open mouth and straining ears, but no one appeared. He heard footsteps splash through a pool of water somewhere behind him and then heard the snap and swish of branches as his pursuer left the roadway and pushed through the underbrush. He waited no longer, but made his way as rapidly as possible to the highway. After that the darkness was no impediment. He went down the highway at a dog trot, gradually losing his fear as the lights of Jonesville drew closer. Near the edge of town he stopped and stepped behind a large tree close to the pavement.

He didn't have long to wait. Within a minute or two he heard footsteps approaching along the highway. The figure passed within ten feet of him, a man mumbling curiously to himself. Edward sighed with relief. It was Floyd Hooks, the dowser. At another time Edward might have hailed him, but tonight he was in no mood for conversation. He let the dowser get well ahead of him before he continued his journey to the sanctuary of his room at Ula Westerly's.

CHAPTER FOUR

❦ ❦ ❦ EDWARD SPENCE FAILED TO GO TO CHURCH THE NEXT morning. He lay in bed staring at the ceiling while the hands of the clock went past the hour he should have risen. When it was too late to go, he got up and made toast and coffee. After he had eaten, he shaved and then put on hiking pants and a pair of leather boots. Below him the house was quiet. Miss Westerly would be at church along with the rest of Jonesville. He stole down the stairway into the gray day and walked rapidly west, leaving the town behind.

It was the second time in eight years that he had missed church. The other time he had been ill, and Manley Foxx had come around to call on him during the afternoon. Today he would have no excuse—none that would satisfy Foxx.

"I went walking by the ocean. I wanted to watch the waves break over the rocks."

That wouldn't do, but it was the best he could offer.

"If you teach school in Jonesville, Mr. Spence, you must be a constant example of good conduct."

That was always the big threat. The big threat for the small transgression. We will squeeze your stomach, Mr. Spence; you will be talked about in parlors; you will have to go elsewhere unless you are more careful.

The ocean was not far. He could hear the crash of falling water. He laughed mirthlessly. How long was eight years? How fat was the illusion which had sucked them up? When the bubble was pricked and the shimmering colors vanished, how could life inside the bubble be justified?

"You, may squeeze my stomach all you please, Mr. Foxx. I have not stayed here because I was hungry."

Without the bubble there was nothing left but a stupidity which could not be explained. But there was no one who wanted an explanation anyway.

No one was on the shore. He had never found anyone on the shore, but this was the first time he didn't hope to find someone. How idiotic it had been to think about it at all. After eight years he had touched a girl's arm and reality had showered around him like falling stones. Ten seconds it must have taken, ten seconds to be an ass.

The water was on both sides of him now. He clambered out along the black rocks with the fierce breeze stinging his face and bits of blown spray lashing at his body.

"I came to watch the water. I wanted to see the white foam riding on the slinky green depths. I wanted to see the snaky kelp crawl over the rocks."

"If you wish to force the issue, Mr. Spence, you can always do so. You don't need to act like a little boy playing truant."

He was not forcing any issue. He was simply behaving as he had to behave. Everything had been calm with the white foam hiding the green water, and then he had gone for a walk in the woods. There had been a catalytic agent with a long nose and he had scraped the foam away.

"I wanted to feel the rocks tremble when the water hit them. I wanted something big and strong to make me feel big and strong."

He sat for an hour on the farthest outpost of land. Then he climbed back along the rocks to the shore and started retracing his steps to Jonesville. Church would be over by now. There would be people coming home. He met Mrs. Whipple at the edge of town. She barely acknowledged his nod as she hurried past him.

Others he met looked at him strangely. He walked swiftly until he came to Miss Westerly's gate. At that moment a blue sedan drove up to the grass parking and stopped. The man at the wheel caught Edward's eye and beckoned. It was Ivor Jones. Edward stepped over to the side of the car.

"Got a little time?" said Jones without preamble.

"Time for what?"

"I want to talk to you. Hop in and we'll go over to my pla" Jones flung the door open and sat staring straight ahead while he waited for Edward to get in. Edward slid in and pulled the door shut.

"All right," he said.

Ivor Jones hummed under his breath as he drove but said nothing until he had stopped the car in his driveway.

"More private here," he said. He stalked across the lawn to the front door, opened it, and with a curt gesture let Edward precede him into the house. In the living room he dropped his hat on the table in back of the lounge and pulled a cigar from his pocket. "You might as well sit down," he told Edward. He bit off the end of the cigar and spat it into the fireplace. "I guess you know why I want to talk to you."

"No," said Edward. "I don't."

"Unh," grunted Jones, running a hand through his shaggy hair. "You can say that, but you know all right." He struck a match to the cigar and settled into a deep armchair. "No use beating around the bush, though. I noticed you weren't at church this morning."

"No," said Edward. He sat on the arm of the lounge tapping his hat against his knee.

"If you had been, you wouldn't need any explanation. Of course, Foxx might not have gone so hard on you if you'd been there." He rolled the end of his cigar against the ashtray. "Now mind you, Spence, I know you're a cut above the average as far as education goes. I don't expect you to take for granted all this stuff Foxx puts out about the Bull Woods. But I do expect you to use a little common sense. Get it?"

"No," said Edward. "I don't get it."

"All right. I'll draw a picture for you in black and white. Jonesville is my town, see? Maybe it's poor politics to say it, but you're smart enough to know it anyway. This has been my town for a long time and it's going to stay that way. We had a little trouble here once a few years before you came. Maybe you know about it."

"I've heard about it."

"All right, then. You must know who was behind it. No use mincing words; it was Oban Kildonan. I've known the man for forty years and I know what he's like. I keep him working because he's the best sawyer in the country and because I can keep my finger on him that way, but I like to keep his ideas isolated. I don't underestimate him, see? He damn' near put a union in here in 1935." Jones bit off half his cigar for a chew and threw the rest of it into the fireplace. "I don't go for that sort of thing. The people in Jonesville are contented; they're my people. I see that they have work and I see that they don't go hungry, and I'm not going to have anyone meddling with them. Is that clear?"

"I know what you're talking about," said Edward.

"Good. Then you know why I don't want you fooling around with the Kildonans. You're the schoolteacher and, whether you like it or not, certain people look up to you. If you make a friend out of Oban Kildonan, others will think they can. Before long I'll have another mess on my hands. I don't want it to get started."

"I'm not making a friend of Oban Kildonan," said Edward.

Jones waggled a finger at him. "Now take it easy. I'm not accusing you of anything. I'm just giving you a clear picture of my viewpoint. There's no use denying that you were at the Kildonan house last night. You were seen."

"I'm not denying it, and I know who saw me."

"Sure. The dowser saw you. You can't blame him for telling. He believes all this stuff about the Bull Woods and thinks he's got a duty to God to tell me everything he sees. It's a good thing for you he did see you because it gives me a chance to steer you off before it goes any further."

Edward slapped his hat against his boot. "It seems to me you're going pretty strong, Mr. Jones, telling me whom I can visit and whom I can't."

"You think so, do you? Well, just think back and you'll see that someone has been telling you ever since you came here. Maybe you think it's Foxx. It's O.K. with me if you do. That's what the rest of the town thinks."

"And anyway, I didn't go there for personal reasons."

"I'm coming to that," said Jones. "You took a man out there with you, a stranger. Who is he?"

"His name is Bleeker Twist."

"That doesn't tell me much. What's his business?"

"He told me he wanted a quiet place to study. I had no reason to doubt him."

"It takes a schoolteacher to believe anything someone says. Is he an organizer?"

"I shouldn't think so."

"Oh, you shouldn't, eh? Well, that's something I'll have to find out for myself. How'd he happen to know about that empty cabin?"

"I told him myself," said Edward stubbornly.

"Uh huh." Jones eyed Edward critically. "If it were anyone else, I'd know something was up. With you I'm not so sure." He used the cuspidor beside his chair and pushed himself to his feet. "Now there's one other thing and I'll have to speak to you as man to man. This is a decent community. I'll have to hand it to Foxx for keeping a tight lid on things, but I know men and I don't have any illusions. There's no reason why a schoolteacher shouldn't be like anyone else where women are concerned. But when you want something like that, Spence, go out of town to get it. Go up to Eureka or take a run down to San Francisco. That's what I do."

Edward felt himself growing hot. "And just what do you mean by that?"

Jones waved a heavy arm. "Don't act so damned righteous. I told you you were seen last night. The girl's a pretty thing and probably easy to have, but you're not going to play around with her and go on teaching school in Jonesville."

Edward stood up. "Did Foxx mention that today, too?"

Jones grinned complacently. "You know Manley about as well as I do. He's got a way of saying things without coming right out and naming names. When he talks about evil, people know what he means. Now take it easy, son. You aren't the first. I had a little trouble with Venderstone, too, but he came around all right. This is all for your own good."

"I think you're going a little too far!"

Jones snorted impatiently. "Use your head. There isn't a small town in the country that would tolerate that sort of thing in a schoolteacher. Maybe you could get away with it in a big city, but not in a place like this."

"But I tell you you're wrong!"

"Wrong?" Jones came over and tapped Edward on the chest with a thick finger. "When a man and woman are alone in the woods, there's only one thing to think. I don't care what really happens. It's the idea of the thing that matters. A man in your position ought to know that without being told. All you have to do is stick to your schoolteaching and go to church regularly. That way you can go right on enjoying life in Jonesville. But keep away from the Kildonans, see? And keep away from that stranger as long as he's in the Bull Woods."

Edward put on his hat. He was suddenly calm with the realization that he didn't care whether he won the argument or not. Indeed, he had intended from the beginning to lose the argument.

"I'm going to do exactly as I please, Mr. Jones. I haven't enjoyed life in Jonesville very much anyway."

"Now don't be an idiot. You've done a good job at the school."

"On the contrary, I've done a very poor job. When I came here, I had plans for adult-education classes, but nothing came of them. A town this size is entitled to receive a supplemental educational program from the state, but it has never been requested. My chief purpose has been to keep the people ignorant. That seems to be what you want, and it seems to be what Mr. Foxx wants. As long as ignorance prevails, you can keep your workers full of fear and superstition about the Bull Woods. I'm not going to help you any more."

Ivor Jones's eyes closed to slits. "My workers are contented and they'll stay that way! I've tried to talk sense to you, but if you plan to go about your own business, you'd better say so!"

"I've already said it."

"Then you can count on your dismissal today!"

"My contract runs until June, Mr. Jones."

"Your contract!" Jones snapped his fingers. "Go read your contract! Read the part about conduct unbecoming to a teacher of small children. You're through right now!"

"All right," said Edward. There didn't seem to be anything else to say. He walked out of the room and out the front door. He could hear Jones muttering angrily as he went down the flagstones to the street.

In his room he sat down on the bed and measured his possessions. There were clothes and books and little else. The furnishings were Ula Westerly's. He pulled a small trunk out of the closet and dusted it off. He spent a half hour methodically emptying drawers and laying his clothing in the trunk in the reverse order of its probable use. In the shed behind the house he found a couple of apple boxes and brought them up to his room for the books. He had almost finished with them when he heard Ula Westerly's footsteps coming up the stairs from inside the house. She knocked and he let her in. She carried a long white envelope in her hand which she tossed on the bed. Then she stood looking around the room.

"So you're packing?" she said.

"Yes."

"I heard about you at church this morning. I knew something was up when you left here last night with that man."

"I'd rather not talk about it."

"Doesn't hurt anything now. That's your dismissal notice I brought you."

"How do you know? Have you been reading my mail?"

"I don't need to read your mail to know that." She peered into the open trunk. "You've been here a long time."

"So I have."

"You sure you know what's yours and what's mine?"

"You can take an inventory before I go if you're worri about it."

"Oh, I'm not worried. I didn't know you were that kind of a man, Mr. Spence."

"Neither did I."

She wandered into the kitchen. "You got any idea where you're going?"

"Not right now."

"Too bad you can't stay here until you make up your mind. But, of course, I couldn't very well let you stay now."

"I'm not asking you to."

"Well, you've been good about paying your rent." She came back into the bedroom. "Is there anything I can do to help you pack?"

"No," he said, "but you can take those English papers and see that Miss Graw gets them. I haven't corrected them yet."

"I'll just take them myself. No need to bother Miss Graw."

"All right. You can throw them in the wastebasket."

"No. I said I'd take care of them myself."

He looked up at her from his box of books. "You'll take care of them?"

"Sure. How do you suppose I knew you were fired? I'm going to take your place at the school." She strolled around the room looking into empty drawers.

"Good Lord!" he muttered.

"Well, and what's wrong with that? Haven't I done substitute work?"

"Yes," he said. "We had to have someone to give the kids permission to go to the bathroom."

"Edward Spence! You'll not talk that way in front of me!"

"Not much longer, anyhow. I suppose I can leave this stuff here until I find some way to move it?"

"Yes," she said. "Just so it's gone by evening." She stood in front of him, skinny and vaguely gray. He noticed for the first time that she was not wearing her Sunday dress but had changed to a filmy gown which hardly suited the weather. Against the light from the windows he could see the contours of her thin thighs.

"I'll be out by evening," he said.

"Well, if you want me for anything, I'll be here." She hesitated. "You ought to be ashamed of yourself, Edward Spence. You could have married Stella Graw."

"That, at least, I have been spared," said Edward evenly. He picked up the English papers from the desk and gave them to her. "This is all I brought home. You'll find whatever else you need at the schoolhouse."

"I'll be downstairs if you should want me. I don't think anyone will be coming around as long as you're here." She went down the stairs, leaving the door open behind her. Edward went over and shut it softly.

CHAPTER FIVE

✤ ✤ ✤ ANDRAMALECH SAT IN THE MIDDLE OF THE CABIN FLOOR and yowled. Bleeker Twist rolled over on an elbow and looked at him from the bunk. Then he got up and ambled over to his suitcase. He tossed a packet of sandwiches on the table and took out a can of cat food which he opened and set on the floor. Andramalech stopped yowling and hunched over the can, devouring its contents with quick jerks of his head.

Twist sat on the edge of his bunk in his green pajamas and smoked a full pipe before he dressed. He put on a pair of old slacks and a sweater, got a kettle from the stove, and stepped outside.

Bits of gray sky showed high above, but little of the light seeped through to the forest floor. The huge trunks were dark pillars lining endless corridors. He found the spring and brought back water for coffee, built a fire from some wood in the woodbox, and ate his sandwiches while the water heated. After breakfast he found a stub broom and swept the cabin, then unloaded the books from his suitcase and put them on a shelf against the wall. He put pencils and paper on the table and sat down.

"Terrible as it may seem, Andramalech," he said, "I can think of no reason for not commencing work."

Andramalech looked up at him and wailed softly.

"Oh, don't take it so hard. It takes time to bring on the mood. I must read for a few hours, stew myself in ideas, get accustomed to this incredible silence. And sometime I'll have to bring in supplies. Perhaps you would like to go exploring? Or is it time for your morning nap?"

Andramalech rubbed against the chair legs and then walked over to the door where he sat down and looked back. Twist followed him and pulled the door open. As he did so, he started nervously. Two men stood outside, their backs to him, staring into the forest. At the sound of the opening door, they whirled to face him. They were tall men with weathered faces. Their dark suits were threadbare and neat.

"Ah!" said Twist, "you gave me a start. I didn't hear you knock."

"We didn't knock yet," said one of them, looking at Twist with narrowed eyes. "We just got here."

"I see. Is there something I can do for you?"

"We came to see Mr. Twist." The faces remained sternly suspicious.

"I am he. Will you come in?"

"We will," said the spokesman, striding into the cabin. He waited until Twist had closed the door before he spoke again. "I'm Aaron Goss. This is George Meadows."

"How do you do? Please sit down. I'll take the bunk here."

The men took off their hats and shuffled them uneasily. Goss finally sat down and motioned Meadows to the other chair.

"Now," said Twist.

"We're from the church," said Goss. "The church always has a committee to welcome strangers."

"Oh, I see," sighed Twist. "How considerate of you. For a moment I thought you were going to serve an eviction notice." He smiled but his smile drew no response from the two men. They sat hunched in their chairs, looking at him.

"It's what we always do with new people," said Goss finally. "Usually there's three."

"Three?"

"On the committee. One is a woman, though, and she wouldn't

come to the Bull Woods. So we two came." He spoke slowly with the cords of his throat weaving about in the loose collar. "We've never had to come here before."

"Well," said Twist hesitantly, "it is quite a walk."

"We don't mind the walk," said Goss in sepulchral tones. "It's the Woods. We wouldn't be here only on the Lord's business. The Reverend Foxx said it would be all right."

"I'm sure of it," replied Twist. There was a long silence. Meadows coughed and shuffled his feet. Goss ran his finger round and round the inside of his hat.

"We welcome you," he said at last.

"Thank you," said Twist. There was another long silence. "Did I understand you to say Mr. Foxx sent you?"

"He didn't need to send us. When there's a stranger, we always go." Goss took out a box of snuff and put a pinch in his mouth. He silently handed the box to his companion, and when it was returned, offered it to Twist. Twist shook his head and got out his pipe.

"But you said Mr. Foxx told you it was all right to come," said Twist. "You must have spoken to him."

Goss nodded slowly. "We asked him because of the Woods. The church folk never come to the Bull Woods."

"Oh, I see," said Twist. "And he told you you could come?"

"He did. He said no harm should come to us while we were on a church mission."

"And what harm might come if you weren't on a church mission?"

Goss and Meadows looked at each other and nodded in understanding. Then Goss leaned forward in his chair and spoke with a hoarse whisper.

"It's what we're here to tell you. You're a stranger and you've been taken in. You should not be here."

Twist's eyes sparkled with interest. He lowered his voice to match Goss's. "You'll have to tell me why not."

Again the two men looked at each other.

"It's not talked about," said Goss. "There is evil in the Woods."

"Ah, now," said Twist. "I must tell you that I heard something about it, but I thought it was superstition."

"That's the schoolteacher telling you." It was Meadows speaking for the first time with a high nervous cackle.

"It's not superstition," said Goss. "It's the living truth. The Woods is full of the evil of the Beast. Everyone in Jonesville will tell you that." He looked at Twist intently.

"Well, well," said Twist.

Goss spoke confidentially. "If you came here not knowing, no harm's done so long as you leave. Did you come here not knowing?" The two men waited breathlessly for Twist's reply.

"Well, as I said, I had heard something of the Woods. I didn't know the story was taken seriously."

"It's serious," said Meadows.

Goss thumped the table with his finger. "We can't tell you more because we don't know ourselves. There are things here." He waved his arm in a slow circle indicating the surrounding forest outside. "Now you know about it, you must go."

Twist puffed on his pipe a moment while he looked at his visitors. He uncrossed his legs and crossed them in reverse position.

"You puzzle me," he said. "Has anyone ever been harmed in the Woods?"

"There was the missionary," whispered Goss.

"I know, but that was a long time ago. I understand he was gored by a bull."

"The bull still lives," said Goss, glancing apprehensively toward the window.

"But has anyone been harmed recently?"

The two men slowly shook their heads in unison. "They haven't been harmed because they've stayed away. Nobody comes here except the ones who are already evil. That's why you must go." Goss dropped his voice still lower. "If you don't, we'll know it's because you belong here." He swallowed hard.

"Oh," said Twist. "Did Mr. Foxx tell you that?"

"It's the Reverend Foxx," said Goss.

"Well, all right, the Reverend Foxx. Did he tell you that?"

"He don't need to tell us. Some things everybody knows."

Twist scratched his head and got up. He paced slowly across the floor. "Now look, Mr. Goss, I'm a stranger. I don't want you to think I don't believe you, but it seems you should be just a little clearer. What is supposed to be in the Bull Woods?"

"There's a tree," Goss's voice was frightened, "where the evil thing rubs its horns."

"Has it ever been seen?"

"Certainly it has. Those have seen it that came close to the Woods of dark nights. There it was with its red nostrils and its shining horns glittering in the shade!"

"Have you seen it yourself?"

"God save me, no! I pray I never see it."

"Well, well," said Twist. "What do you men propose I do?"

"We told you already. Get away from here. Come to the church. You'll be welcome there."

"Hmm, I'll think about it."

"Not too long," said Goss. "Not for another night or we know you belong here."

"But suppose I should stay and find out what it is that troubles you?"

The two men looked at him, horrified. "There's nothing you could do. The schoolteacher came here last night and look what's happened to him."

Twist looked at Goss sharply. "You mean Mr. Spence?"

"That's his name, all right."

"What's happened to Mr. Spence?"

"He'll be leaving town, that's what. He can't teach school here no more."

"Oh," said Twist slowly. "I'm glad you told me that."

"So you see what happens when one comes knowing." Goss spoke darkly with lowered eyes.

"Yes, I do see," murmured Twist. "I see quite clearly. Did you men have anything else you wanted to tell me?"

"That's all," said Goss. "We want to bid you welcome to the church." He got up and clapped his hat on his head. Meadows imitated him. They stood hesitantly by the table, looking at Twist, and, while they hesitated, something scratched at the door. Both men jumped and stared at the door wide-eyed.

"What's that?" cackled Meadows.

"It is probably Andramalech," said Twist.

"Andramalech!" Goss's face paled.

"My cat," said Twist. He walked over to the door and opened it. The cat slid in and walked around the room at the base of the wall until he came to the bunk. He leaped onto it and began licking his paws.

"A cat," sighed Goss. "Come on, Meadows. For your own sake, you'll take the warning, Mr. Twist?"

"I shall give the matter my best thought. Good day to you." With their faces still set, the two men strode away with quiet dignity. Twist closed the door and paced rapidly up and down the room for a moment. He stopped at the bunk and looked down at his cat.

"How odd," he said to the purring animal, "that two millworkers, obviously poor and uneducated, should jump at the mention of your name. It does not occur in the Bible. It does occur, however, in one of the great English poems—a work of which Satan is the undisputed hero in spite of Milton's best efforts to prevent it. The pastor, at least, seems to know his demonology." He looked down at the cat and smiled. "Let us have a look at this beast!"

He took his jacket from a hook on the wall and went outside. Andramalech trotted at his heels like a dog. He went down the path by the spring and continued on into the forest, peering among the trees for an opening. The path grew fainter as he progressed and finally petered out altogether. He walked on, following a great circle through the trees. He paused frequently to listen but heard only the murmur of the treetops, so distant that they seemed alien to the great trunks which supported them. He gradually narrowed the circle until he had reversed his direction. Then he stopped and stared.

Not far ahead something pale and sinuous rose from the forest floor. He strode on until he came to the edge of a small clearing. In its center was a tree dwarfed to almost human size by the mass of the dark redwoods around it. The satin-smooth bark glowed pink from the light pouring through the opening high above, and the small green leaves were bright against the sullen background. It was a naked dancer alone in the forest, a wood nymph, a satyr with bare arms thrown upward.

Twist walked across the clearing. Close at hand the tree was larger than it had at first seemed. His arms could not quite embrace its trunk. Near the base the thin outer bark fluttered like shreds of discarded garments, but above it the undercoat was a sheath of silken skin. Twist stepped around the tree slowly, then bent close to examine the texture of the bark. At a little less than waist height were faint welts running horizontally around the trunk. He could feel the roughness with his fingers. Closer scrutiny disclosed other welts, some of them running almost completely around the tree. Most of them were about three feet from the ground but a few were higher, and some were almost at the roots. He backed off a few paces and looked at the tree with half-closed eyes. A sharp horn could have made those welts.

"But," he said to Andramalech, "would a beast walk completely around the tree, scraping the tip of its horn against the bark?"

The cat looked at the tree and yowled.

"I think not," said Twist. "And if not all, not any." As if in answer, Andramalech reared up on his hind legs and sank his claws into the bark, pulling them down to leave long scratches. Twist lifted him to his shoulder.

"Please do not create more mystery where we have one already. We have discovered that there really is a tree and that it has strange marks on it. Let us leave it at that for the moment." And with the cat on his shoulder, he headed back for the cabin.

CHAPTER SIX

❦ ❦ ❦ TWICE DURING THE AFTERNOON EDWARD WALKED ACROSS
Jonesville to a battered shack on its outskirts, and on both occasions he found the shack empty. The third try was made after
darkness had fallen and this time a light glowed in the window.
He crossed a yard littered with piles of collected junk and
rapped at the door.

The man who opened it was as disheveled as his surroundings.
The thin brown hair hung straight down around a pallid face.
Two black eyes glittered with an unnatural light, and the loose
mouth displayed a jagged line of yellow teeth. His faded denim
trousers and jacket looked quilted from the number of patches.
He stood with a half-eaten loaf of bread in his hand, staring at
Edward.

"Good evening, Floyd," said Edward gently.

"Evening," replied Floyd Hooks. He put the bread to his
mouth and tore off a section.

"Would you care to earn a couple of dollars?"

The dark eyes sparkled. "Dollars?"

"That's right. I need someone to haul a trunk and a few boxes
for me. Can you do it with your wagon?"

Hooks masticated the bread and swallowed it. "When?"

"Right now, if you can come."

Hooks took another bite out of the bread and chewed in
silence, watching Edward suspiciously. He swallowed again.
"Where you going?"

"I want you to haul them to Oban Kildonan's cabin. Can you do it?"

Hooks looked vaguely frightened and pushed the lank hair back from his eyes.

"I'll go with you," Edward added. He pulled a wallet from his pocket and took out two $1 bills. Hooks eyed the money greedily and reached out a gnarled hand. Edward let him take it. Hooks stepped back inside the shack and closed the door, leaving Edward on the outside. Edward heard the sound of a board being lifted from the floor and then a sound of change rattling in a tin can. When Floyd appeared again, he had a dark hat pulled over his eyes. The loaf of bread was bulging from a jacket pocket.

"You wait," he said and disappeared behind the shack.

About ten minutes later Edward heard the squeak of wheels and then the horse and wagon pulled up from around the side of Hooks's house. Edward climbed up to the seat beside Floyd and they started back across town to Miss Westerly's.

A light was on in the lower part of the house, but Edward used the outside stairway to bring down his trunk and boxes. After they were stowed in the wagon, he went back alone to make a last check of his room. He had gone through the drawers of the dresser and was turning away from the closet door when he realized he was no longer alone. Stella Graw was standing just inside the landing. Her abrupt appearance startled him, but one glance assured him that it was not her intention to do so. She was pale and visibly agitated but seemed unable to speak. It was as though the effort of will which had brought her to his door had cost her so much resolution that none remained with which to state the reason for her visit. She was buttoned up in a white raincoat which her gloved hand clutched together at the throat. A few wisps of hair strayed from beneath her felt hat, softening her usual orderly correctness. Edward closed the closet door.

"Hello," he said. She failed to return his greeting. "I suppose you've come about the school work. I've turned everything I had over to Miss Westerly." Stella spoke with effort.

"It isn't the school work." She was blocking the exit. He didn't know whether this was by accident or design, but in either case conventional courtesy would have prevented him from walking away from her.

"Is there something else then?"

"You're going away," she said.

He gestured toward the shelves and desk which no longer held any of his personal belongings. "As you see."

"I heard about it in church," she said.

"Apparently everyone heard about it in church," he replied impatiently. "I'd just as soon forget it."

"Yes," she said. "I've been playing the organ and I got to thinking. I heard you were leaving." She paused, looking at him round-eyed. "You're going right away?"

"I'm leaving here right away."

"But Jonesville? You're leaving Jonesville?"

"Is there anything to stay for?"

"I don't know," she said. "I guess not." She still stood in the entrance, increasingly nervous. She cast a glance down the stairway behind her as though she wanted to leave but didn't know how to bring about her departure. "I shouldn't be here," she said.

"I doubt that your telling me good-by will be considered such a transgression," he said bitterly.

"I wasn't thinking of what other people might say," she said.

He stood in the center of the room, shifting restlessly. Hooks was waiting outside with the wagon, and Edward wanted to be on his way.

"Well, if there's anything you want to know . . ."

"I was just thinking about being here."

"Yes?"

"You were in the Bull Woods last night."

"That seems to be general information."

"Mars Venderstone was back at church this morning."

"I understand that too." The two things seemed to go together. Mars was back at church; Edward was in the Bull Woods. Sort of a cause-and-effect relationship.

"You saw that girl." Her voice was a whisper.

"Look," he said as calmly as he could. "I don't want to talk about it. It's my business. And I'll be leaving town anyhow, so it doesn't matter." She stepped toward him.

"But you didn't have to do it, Mr. Spence. You didn't have to!" She stopped a few feet from him. Did she know about those incredibly stupid words he'd cried out to Ailsa. Did the whole town know? He flushed with anger and embarrassment.

"I've got to go now," he said.

"But if you're leaving town . . . if I don't see you again . . ."

"Yes?" he said sharply.

"What would it matter now if . . ."

"If what?"

She stared at him a moment, breathing deeply, then backed away to the landing of the outside stairway. "It's nothing," she said quietly.

He followed as she started down the stairs. "I don't understand you."

"I know," she said. "It's nothing."

Nothing, he thought. That word had sounded in his ears on another occasion very recently. It was as though she were mocking him. She didn't wait at the foot of the stairs but walked rapidly away in the darkness. For a short distance the glow of her raincoat marked her departure. He watched until she was gone, and then hurried out to the street and climbed to the wagon seat beside Hooks.

Hooks drove back to the highway and let his horse plod slowly through town. People walking to the motion-picture house watched them curiously as they passed. Edward looked straight ahead and said nothing until they'd left the town behind them. Inwardly he was seething, but at the same time he felt definite relief now that the first step was almost accomplished. He looked at the driver.

"I understand you saw me last night, Floyd?"

Hooks darted a glance at him. "In the Bull Woods," he said.

"That's all right," said Edward. "Then did you tell someone?"

Floyd nodded. "Tell Mr. Jones. He give me a dollar."

"I see. Do you go to the Bull Woods often?"

"Sometimes for wood," said Hooks, shaking the reins over his horse.

"You aren't afraid?"

Hooks chuckled shrewdly. "Nothing hurt Floyd." He peered at Edward from under his hat brim. "You afraid?"

"No," said Edward.

The horse plodded slowly on until they came to the Kildonan road. After they turned, the horse's hoofs made no sound, and there was only the irregular squeak of the wheels to accompany them. The sound seemed disproportionately loud in the silence of the trees. Edward held his breath as the Kildonan house hove into view, but no one appeared in the doorway to watch them pass. Hooks drove as far as the road permitted and pulled the horse to a stop. They climbed down from the seat and unloaded the trunk and boxes.

"You want help?" asked Floyd.

Edward thought a moment. He had had no way of telling Twist that he was descending upon him and was simply relying upon a return of hospitality as a guarantee of welcome. He felt sure, however, that Twist would not resent his staying a few days until he had decided where he wanted to go.

"We'll take the trunk," he said.

They lifted it between them and started along the path. Edward had brought his flashlight tonight and they made good time until they had covered half the distance. Then quite suddenly Floyd came to a halt, jerking Edward to a standstill as well. Edward looked back at him.

Hooks was standing with his hand raised for silence. His

mouth gaped open and his eyes glittered as he listened. Softly he set his end of the trunk on the path and walked several steps into the trees. Edward came up beside him.

"What is it, Floyd?"

Hooks raised an arm and pointed. Edward turned his beam in the direction indicated but could see only the receding columns of the redwoods.

"What is it?" he repeated.

"The white thing!" whispered Floyd. "The white thing!"

"What do you mean?" asked Edward crossly, an uncomfortable chill running down his spine in spite of himself.

Hooks looked at him with gleaming eyes. Then without a word he turned and ran back along the path into the darkness. Edward followed a few paces with the beam of light searching the path, but the dowser had disappeared. He waited for several minutes and then heard the squeak of the wagon wheels. Edward cursed softly and swung the beam of his torch in a circle around him. It revealed nothing but the trees. He bent down and lifted one end of his trunk. It was not too much for one man to carry a short distance. He wedged the flashlight under one arm and hoisted the trunk onto his back, then plodded on down the path toward the cabin. He kept expecting to see the light from the windows through the trees, but none came. When he finally arrived, the cabin was dark. He set the trunk down before the door and knocked, thinking Twist might have retired early. There was no answer.

He was unwilling to enter during Twist's absence, so he decided to make another trip for one of the boxes on the chance that Twist might return in the meantime. He went back along the path at a swift walk. The boxes were where he and Hooks had left them, but all signs of Hooks and the wagon had disappeared. He picked up one of the apple boxes and started back. It was lighter than the trunk but awkward to carry, and he stopped midway to rest. He sat on the box, listening intently to the silence around him. That was when he heard the laugh.

It was so faint and far away that for a moment he was uncertain. He held his breath, his mouth open. It came again, a low, mirthless chuckle. Then as he rose to his feet, he heard a wild yell of terror. It was far away too, but the sound carried clearly —a man's voice crying out in deep-throated agony. It came twice more, and then there was utter silence.

For a few seconds Edward stood rigid. Then he started running toward the cabin. The sounds had come from that direction. The cabin was still dark when he burst into the clearing, but his trunk was no longer at the door where he had left it. He pounded on the door and, getting no response, threw it open. The shining eyes of Andramalech glared at him from the bunk, but there was no sign of Twist. His trunk was sitting in the middle of the room.

He turned back to the forest and ran on down the path by the spring, stopping to peer through the timber. A light shone dimly in the distance. He could catch its faint reflection on the towering trunks. He plunged into the forest, running silently on the thick humus. After a few moments he paused and switched off his torch, hoping to catch a second glimpse of the fugitive light ahead. There was only darkness now.

"Ho!" he shouted. "Ho, there!"

"Ho!" The answer came from somewhere behind him. He dropped down at the base of a tree and waited. A light was coming, a lantern, judging from the way the shadows swayed back and forth. He watched until it came into view and then turned the beam of his torch on the person carrying it. It was Oban Kildonan. He stood up and called out again. The burly figure walked toward him, holding the lantern high until he saw who it was.

"Aye," he said angrily, "so 'tis you yelling your head off in the forest. What ails you?"

Edward shook his head. "Not me. Something out there. I'm looking for it too."

Kildonan stared at him a moment, started to speak, then

looked thoughtfully in the direction of Edward's beam. "We'll see," he muttered and started on.

They had gone another fifty yards when the light of the electric torch caught something pale ahead of them. Edward stopped short and played the beam slowly back and forth.

"That's only the madrone tree that grows there," whispered Kildonan. "Come ahead." They moved forward again, when another voice cut the silence.

"Ahoy, there!" It was close at hand. As they turned in the direction of the sound, a match flared in the darkness. Bleeker Twist was lighting a darkened lantern. He squatted at the base of a tree, staring into their lights before he got up and came forward. The three men stared at each other silently. Then Twist turned again to the forest.

"If it was not one of us, then something is still to be accounted for." The three of them walked on toward the madrone tree. They came to the edge of the clearing and stopped. They could see it plainly now. A man lay face down on the dark earth at the base of the tree, his arms and legs sprawled wildly. His hat lay near him.

The three men approached silently until they stood over the prostrate figure. Twist dropped to one knee, setting his lantern beside him, and put a hand on the man's shoulder. There was no response to his touch. He ran his fingers under the chest and then with the other hand gently touched the back of the man's head. When he drew his fingers away, they were dark with blood.

"He's dead," he whispered. "Not long dead. The body is still warm." He put his hand on the shoulder again and rolled the body over to see the face.

"It is familiar," he said. "Do you know him?"

"Yes," said Edward and Kildonan in unison. Then Oban added, "It is Mars Venderstone. I shall need a new setter for the head rig when the mill opens again."

Twist rose slowly to his feet and held the lantern high to look about the clearing. The deep layer of humus showed no sign of footprints except where Venderstone's boots had plowed into it during his death struggles. Except for the hat, the clearing was empty. He looked at the madrone tree and exclaimed sharply, stepping forward to examine it. There were fresh marks on the tree. The pink bark had been cut and bruised. Faint beads of sap glittered in the light. The three men looked at each other uncomfortably.

"This is not an affair for us," said Twist. "Is there an officer in Jonesville?"

"There is a constable," muttered Kildonan, "but I do not want him here. Venderstone is dead on my land."

"We have to notify someone."

"The sheriff is in Ludlow not twenty miles away. Banders is his name. This would be for him to see."

"Can you reach him?"

"By telephone. I will have to drive into town."

"Then I suggest that be done," said Twist. "Mr. Spence and I had better wait here until you return. You can meet the sheriff and show him the way."

Oban nodded slowly, looking down at the body. "I'll do it. Mind you that nothing is disturbed. I'll not have it said this is the work of evil spirits." He paused. "He was a good lad and strong as a bull, and why he was here, I don't know."

Oban turned his back on Edward and Twist and stolidly strode away into the forest.

CHAPTER SEVEN

✿ ✿ ✿ AFTER THEY WERE ALONE, EDWARD AND BLEEKER TWIST withdrew to the edge of the clearing and found seats on a gnarled redwood bole. They couldn't see the body except as a shadow on the ground. Twist set his lantern down a few feet distant and pulled out his pipe. Neither spoke for a long while. Occasionally they glanced at each other questioningly when some sound in the forest didn't yield to ready explanation. These were few, and since they weren't repeated, it was safe to assign them to ordinary causes.

"We often believe things subconsciously even while we deny them verbally," Twist said finally. He spoke softly, and since his statement was in reference to nothing said previously, it appeared to be addressed to no one but himself.

"What do you mean?" asked Edward.

"Just a trivial idea I was playing with. That lantern there," Twist cocked his pipestem at it, "gives us a sense of security. We feel safer while it burns than we would in darkness. And yet, just the opposite must be true. If there is a dangerous man in the locality, the lantern shows him where we are. If he should attack, he would have the advantage because his eyes would be accustomed to the darkness while ours would have to overcome the effect of staring into the flame there."

"We could blow it out," suggested Edward.

"By no means. Then we would sit here shuddering. If there

is anything in the inheritance of ancestral habits, we might surmise from our love of the lantern that primitive man had much more to fear from beasts than from other men. A campfire or a blazing torch was probably the best defense early man had against a cave bear. Against other men the defense wouldn't have worked so well."

"A possible explanation," said Edward.

"I was thinking of the other explanation, however."

"Which other?"

"I didn't mean to labor the point so. I was simply wondering if it isn't still a beast we fear." He chuckled. "That's what I meant when I said we often subconsciously believe what we consciously deny. We haven't talked about it, and yet I'm sure we would both take the viewpoint that some human agency is concerned with Venderstone's death. That's what we would say we believed. However, we sit here with the lantern burning. Why? To ward off a beast, of course." He again laughed softly, as though in appreciation of the point he'd made. They continued on in silence a few minutes, with Twist puffing on his pipe while Edward mentally recounted the events of the evening—the queer behavior of Hooks, the shouts of terror, the laugh.

"Did you hear the laughter?" he asked.

"Laughter? When was that?"

"I mean earlier, before Venderstone shouted. I suppose it must have been Venderstone doing the shouting."

"No. I heard no laughter."

"Where were you, by the way? You weren't at your cabin when I first got there."

"I'd been to town. I found your trunk in front of the door when I got back. It had your name on it, so I knew it was yours. Just as I set it down inside the cabin, I heard the shouts, and knowing you were in the neighborhood, I was afraid you were the person in trouble, so I started out on a run."

"Odd we didn't meet on the path. You didn't see Floyd Hooks by any chance?"

Twist shook his head. "I don't know Floyd Hooks and I didn't see anyone. I came directly through the woods. Went to town the same way. There seems to be a faint trail which comes out of the woods in the neighborhood of that immense church. It's much shorter than going around by the highway."

"I suppose so," said Edward. He knew the trail Twist meant. He had followed it a few times himself. He wondered if his own footsteps might have been sufficient to make it, or were there others? "You were in town after supplies?"

"That was part of my purpose. I also went to find you."

"Find me?"

"I heard that you'd lost your job at the school, and I thought you might lose your room also. I intended to offer my upper bunk in case you wanted it."

"So even out here in the woods it was known I'd been fired."

"Yes," said Twist.

"And what did Miss Westerly have to say when you called for me?"

"I didn't see Miss Westerly. She wasn't home I went up your stairway and peeked into your room through the window. Your books were gone, so I surmised you'd gone also. I hoped you might be on your way out here, so I hurried back with my bag of groceries. That's about it. I found your trunk and then heard the poor fellow yonder." He struck another match to his pipe.

Oban Kildonan finally returned with William Banders, the sheriff, and his two deputies. The officers spent a long time going over the ground immediately surrounding the body. One of them took flash pictures. Banders finally approached Edward and Twist. He hid his uneasiness rather poorly behind a brusque manner of speech while he carefully catalogued the replies to his questions in a notebook. When he'd finished, he shoved the notebook in his pocket and became more informal. He kicked at a root with a booted leg.

"This is going to raise hell," he said. "I live in Ludlow, but I hear some of the stories that come out of Jonesville. Queer stuff about these woods. I don't suppose you men take any stock in them?"

"Well," said Twist, "I haven't so far."

Banders laughed shortly. "But after tonight you don't know— is that it? Don't know as I blame you. That tree there—" He paused to look across the clearing to where his deputies were still at work. Both of them had gasoline lanterns which threw a clear white light over the scene. "That tree there, those marks on it. According to the story some wild bull rubs his horns on it. Wild bull is right. What I'm wondering, though, is whether there might be a wildcat or a mountain lion that's wandered down from the hills. There's some marks on that tree that I'd swear are claw marks."

"There certainly are," said Twist solemnly. "My cat made them."

"Your cat?"

"Andramalech's his name. We were here this afternoon. You see, I heard about the tree too. Something very queer about that tree. But the claw marks belong to my cat. You'll see when you measure them."

"And what about those other marks?"

"That I can't say except for one thing. The marks I saw earlier were old ones. Those on the tree tonight are fresh."

Banders rubbed his chin thoughtfully, then took his notebook out and penciled in the additional information. "My experts out there will probably have more to say about it when they're through. Stuff like this is out of my line. If you men want to go, you might as well. There'll be an inquest in Jonesville tomorrow, and you'll be expected to be there." He swept a stern glance across their faces to make certain they understood. No objection was raised, and so he turned on heel and joined his deputies. Oban Kildonan picked up his own lantern and nodded to Twist and Edward.

"I'll see you tomorrow," he said, and departed without waiting for a reply.

"And we had better go too," said Twist. "I understand you are not completely moved yet."

"No. I still have some boxes up the path."

They found the rest of Edward's belongings where he had left them and carried them to the cabin. Then they sat down and looked at each other. Twist thoughtfully stroked his nose.

"Well, Edward, unless something turns up, you seem to be in the soup."

Edward looked at him in alarm. "What do you mean?"

Twist chortled. "At the moment you are an excellent suspect. Banders is not a local man and will not be swayed by legends. He will look for a human killer. He will remark the fact that in spite of the stories of evil, no harm ever came to anyone in these woods until the day you were dismissed from your position and came yourself to live in the Bull Woods. From the trend of his questions, I gathered that you cannot establish any proof of your whereabouts at the time of the murder."

"Nonsense!" said Edward angrily. "He may also remark the fact that no harm ever came to anyone until you moved into the Bull Woods. And since you were not in your cabin when I first got here, it seems you can't establish proof of your whereabouts either."

Twist laughed appreciatively. "Very good. It is fortunate that there are two suspects—perhaps a third in Oban Kildonan. But the fact remains that I had no motive, whereas you did."

"Motive? What motive?"

"Ah, Edward, the most powerful motive in the world. Jealousy!"

"That isn't true!" said Edward, rising to his feet.

Twist remained complacent. "Are you trying to tell me you were not relieved at finding Mars Venderstone dead?"

"I most certainly am!" cried Edward.

"Don't be ridiculous. Probe yourself with the lance of objectivity and see what you really feel. That you are horrified at the

 83

manner of his death, I'll not deny. But that is far different from being displeased that he is dead."

"If that's what you think, I'll not stay here another minute!" Edward strode across the floor in the direction of his trunk.

Twist took out a pipe. "I'd advise you against any more hikes through the woods this evening. From the abrupt manner in which Sheriff Banders departed, I gather that he intends leaving one or both of his deputies near the scene of the crime all night. It is possible that the killer may return to destroy evidence. That is certainly what they would think you were doing."

Edward sat down on his trunk and looked at his host. "Do you think I killed him?"

Twist chuckled again. "I am quite certain that you did not, but, unfortunately, I do not represent the law." He arose and sat on the table facing Edward. "I'm serious about this business of motivation. Before my arrival in Jonesville last night, I met Mars Venderstone and Ailsa Kildonan in a parked car near the Kildonan road. You failed to notice that Ailsa and I had met before. Did she not greet me by remarking that I was the man with the cat? Most men in your place would have been immediately curious as to how I, a stranger, had met her. And yet you didn't even ask for a very simple explanation." He tapped his head. "Failure to act in a normal manner means something. It meant, Edward, that you were under such emotional strain at the time that you paid no attention to the words being spoken. You came with me last night for more than an opportunity to see a pretty girl. There is a deep attachment there."

"That's untrue," protested Edward. "I haven't spoken to her more than a dozen times in my life."

"That does not preclude an attachment." Twist rose and walked the room uneasily. "I feel miserably guilty. It was my doing that brought you here. You had told me the Kildonans were outcasts from the social life of Jonesville, but I failed to evaluate the situation. There are outcasts in every community, so I took it with a grain of salt. I had no idea that the consequences could be so disastrous." He pointed a finger at Edward. "It was because of your contact with the Kildonans last night that you lost your job, is it not so?"

"How do you know that?" demanded Edward.

"Because I was told as much this afternoon. I haven't had time to tell you of my visitors. They were emissaries from Mr. Foxx." Twist shuddered. "Edward, in this room today sat two men. They were poor—desperately poor—they were unlettered and ignorant. But they were as implacably sincere as a Jonathan Edwards. They believe with all the might of their ignorance that these woods contain a demon. And they believe that by coming here in full knowledge of the demon's presence, you have linked yourself with the powers of evil and are in for a bad end."

"A bad end? Me?"

Twist nodded. "The same applies to me now that I have been warned." He paced the floor silently a moment, then spoke in a quiet voice. "The various beliefs to which men cling do not gain their power according to whether they are true or false; they gain their power solely from the sincerity with which they are believed and acted upon. A clever person could take advantage of that."

"How do you mean?"

"I mean that in spite of what Banders may discover, many people in Jonesville will ascribe what happened tonight to the powers of evil. That is a safeguard for the killer. What I do not understand at the moment is why it was Mars Venderstone who was killed. His presence in the woods is so far unexplained." Twist looked at Edward critically. "When you left town this evening, you must have come by the highway?"

"That's right," said Edward.

"So that everyone in town had opportunity to see you leave. They also know why you were going and undoubtedly could guess where. So after you arrived in the woods, you were suddenly left alone. Now, isn't it just possible that Mars Venderstone was so unfortunate as to stumble into a fate reserved for yourself?"

"Good heavens, what an idea!" Edward came to his feet.

"Merely a thought," said Twist. "On the other hand, is it possible to explain Venderstone's presence?"

"I don't know," said Edward.

"Your voice indicates doubt. What are you thinking?"

"It doesn't matter. It's absurd."

"Thoughts do not occur without a basis. Venderstone has an interest near here."

"Yes."

"And what would that be?"

"You want me to say Ailsa Kildonan."

"You are the one who has said it."

"But why at the madrone tree?"

"Ah, now! That is the question. What is the meaning of those marks? If we cannot believe them made by a mythical beast, we must believe them made by a human agent. I must confess, the first choice contains the least horror. What sort of mind is it that pantomimes the essence of evil while it commits murder? Can you contemplate it and sleep peacefully in the Bull Woods?"

"No," said Edward, "I cannot." And he poured water into the coffeepot and started building up the fire in the stove.

CHAPTER EIGHT

✤ ✤ ✤ THROUGH THE WINDOWS OF THE MILL OFFICE WHERE the inquest was being held, Edward could see the face and figure of Aaron Goss. Mr. Goss stood immobile throughout the morning hours, staring with drooping eyes into the mill office while water dripped slowly from his hat brim. Others came to stand beside him, then moved away again, and always in the background was the uneasy shuffling of people waiting for the decision.

Far behind them on the south edge of town where the cemetery lay, the Tree of the Dead towered upward into the mist. It was a bare trunk, all branches hewn away, dominating the tombstones and the endless expanse of stumps which lay about it. In tall rigidity it echoed the dark figure of Aaron Goss.

Inside the mill office a nervous bustle characterized the passing hours. Peasley Muse, the coroner, trotted to and fro between the outer office, where the witnesses and the body waited, and an inner office, where Edward could hear the rumbling voice of Ivor Jones and where, through the opening door, he once caught a glimpse of the lean frame of Manley Foxx. Beads of perspiration dotted Peasley Muse's forehead, although the mill office was cold. He played incessantly with his nose-pincer glasses, clamping them on to fumble among his papers and flipping them off with a quick lift of his eyebrows, catching them always at mid-waist level.

The coroner was an undertaker by profession, and his examination of the body was his most efficient activity. He kept returning to it in moments of indecision, as if to gather reassurance from the cold and shrunken features. Then back at the witnesses again, his hands clutching wrinkled papers, his glasses going on and off, repeating again and again the same series of questions.

"Was there any indication whatsoever of a light in the direction of the cries?"

"No."

"Did the cries all seem to arise from the same place?"

"They seemed to."

"Is it possible they could have come from slightly different places?"

"Possibly."

"And no light at all from the moon and stars?"

"None."

"How far apart, in space, would you say the cries were?"

"They seemed to come from the same place."

"But there could have been a slight difference?"

"Possibly."

"If the man had moved—say twenty yards between cries—you couldn't have told the difference?"

"I doubt it."

"So he could have been running?"

"He could have been."

"Is there much underbrush?"

"Hardly any."

"But roots?"

"Yes."

"And the man was running?"

"He could have been."

"And you saw no indication of a light of any kind?"

"None."

More fumbling with papers, notations with the pencil, back to the body, back to the inner office, a handkerchief wiping away the perspiration, and outside the stern face of Mr. Goss staring in and waiting.

"Have you examined the body, Dr. Brill?"

"I have."

"In your opinion, what was the cause of death?"

"Death resulted from one or more blows on the head."

"Is the skull fractured?"

"It is."

"In your opinion, could such a fracture result from a man falling and striking his head on a root or running into a tree?"

"He would have to fall with considerable force."

"But is it possible?"

"There was more than one blow on the head."

"Could they have been dealt simultaneously?"

"I do not know what you mean."

"Could he have fallen against a forked root at the base of a tree and so have struck two parts of his head at once?"

"I do not know what happened."

"I am not asking what happened. I am asking whether, in your opinion, such a thing is possible?"

"I suppose it is possible. But I understand there were no roots near the body."

"We are merely examining possibilities. A man running can continue running a short distance even though he has been struck a fatal blow, can he not?"

"If the blow does not produce death at once."

"So it is possible?"

"Yes, it is possible."

"What was the shape of the object which struck the head?"

"In my opinion, cylindrical."

"A root or a tree trunk is cylindrical, is it not?"

"Yes, but the position of the wounds—"

"Thank you, that is all."

At noon a recess was declared and witnesses were excused for lunch. Bleeker Twist and Edward walked down the wooden steps in front of the office, and the crowd parted to let them pass. Mr. Goss silently took out his snuffbox. They went to Larry's Bar where they each had a sandwich and a glass of beer. The few loiterers at the bar looked at them curiously. Edward didn't know whether the glances were caused by his connection with the death or because they found his presence in the saloon unusual. He had never been there before.

After lunch they were back at the mill office again.

As afternoon wore on, the crowd outside grew. It milled slowly and sullenly around the tall figure of Aaron Goss. Peasley Muse watched it and his agitation increased. His questions became sharper, his passages to the inner office more frequent, his meditations over the corpse longer. Papers fell from his hands to the floor.

"Is there much slash in the Bull Woods?"

"None at all. My woods have never been logged."

"Not many loose sticks around?"

"No."

"Such sticks as there are—would they be green wood?"

"They would be dead."

"Heavy?"

" 'Tis the rotten branch which falls of itself."

"You mean they would be light in weight?"

"Aye."

"You were at your house when you heard the cries?"

"At the woodpile getting a log for the fire."

"Your wife and daughter were in the house?"

"They were."

"They heard the cries?"

"They say not."

"And the cries seemed to come from the same place?"

"I've already said so."

"But they could have come from slightly different places?"

"I've said that, too."

"To be sure."

Banders came in and stood with his hands in his pockets. He listened quietly a few minutes before he went outside and got in his car and drove away. Peasley Muse went back in the inner office and stayed a long while. When he came out again, he wore his hat and overcoat. He paused a moment by the body where he twitched his eyebrows and moved his hand to catch his glasses. He slipped through the door to the office porch and stood squinting at the crowd. Then he propped the outer door open and beckoned the crowd forward. Mr. Goss stepped slowly and deliberately up to the foot of the steps and the others moved with him.

"Verdict of the Coroner's Court," he announced, then broke into a series of dry coughs. From inside the office a clerk brought him a glass of water. He drank half of it, shook the paper out flat and began again.

"It is the duty of this court to fix the cause of death. We have carefully examined the condition of the deceased. We have carefully weighed the testimony of witnesses." His voice broke into a squeak. He reached for the water glass and drained it, then continued so rapidly that his words were barely distinguishable.

"The evidence shows that the deceased met death at approximately 9:15 P.M. on the night of February 23 in a strip of timber known as the Bull Woods. Death resulted from a blow or blows on the head of sufficient force to fracture the skull. The evidence fails to show that any other person was in the immediate vicinity of the deceased at the time of death. No weapon has been produced in evidence. The evidence does show that the deceased could have been running through the forest in an area of many trees and roots which could result in a fall." Peasley Muse swallowed and wet his lips with his tongue. "In view of these considerations, the court must issue a verdict of death by misadventure." He paused and looked at the silent crowd. Then he added: "It is not the responsibility of this court to inquire into the reason for the deceased's presence in the forest or the cause of his flight. All witnesses are excused."

The coroner flicked his glasses into his hand, shoved the paper into his pocket, and scuttled down the steps and around the side of the building to his car.

CHAPTER NINE

🌷 🌷 🌷 "YOU HAVE BEEN PACING THE FLOOR FOR AN HOUR," said Edward. "Will you rest for awhile?"

"My dear fellow," said Twist, "I have not been pacing the floor for an hour. I have stopped twice, and on both occasions you have started pacing the floor yourself. If you want to resume again, I shall yield."

"I'm trying to decide where to go."

"That is evident from the array of road maps you collected in town today. You have not decided yet, of course."

"What makes you so certain?"

"Because at the moment you don't want to go anywhere. You want to stay here. You are still chained to Jonesville by the same bonds which have held you the last eight years."

"I don't see that. I've lost my job."

"Nonsense! You are a man with no family responsibilities who obviously hasn't liked this place from the beginning. The job had nothing to do with it. It is far more likely that I shall leave myself. For the time being I am free to do so."

"Then why don't you?" said Edward crossly.

"Because a corpse has entered my life. I had immense plans for work, and now comes this distraction. As always, the laboratory is more interesting than the study." He waved at his shelf of books. "In those pages what can compare for interest with the situation at my doorstep?"

"I find your attitude ghoulish."

"Of course! That's because you are the slave of convention. It is among such as you that the greatest deviations appear." He skipped across the room to the books he had indicated and plucked a volume from the shelf. "Do you know that almost universally the bull is the symbol of sexual virility?"

"I thought the goat had that honor."

"The goat symbolizes sexual license and promiscuity, a sign of degeneracy. But the bull is the life force itself. It is undiluted male strength." Twist opened the book and flipped through the pages. "And in at least one great religion the bull was also the symbol of evil. I assure you, the choice of the bull was no accident." He found the page he was looking for and laid the open book on the table. "Are you familiar with Mithraism?"

"No, I am not."

"A very superior religion. Up to about the fourth century it had almost as many converts as Christianity. About that time the Christians gained political supremacy and had it suppressed, but it was still practiced in parts of the Balkans and northern Europe up to the seventh and eighth centuries."

"And what has that to do with Jonesville?"

"Simply that it was the Mithraic religion which used the bull as a symbol of evil. According to legend, Mithras was the arbiter between Ormuzd, the all-powerful god, and the world. He is supposed to have slain the bull, thereby permitting mankind to embark upon the road to righteousness." Twist perched on the table edge. "Mithraism was an outgrowth of Zoroastrianism, which was plagued from the beginning by the inequities of history. In ancient times it felt the pressure of Judaism. Many scholars attribute much of the Old Testament to tales borrowed from the Avesta during the Captivity. Later it was trammeled by the successors of Alexander the Great, and still later it was swept out almost completely in the East by the rise of the Mohammedans. All that remains of it now are the Parsees, who bury their dead in trees."

94

"In trees?" said Edward.

"Or in their towers of silence."

"That's odd," said Edward. "We have a Tree of the Dead in Jonesville. You may have noticed it while we were at the inquest. It stands at the entrance to the cemetery."

"You mean that great redwood trunk with no branches?"

"That's it."

"And why is it called the Tree of the Dead?"

"Because whenever a lumberman dies, his boots are fixed to the top of it. I have always looked on the ceremony as a purely local custom."

"Is it not the custom in other lumber towns?"

"Not that I have heard of."

"Well, well," said Twist. He took several more turns about the floor. "Well, well. Mr. Foxx is a Christian, I trust?"

"At any rate he bases his sermons on the Bible. In Jonesville religion is intensely localized."

"I have gathered as much from its effect on the people."

"Are you suggesting that he is preaching Mithraism?"

"Oh, dear no! Nothing of the sort. In Mithraism the bull is slain, not kept alive."

"I don't see what you're driving at."

"No? Then I shall tell you." Twist paused to load and light his pipe. "Let me tell you first that every conscious activity of every individual is expressed through symbols. Every word we speak is a symbol; every gesture is a symbol; every work of art, every philosophic concept—all are symbolic. You may ask, symbolic of what?" Twist slowly tapped his forehead. "In the depths of the mind there is a reality which most of us never know. It is this reality which expresses itself in terms the conscious mind can grasp—in symbols." He paused again and waved aside his previous statements. "So much for that. I merely give you a premise. The point I started to make was that because men are more alike than unlike, the same symbols arise spontaneously over and over throughout history. Thus with the bull. Mr. Foxx does not need to know about Mithras to set up the bull as a symbol of evil—or as a symbol of sexual virility. Nor do you have to be a Parsee to have a tree of the dead in Jonesville. Do not millions of people celebrate Christmas each year without realizing that it was originally a Mithraic holiday? Where in Christian legend can you find a reason for the Christmas tree? These symbols arise, and we accept them because they answer some deeper need. But occasionally," Twist waggled his finger imperiously, "occasionally the symbol is perverted. And that is what I find in Jonesville."

"Perverted?" said Edward. "How?"

"When the original bull roamed these woods, it was the missionary who was killed. In effect, the spirit of evil killed the man of God. That is the reverse of the normal legend."

"Unfortunately," Edward pointed out, "you are dealing with what really happened."

"Nonsense! When did legend hesitate to twist events to its own purposes? Next you will be telling me that Romulus and Remus were really suckled by a wolf. The only fact of importance in your local legend is that it has permitted the spirit of evil to live on. Indeed, it has made the bull a local deity. Even more, it permits a manifestation of the demon's presence through the horn marks on the madrone tree." Twist suddenly shot a finger in Edward's direction.

"You described that tree to me the first evening I was here."

"Yes."

"Do you recall that description?"

"Yes," said Edward, and felt his face flushing.

"Ah, I see you remember the gesture you used, the stroking movement. What was in your mind?"

"I don't think anything was," muttered Edward. "I was just thinking of the smoothness of the inner bark."

Twist snorted. "You are more a product of Jonesville than you realize. I don't think I have to interpret your gesture. You know its meaning too well."

96 🎵

"You're reading a meaning into something that has no meaning."

"Wrong! Everything has a meaning."

"And besides, none of this has anything to do with what seems to be worrying you, which is how Mars Venderstone met his death. He certainly wasn't killed by a symbol!"

"You're right about that; he wasn't killed by a symbol. But we need to know these other things in order to understand what has happened. Didn't you find the coroner's verdict remarkable?"

"I've never seen a man as nervous as Peasley Muse."

"Quite so."

"And the verdict is a farce. Misadventure! Muse overlooked the laughter entirely."

"Because you were the only witness who heard any. And what a scene the verdict conjures up in the mind! Venderstone's skull showed the effect of far more than one blow. We are asked to believe that he went charging through the trees, beating his head first against one trunk and then against another until he finally struck one with sufficient force to kill himself. No, the decision would have been the same in any case. Tell me now, what do you know about Ivor Jones?"

"I know he had me fired."

"What else?"

"He owns the town. So far as I know, he established it when he built the sawmill and has been its boss ever since. His phobia is trade-unions. I don't think he worries about anything else."

"Ah, yes. The fear of violent revolution. It is an extremely common malady which if widespread enough generally succeeds in bringing about the condition its sufferers most dread. Is there a union at the mill?"

"No. Nothing even suggestive of one. Ivor Jones is a good politician. He mingles with the men and keeps posted on their troubles. He has no interests outside of Jonesville."

"Has he ever had union troubles?"

"During the thirties, when everything was organizing. There was a strong drive throughout the whole Pacific lumber industry, but it didn't get far here. Jones led his own workers to drive the organizers out of town. I've heard there was violence of sorts, but it was pretty successfully hushed up. He likes to pretend there has never been any trouble."

"When did Manley Foxx arrive?"

"Shortly after the trouble. Before that there hadn't been any church. Anyone wanting organized religion went to Ludlow. Foxx found a fertile field. Jonesville needed a social and emotional outlet; he and his church supplied it."

"Who paid for the church?"

"Jones supplied the timber. It must have taken half a season's cut. He also supplied the labor to build it."

"A religious man?"

"I don't think so. He attends church regularly, but I think it's for the value of the example."

"What about his educational background?"

"None to speak of. He can read and write and he's developed a veneer of speech to help him in business. But he doesn't know what education means. He has Ula Westerly teaching school in my place."

"Your former landlady?" Twist smiled. "How delightful."

"It's not funny," said Edward. "She'll have the children screaming in their sleep before the week is out. She has visions. In fact, she had a vision that someone was going to die. I didn't pay much attention because I've heard about her visions so often."

"Another character I must meet again," said Twist. He struck a match to his dead pipe. "A pattern begins to emerge, a familiar pattern with a bit of new embroidery. Mr. Foxx is Ivor Jones's answer to the threat of unionization. He has given his employees religion to occupy their spare time. It has been often and successfully tried." He paused, grinning at Edward. "Now, the question is this: Does Mr. Foxx know he was brought here solely to take the millworkers' minds off their economic troubles and give them spiritual troubles instead?"

Edward shrugged. "Your guess is as good as mine."

"Why guess? What is your feeling in the matter? Is Mr. Foxx a sincere man?"

"He is fanatical in his devotion to his own ideas."

"That is the impression I gathered from Mr. Goss. And that means he places his church first and Jones second." Twist paused with his hands on his hips. "What a beautiful situation! Ivor Jones must have thought himself a very clever man all these years. Now suddenly he has murder on his hands." Twist stroked his chin thoughtfully and spoke quietly. "I see now an explanation for the coroner's agitation and for the sheriff's obvious chagrin. The death becomes a thing of political importance. If Jones permits it to be called murder, he has placed a powerful tool in the hands of Mr. Foxx. Foxx can then assign the death either to his mythical monster—if his fanaticism is great enough —or to one of the nonbelievers who lives in the Bull Woods. To the Jildonans, or to you, Edward, or to me."

"You are simply theorizing," said Edward.

"To be sure I am theorizing. I am attempting to explain the observable facts. If you can think of a better theory, I should like to hear it."

"Maybe Jones knows who the murderer is and doesn't want him taken."

Twist slowly shook his head. "Very doubtful. His motivating drive is greed for wealth and power. To shield a murderer would jeopardize his position. But his position would likewise be endangered if he permitted an innocent man to be accused of murder. It would disturb the security of his employees. So Jones must have insisted that the coroner find a natural cause for Venderstone's death. And that's what the coroner did, at great cost to his nervous system."

"And in the meanwhile, the murderer goes free."

Twist's eyes glittered. "True enough. But on the basis of evidence submitted so far, no one could be convicted anyway. Do you know, Edward," Twist contemplated his companion thoughtfully, "one thing about Jonesville strikes me above all others. That is the presence of black evil. Not the evil of dark deeds— Venderstone's death is the first overt act—but the evil of suppressed minds. When the natural channels of expression are closed, a perverted outlet will be found. We have already seen a symptom in the perversion of the legend. It will have left its mark upon the people. Ha! What is that faint flush I detect upon your face? You are not immune yourself, I see. Tell me about it."

"Nonsense," said Edward.

Twist looked at him warily. "You will contain yourself until someday you will burst."

"I contain nothing which is not highly imaginary."

"And you think for that reason it is not important?" Twist shook his head sorrowfully. "But I will not press you. When you want to tell me, you'll do so."

"Nonsense," said Edward again. It was all he could think of to say, and it reminded him of certain pupils he had had in school who sought refuge in constant and categorical denial. He got up stiffly and walked over to the window, where he stood looking out into the night. But the gesture was empty because he could see nothing beyond the pane of glass. He felt foolish and knew that Twist must be regarding his back. The knock on the door was a relief. He turned as Twist threw the door open.

Ailsa Kildonan stood on the threshold, her face pale, her breathing rapid. She looked at the men for several seconds before she stepped into the room.

"I've got to talk to someone," she said. "I killed Mars Venderstone." She spoke quietly, and there was a faint smile on her lips.

CHAPTER TEN

🌱 🌱 🌱 IVOR JONES WALKED BACK AND FORTH ACROSS THE length of his shadowy living room. He paused occasionally before the embers of a dying fire but made no move to rebuild it. He paused, too, before the window to peer out into the advancing evening. His footsteps were heavy and his shoulders sagged. He walked with his thumbs hooked in his belt and his eyes on the floor. The only light in the room was that which came from the fireplace, but he moved easily from long habit among the heavy furniture. Once he stopped to lift the cover of the redwood snuffbox and lay a pinch of snuff inside his lower lip. Then he resumed pacing, watching the receding daylight from the window and waiting for night.

It was a hard thing he had to do, and he sighed with the burden of it, but he moved toward the time of action with the same determination that had kept him master of Jonesville since the first redwood log had rolled into the millpond. He waited for the night and spat frequently at the fading embers. When it was dark, he went to the bedroom and put on an overcoat. Then he went outside and swung open the doors of his garage. They made no sound on their well oiled hinges.

He started the motor and backed the car out of the driveway, swinging it so that it faced away from town. Without headlights he drove slowly away from the house, turned on the first crossroad and turned again at the next half-mile intersection. When he reached the highway, he was well north of Jonesville with the Bull Woods towering on both sides. After swinging into the Kildonan lane, he had to use his headlights, but only briefly before he stopped the car in front of the house. Then he got out, closed the door softly, and walked across the yard.

Oban Kildonan answered the knock and stood looking at his visitor coldly.

"I came to talk to you, Oban, if you'll let me come inside and take a chair." Jones waited for his request to be granted.

Oban Kildonan stepped aside. "I never yet refused a man a place by my fireside when he came with peace in his heart. You can come in, but mind your words, for I've a sick wife and won't have raised voices."

Jones stepped inside and drew his coat from his shoulders. "I'm sorry to hear about Ellen. Is there anything I can do?"

"There is nothing. It's the damp weather that affects her the same each year. She's not a young woman anymore."

"I'd like to see her before I go," said Jones. He took a seat by the fireside and fumbled in his pocket for his snuffbox, but he had forgotten to bring it. Oban produced a round box from his pocket and handed it to his guest.

"You'll have things on your mind to forget your snoose. Take this and tell me what brings you."

Jones helped himself from Oban's supply. "I came because of the death of Mars Venderstone."

"It would take such a thing to make you set foot inside my door. You're thinking now you're without a setter for the head rig and you're wondering what can be done."

Jones brushed the remark aside. "I'm not worried about that, I can get a new setter, maybe not as good, but there are young men willing to learn. I came because I'm worried about you and your family, Oban."

Kildonan chuckled mirthlessly. "That's likely. In twenty-five years you've not so much as inquired into the state of our health.

You've taken my labor and glad to get it, but you care nothing for what takes place outside the mill."

Jones lifted a finger. "You're wrong, Oban. I know what goes on. Just because I haven't come visiting doesn't mean I haven't kept tabs on you."

Kildonan chuckled again. "Aye, you've kept tabs, all right. You'll watch to make sure no one comes near me. You've done me ill, Ivor Jones, and you cannot say otherwise tonight."

"I've done you no harm," said Jones, raising his eyebrows imperiously. "I've kept you at work when another man would have paid you your time ten years ago."

"I've earned my time and more."

"I don't say you haven't. But you can't hold it against me because I want to run my own mill the way I want it run. You would have given me to the Bolsheviks if you could."

"'Tis no more use trying to make you understand now than it ever was. You're greedy and a coward, but it's a dead subject. I'm living out my years on my own land and I'll work for you in season. There's nothing to fear from me."

Jones heaved himself to his feet. "I don't fear you, Oban, and never have. But I don't like what's happened to young Venderstone. You know I had nothing to do with that."

"I'll not say you did. But I saw you and the preacher at the inquest today fixing things to suit your business. Murder has been done and you know it."

"He could have struck his head as the coroner suggested."

Kildonan grunted his disgust. "And who suggested it to the coroner?"

"The facts," snapped Jones.

"Don't play with me, Ivor Jones. I know you."

"All right," said Jones angrily. "And what would happen if the coroner said murder?"

"There'd be some coming after me because if aught is amiss in the Bull Woods, the fault is mine. And they can come for all of me." Kildonan's face darkened. "You've let a monster roam my woods these many years, and now you're saying you do not like it."

"The monster, as you call it, is no invention of mine. I have had nothing to do with it."

"Not of your doing, but could have been of your undoing. Instead you did nothing, and now you've lost your setter."

Jones leaned forward. "I didn't come to argue with you, Oban. I came here to give you a warning."

"So now it's a warning, is it? A warning of what? Are you planning to fix me with the death of Venderstone?" The shaggy brows contracted angrily under the black hair.

"You've got to listen to me. We were friends once, a long time ago. We were the best team of fallers in the country. We trusted each other."

"And whose fault is it I no longer trust you? Don't go sentimental on me, Ivor Jones. There's no sentiment in your nature and it doesn't suit you to put it on."

"I'm not putting anything on and I'm not being sentimental! I'm going to tell you something and you're not going to believe me, but I want you to remember that I'm a man of my word. You've got to get out of here, Oban."

Oban stared at him a moment, then threw back his head and laughed. "So it's that you're coming to! You're after the Bull Woods again! You've run low on your stumpage and cannot stand to see the green timber so close to your mill. Why not offer me a price? I know the worth of my trees. You think you can frighten me out so easily?"

"I don't want your timber," said Jones testily. "I've got all the stumpage the mill can handle for the next ten years, and if I live past that time, someone else can worry about it. I want you and your family to go away, go someplace where you'll be safe."

"And well I remember in the old days you speak of, we were not against pirating a good tree when the woods were clear. What do you take me for?"

Jones shook his gray head angrily. "I knew you'd laugh at me before I came. I'd like you to know it wasn't easy coming. And I'd like to remind you that if you go, I'm going to lose my head sawyer. I won't get another like you, Oban."

"You needn't worry, for you will not lose me. This is my home and here I'll stay till the dark earth closes over me."

"It might do that sooner than you think." Jones shoved his chair closer to Kildonan's and sat down again. "I can fire you, Oban."

"And lose half your cut? You might fire me to get my trees, but you'll not fire me while I stay. And stay I will. I told you before, this is my home."

Jones started to reply hotly, then controlled himself with an effort. "You can do this, then. Go away until I send for you. This thing will pass in time."

"You'll still try anything to gain your ends, won't you, Ivor? I've no reason to trust you. You sold on us years ago to get your start, and you'd do it again."

"You're a fool as always! If you think it's my conscience bothering me, you're wrong! I gave value for what I received and that's all that's necessary."

"Then maybe you'll tell me what ails you?" rumbled Kildonan.

Jones stood up again, jamming his hands into his pockets. "Do you know how Venderstone died?"

"He died from a crushed skull. I saw it myself. What else he died of, I'll bide my time before saying."

"You can't say what thing delivered the blows."

"A two-legged thing! I'll tell you that, and you know it's the truth!"

"But you know what they'll say in town. Venderstone was back at church Sunday. He was liked. They'll say you turned against him when he came back to church."

"And how can they say that? I haven't seen Venderstone since the mill closed."

"He's been in your house."

"In my house? The man hasn't been near my house until he died in the Bull Woods!"

Jones paused, frowning. His face was puzzled. "He was away from church for two weeks until Sunday."

"And what do I care for that? Are you saying 'twas my doing?"

"You were always near him at work; you can't deny it."

"You'll have a hard time running your mill with the setter and the sawyer far apart. What are you trying to say?"

"I'm saying that people will think you put ideas in his head, and when he threw them back at you, you didn't like it. That's what they'll say!"

"You're giving me the fear of the mob, are you? Me, who went through the wild days with the Wobblies and fought my way clear a hundred times! What's in your mind, Ivor Jones? There's no mob unless you say so."

Jones paused a long time before he answered. "I'm a rough man, and if I was in the right, I wouldn't hesitate to kill. But I've never had to. Mars Venderstone died and I had nothing to do with it."

"That I can believe. You wouldn't spoil a man who made you good money."

"Forget that, can't you!" snapped Jones. "I'm trying to tell you that things have happened in Jonesville that are past my control."

Kildonan bent forward, peering at his guest. "And that is a thing I never thought I'd hear." He laughed heartily and leaned back. "Who has you by the tail, Ivor? Is it the preacher you set on me years ago?"

"No one's got me by the tail!" replied Jones irritably. "All I say is that Venderstone died in the Bull Woods and no one has been found to say how. Maybe it's the last, but maybe it's just the beginning, and you're safest out of it. That's what I came to tell you and you can do what you please about it."

"You're not worried for my safety, Ivor. I never knew you to think of anyone but yourself. Are you afraid there'll be more killing and the blame will come to roost at your own door?"

"And what if I am?" demanded Jones. "I'm not the one who's getting killed."

"But you think you know where the danger lies, and you're too cowardly to speak out."

"I'm afraid of no one, and I'll speak when I please!"

"Why don't you go to Foxx and tell him the same? Tell him 'tis time to stop feeding the people lies and time to leave Jonesville alone."

"There's no reason for it. He's interpreted this thing according to his beliefs, just as he'd be expected to do."

"You cannot see the truth for your dollars, Ivor. You're afraid of trouble if the preacher goes. Aye, and you'll have it, too. You'll pay high when God goes and leaves the people with time on their hands to think of their empty purses. And mind you now, if there's more goes wrong, I'll know where to look."

Jones glared at him balefully. "If you won't listen to me, there's nothing more I can do. I understand you've rented your cabin. At least you might tell this stranger he'd best be off."

"I'll tell him to be on his watch. Whether he chooses to go or stay, 'tis no affair of mine."

Jones sighed and picked up his overcoat. Then he put it down again. "I nearly forgot. You promised to give me a word with Ellen."

"I made no such promise, and I'll not have you worrying her with your warnings."

Jones turned on him impatiently. "I don't intend to worry her. I just want to say hello. We were all young together and you can't rub out the past."

"Nor forget it, either."

"She can't have had many visitors. It may cheer her."

Oban shrugged. "Well, so you mention nothing of this, there's no harm in it. But if you do, out you go. My limbs have not grown fat with easy living."

"I'll simply give her my regards," said Jones. "Where is she?"

"She's in the rear with Ailsa. Come this way. You might tell her you came a-purpose to see her."

"I'll tell her that," said Jones. He followed Oban through the hallway to where it ended in a set of doors. Oban opened one of these softly and stepped through with Jones behind him.

"She's asleep," he cautioned, stepping toward the bed. "Has she been asleep long, Ailsa?" There was no reply to his question. He looked around the dim room and then stepped back to the hallway. "Ailsa," he called; "Ailsa!" There was no reply.

In the bedroom Ellen Kildonan opened her eyes as Oban stepped back to the bedside.

"Where is Ailsa?" he asked her.

She raised her head slightly to look around the room. "She was here," she said weakly. "She brought me a drink of water." Then she gazed at the dark window. "What time is it?"

"It is near eight o'clock."

The eyes of the sick woman became puzzled. "I have slept a long time. 'Twas daylight when she gave me the drink. The poor thing must have grown weary sitting beside her mother and has gone for a breath of fresh air."

Oban stepped to the window and looked out into the night. Then he turned back to the bed.

"Here's a friend come to say good evening, Ellen," he said, and as Jones stepped forward, Oban softly left the room.

CHAPTER ELEVEN

❀ ❀ ❀ AILSA KILDONAN LAY ON THE BUNK WITH HER EYES closed and her dark hair tumbled about her face. In the bunk overhead the Siamese cat squatted on his haunches, peering down at the sleeping girl. Edward Spence sat at the table, slowly kneading a wad of paper in his hand and watching with frightened eyes.

At the foot of the bunk Bleeker Twist tapped a pencil against the back of his left hand, then walked over and laid it on the table. He returned to the bunk and leaned over Ailsa, taking her hand in his. He lifted it a few inches from the blankets and released it. Her hand stayed motionless where he had let it go, the fingers slightly spread. He bent the little finger down against her palm. The finger remained as he placed it. He pushed the hand back against the blanket and straightened up.

"You are asleep, Ailsa," he said softly. "Remain as you are until I speak to you again. Rest. No one will bother you." He watched her even breathing a few seconds before he walked across the room to where Edward sat.

"Are you sure you want to stay?" he asked.

"I'll stay," said Edward in a whisper. "I've seen this much and I'll see the rest."

Twist nodded, as though well satisfied. "In most states a man who hypnotizes a woman puts himself at great disadvantage with the law should any accusations be made. I appreciate a witness.

You can at least vouch for the purity of my actions." He walked back to where Ailsa lay sleeping and gently called her name.

"Can you hear me?" he asked.

There was a visible effort on the part of the girl to move her lips, but she made no sound.

"Do not be surprised," Twist said. "You are asleep, but if you try, you will find that you have no difficulty in speaking. See how easy it is. Tell me your name."

"Ailsa Kildonan." The words came effortlessly this time.

"Ah, to be sure. What a remarkable person you are to be able to answer questions while you sleep! Can you hear me quite clearly now?"

"Yes," came the low answer.

"Good, good," said Twist, as though he were coaching a reluctant pupil. "You can no doubt remember, too, in your sleep. Tell me this, Ailsa. Where are you?"

"I am in the cabin by the spring," she said.

"That's exactly right. How did you get here, Ailsa?"

"I walked by the path."

"And you came straight here?"

"Yes."

"And where were you before you came on the path?"

"I was in my father's house."

"In your father's house, to be sure. What were you doing there, Ailsa?"

"I was sitting with my mother. My mother is ill."

"Indeed? I'm sorry to hear it." Twist's tones were so conversational they made Edward's blood run cold. He had always imagined a scene of this kind played in a darkened room by a man who spoke in hollow tones and wore a goatee. The cabin was well lighted by the gasoline lantern they had brought from town, and Twist looked like any backwoodsman in his dirty breeches and checkered wool shirt. "Did you leave your mother alone?" he continued.

There was a perceptible pause before she answered. "My father is in the house."

"I see. That makes it quite all right, doesn't it? By the way, do you know who is in the room with me?"

"Yes," she said.

"Who?" he asked.

"Edward Spence," she said. Twist smiled, and to Edward's amazement the girl's lips also parted in a smile, as though they shared some joke together.

"So you know Edward Spence?"

"Yes, I know him."

"Do you know him well?"

Again there was a pause. "I don't know what you mean," she said finally.

"Hmm, well, it doesn't matter. That's rather a hard question for a girl to answer, isn't it? Now tell me this. What was it you said when you first came into this room about an hour ago?"

Ailsa stirred restlessly. "Must I?"

"Yes," replied Twist, and his voice was suddenly commanding. "You must say it again. Tell me."

There was a long pause; then very faintly she said, "I killed Mars Venderstone." Edward could not have understood her had he not known what words to listen for.

"There," said Twist, conversational again. "That wasn't hard, was it? Now tell me what happened after you told us that."

"I fell on the floor," she whispered.

"Do you mean you fainted?"

"Yes," she said. "I fainted."

"Now, Ailsa, did you really faint?"

"I fell on the floor."

"But did you really lose consciousness?"

The girl ran her tongue along her lips.

"Perhaps you just pretended to faint. Could that be? Did you just pretend to faint?"

"Yes," she said. "I pretended to faint."

111

"Very good. I see that you remember everything. Then what happened?"

"Then you and Mr. Spence carried me to the bunk and put a cold cloth on my face."

"Yes. Then what?"

Again her lips parted in a smile. "Then I pretended to wake up." Once more she and Twist smiled together, conspiratorially. Edward slowly crumpled the paper in the palm of his hand and felt drops of perspiration run down his neck behind his ears.

"It was a good joke, wasn't it?" said Twist. "And do you remember, we made you a cup of coffee?"

"Yes."

"And we talked."

"Yes."

"Do you remember what we talked about?"

"About . . ." She suddenly rolled away from him. "I'm tired," she said.

He bent down and put a hand on her shoulder. "Of course, just relax now. You are sound asleep and resting. You can't be very tired. Would you rather we talked about something else?"

"Yes," she said, slowly rolling over on her back again.

"Good, we will talk about something else. But I think you would rest easier if you told me one thing first. Where did you meet Mars Venderstone last night?"

The girl's hand lifted from the blanket and the fingers opened and closed nervously. Her head turned slowly from side to side in a negative gesture.

"You can tell me," said Twist softly. "It's as easy as the other. Where did you meet Venderstone last night?"

Edward hurled the wad of paper to the floor and stood up. "I've had all I can stand of this!" he cried.

Bleeker Twist dropped to his knees beside the bed and placed his mouth close to Ailsa's ear while he murmured words inaudible to anyone but the girl. Then he arose and turned to Edward, who stood white-faced in the center of the room.

"My friend, let me impress upon you that she is in a very suggestible state. If you have fears, you should take care not to express them aloud. They are easily transferred."

"Then wake her up," said Edward. "There's no sense to this. You can make her say whatever you want her to and it will mean nothing. You're simply suggesting to her that she met Mars Venderstone last night. You have no way of knowing that she did!"

Twist regarded him steadily. "I am sorry if this hurts you. Man is not an original creature, Edward, and you are fundamentally a very moral man. Your most wicked thought is only a deed of the moment to those who require stronger stuff than dreams for nourishment. Once more I invite you to stay or go, but if you stay, I prefer silence until I am through. I will not harm the girl."

Edward glowered at him indecisively, then sat down again, resting his head in his hands. "There is nothing I can do. I can't take her away from you."

"Exactly. I am glad you see that." He turned back to the sleeping girl. "Ailsa," he said, and his voice was gentle, "you were about to tell me where you met Mars Venderstone last night. Can you tell me now?"

Ailsa lay very still for a few seconds while Twist waited patiently. "I did not meet Mars Venderstone last night," she said at last.

"Ah, now I am sorry I asked you. You see, I thought you must have. You told me you killed him. Did you mean it when you said you killed him?"

"Yes," she whispered. "I meant it."

"Did you see him at all last night?"

"No," she said.

"Did you touch him?"

"No."

"I see what you mean now. Are you trying to say that you were the cause of his death?"

"Yes," she said. "I was the cause of his death."

"There, now. That makes a difference, does it not? Why do you think you caused his death?"

Several more seconds passed in silence. "I cannot tell you that."

"Would it embarrass you?"

"Yes."

"I don't want to do that. I will ask questions which aren't embarrassing. They won't bother you at all. When did you see Mars Venderstone last?"

"Saturday night."

"Of course. That was the evening I met you on the highway. Remember?"

"Yes," she whispered.

"So if you did anything to cause his death, you did it since then, didn't you?"

"Yes."

"Now, Ailsa, I think it would have been very difficult for you to have done such a thing. Perhaps it is your imagination. Did you quarrel?"

There was a long pause before she whispered in the affirmative.

"Why did you quarrel?"

Again the fingers twitched nervously. "I cannot say."

"Was it because Mars had called on another girl?"

"No."

"Then he must have told you something you didn't like. Did he make you angry?"

"Yes."

"I'll not ask you how. But I do want you to tell me what you said to him. You can do that easily."

"I told him to go back to church."

"Oh," said Twist. He paused for several seconds, then leaned close to her. "He did go back to church, didn't he?"

"Yes."

"Why did he go?"

Her head turned slowly away from him until it faced the wall. "Foxx," she whispered.

"Do you mean he wanted to hear Foxx's sermon?"

"No," she said, still facing the wall.

"Why, then?"

Her head turned slowly to its original position. "To watch Foxx."

Again Bleeker Twist waited. He glanced over to where Edward sat white-faced at the table, then turned back to the sleeping girl again.

"Has Mr. Foxx ever spoken to you?"

"Once."

"When was that?"

"It was years ago."

"But has he spoken to you recently?"

"No."

"Has he been near you recently?"

"No," the denials came quickly and clearly.

"But did Mars Venderstone think he had?" The question fell rapidly on her last denial.

She stiffened. "I think so." The voice was faint.

"Is that what you believe caused his death?"

Her lips suddenly shut fast. Her eyelids fluttered as though to open. Bleeker Twist bent forward.

"Do not answer if you do not wish to." He stroked the side of her throat. "You must relax. Perhaps you should rest awhile now. You are tired from talking."

She stirred uneasily. "I must go. I hear Father calling me. He will wonder where I am."

"Indeed?" said Twist. "Rest a moment while I see." He walked over to the door and opened it. Both he and Edward listened intently. Twist walked back to the bunk.

"Do you still hear it?"

"Yes, it is Father. He is coming down the path."

Twist returned to the door and stood for several seconds. Then he went back to Ailsa once more, quickly this time, and dropped to one knee beside her, laying a hand on her forehead.

"You are going to wake up," he told her. "You will awake as from a deep sleep and remember nothing of what we have said. Do you understand? You will remember nothing." The girl's head nodded. He lowered his hand to her wrist. "You are awakening, Ailsa. You are almost awake." He shook her arm gently. "Your eyes are opening. When you can see me, you will be wide awake."

Ailsa looked at him with sleepy eyes, then yawned. Twist rose to his feet. "I'm sorry to wake you, Ailsa," he said, "but your father is coming. I didn't know whether or not you'd want him to find you here."

She swung her feet to the floor. "Father? Here? I'm supposed to be home with Mother." She leaped up and took her jacket from the back of a chair. "I've been asleep a long time. It's dark out." She ran to the door and paused. "Please don't tell him I was here. I'll be back at the house before he gets there." And with a puzzled look at Edward, she stepped out the door and ran into the darkness of the forest.

Twist closed the door and swept the cabin with a glance. He patted the lower bunk back into shape and then dropped Andramalech on it. He sniffed.

"The girl wears perfume. Open the door again, Edward." Edward opened the door while Twist pushed open the windows.

"For a man with no evil intentions, you act uncommonly guilty," said Edward.

"I simply don't want my neck broken. There is a very strong relationship between Ailsa and her father."

"And anyway, how do you know Oban is coming?"

"The ears of the subconscious are very acute. Ah, that's a nice breeze. A few moments should do it." He waited by the window while the fresh air poured into the cabin. While he waited, there were footsteps outside, and Oban Kildonan presented him-

116 🐦

self in the doorway. He was breathing hard from the speed of his walk and his face wore a worried scowl.

"I am looking for Ailsa," he said without preamble.

Edward started to speak but Twist cut him short.

"Ailsa?" he said. "Ailsa? Perhaps it was she we heard pass by a few moments ago. We opened the door to see. We have been rather nervous since last night."

"And no more nervous than I," returned Kildonan, "where my own are concerned. Which way went these footsteps you speak of?"

"Toward your house it seemed. You must have passed her."

Kildonan frowned into the darkness. "She goes by the woods as often as the path. Look you, I've a guest at the house and cannot stay. If you see her, say that her father wants her at once." He hesitated, then started back up the path as rapidly as he had come.

"And so we have our farce along with our tragedy," said Twist as he closed the door. "I was afraid your honesty would overcome you for a moment, Edward."

"I don't see that your story helped her any. You implied that Ailsa had been running around alone in the forest."

"But that does not seem to be so uncommon. It was association with us that she wanted to keep from her father. Ailsa, too, has a repressive influence in her life. Come now, don't look so dour. I tell you I didn't injure the girl in any way. I didn't even complete my experiment with her, although, I must confess, I would have been a trifle disconcerted to have had Oban arrive while his daughter was still stretched out on the bed with me bending over her. I think I should have had some difficulty explaining."

Edward walked around the room moodily. "Look," he said. "I'm sorry about that outburst. You don't think it did any damage?"

"Not a bit so long as I was present. Don't let it worry you."

"I haven't had much experience with that sort of thing. It upset me."

117

"New experiences often do that. Let me recommend some reading to you so that next time you'll have a better idea as to what is going on." Bleeker Twist pulled from the shelf of books a volume entitled *Poetry of the Mind*, which he laid with considerable modesty on the table before Edward. "This is authoritative. You will note that I wrote it myself."

"Oh," said Edward, picking up the book carefully. "I didn't know you had gone into the subject so thoroughly."

"I see your years as a teacher have given you undue reverence for the printed word. You'll believe what I write whereas you'll doubt what I say." He plucked the book from Edward's hands and whirled it to the back pages. "See, no bibliography. The whole book is from my own mind based on my own experiences. I've accepted nothing as valid which I did not experience myself." He put the book back on the table, clasped his hands behind his back, and walked nimbly about the room. "I beg of you, don't start reading the book now. Save it for a dull evening. We must recapitulate what we have learned."

Edward closed the volume and looked at his companion. "I'm sure that if I stay with you much longer, you'll drive me insane. As far as I'm concerned, all we learned from Ailsa was that she was lying when she said she killed Mars Venderstone."

"Not at all," said Twist. "She believes she caused his death. And far more important, she has furnished a connection between the church and the madrone tree."

"I don't see that."

"You do not? She tells us that Venderstone returned to church to watch Mr. Foxx. Then he is found dead by the madrone tree. Perhaps I oversimplify." Twist stopped suddenly. "Edward, do something for our cause, will you?"

"What's that?"

"Oban Kildonan mentioned that he had a guest. If you move quickly, you might be able to get to the house while the guest is still there. I should like to know who calls upon the Kildonans this evening."

Edward got up slowly. "I can hardly walk up to the door and ask Oban who his guest is."

"Good heavens, man! Who said anything about walking up to the door? Peek in the window. If the guest has a car, look at the registration plate. Don't be so infernally afraid you are going to offend someone. We have a situation which must be unraveled or you and I must move out of the Bull Woods at once. Go on now. A little snooping will be good for your soul."

"I'll see what I can find out," said Edward, and getting his jacket, he stepped out into the night.

CHAPTER TWELVE

❀ ❀ ❀ THE SOFT FOREST FLOOR NOISELESSLY ABSORBED ED-
ward's footsteps as he walked along the path toward the Kildonan house with his torch stabbing into the darkness. He
walked swiftly and paused only once when he thought he heard
a sound ahead of him and stopped for fear he had overtaken
Oban Kildonan. But the sound was not repeated and he went on
until he arrived at the clearing surrounding the house. Here he
switched off his flashlight. A light was on in what he took to be
a back bedroom. He could see the corner of a dresser through
the half-drawn shade. He started circling the house to get a view
from the front.

He was halfway around when he heard the front door slam.
He stopped cautiously, watching a dark figure cross the yard at
right angles to him. Then he caught a glint of light on polished
metal as a car door opened and closed. He waited for the dash
light to go on and reveal the occupant. The dash stayed dark,
however. He heard the motor start and then the parking lights
came on as the car started moving. It swung sharply away from
him to make the turn into the lane leading to the highway. He
ran across the outer fringes of the yard, hoping to identify either
the car or the owner before it gathered speed, but he hadn't gone
fifteen yards before he realized he was too late.

He paused, exasperated, and had a vision of himself returning
to tell Bleeker Twist that he saw a car drive away but didn't

know who was in it. The sense of inadequacy the picture gave him was more than he could endure. With almost reflex action he lifted the flashlight and switched the long beam on the front seat of the car. He saw Ivor Jones's gray head whirl in the direction of the light just before he turned it off. Then Edward heard the car stop and he stood still, scarcely breathing.

"Who's there?" came Jones's voice through the darkness.

He did not answer. He thought, even while he waited, that there was no reason why he shouldn't. He could apologize and say he was on his way to town for supplies, except that Jones might offer him a ride. Or he could say he was calling on the Kildonans; that was no crime.

"That you, Oban?" came Ivor's voice again. Edward retreated silently to the seclusion of the nearest tree. He heard the car door open again and then another flashlight sent a beam in his direction. He hugged the giant trunk closely as the light played on both sides of it. Then he heard Jones grunt and climb back in his car. The full headlights came on this time and the car lurched forward with more speed than the road safely allowed. Edward traced the glow of the headlights through the trees to the highway. Then he looked at the house.

A front window was open and through it he could catch intermittent glimpses of Oban Kildonan as he strode to and fro in his living room. He could hear the rumble of the bass voice and softer accents of another, answering voice. Edward moved closer to the window. He had completed his assignment, but he was fascinated, as always, by the opportunity to observe Ailsa while remaining unseen himself.

He crossed the yard to the corner of the house and crept along the wall until his head was close to the open window, taking care not to let the direct light from the interior strike his face. Standing with wide eyes and mouth slightly open to permit silent breathing, he peered in.

Ailsa was sitting in a deep chair by the fire, slowly twisting a heavy strand of hair around and around her finger, watching her father as he walked to and fro. Edward could see Oban only when he passed the fireplace at the extremity of the room. But his eyes were for Ailsa. Even though he had seen her so recently at the cabin, he drank in her image hungrily. At the cabin Bleeker Twist had been present and had been a restraining influence even on his thoughts. Now he could stand in the darkness alone and let his mind do with her what it would. So absorbed was he that for several seconds he neglected to listen to the conversation which came clearly through the open window. When he did begin to listen, the words served only to excite further his thoughts.

"I cannot have it, Ailsa," Oban said, and his voice was gentle but firm. "You will walk no more in the woods at evening. It is wrong of you to leave your mother without telling me and wrong to go alone at such a time."

"I'll do as you say," replied Ailsa, "but I've never been harmed in the woods."

"That's good of you to promise. I want you close to me until this thing is past. I don't know what Ivor Jones had in mind this evening with his warning, but he's not a man to speak idly."

"Warning?" said Ailsa.

"Aye, he came to tell me to take my family out of here." Oban's laugh rumbled. "As if I would play up to his tricks! But he's a man to be watched. He grows angry when he does not have his own way. I know him well."

"Did he say what the danger was?"

"No, he did not say. He was afraid to say for fear I'd laugh in his face, but it has to do with the preacher. He's let the man grow too big and now doesn't know what to do with him." Oban laughed again. "Good justice it is, too. He has drawn the will from his workers and now they will follow like sheep whoever has the voice to lead them."

"But, Father," said Ailsa, "if he knows what it is, he'd have to stop it."

"You don't know the man, Ailsa. His conscience is gilded and has no feeling in it. He'd have us go to save himself worry, but he'll not throw out the preacher who keeps his workers in ignorance." Oban stalked back and forth in silence a few minutes. "I do not tell you this to give you fear. No Kildonan was ever afraid of any man. But you must keep out of the woods until we see what foolery he speaks of."

Ailsa slowly twisted the lock of hair. "There are still men at the mill who'd listen to you if they dared."

"If they dared," he said contemptuously, then shook his head. "And perhaps that's what did for Mars Venderstone, that he was close to me at work and often we talked while waiting for the logs to come in." He paused suddenly before his daughter. "And do you know what Mr. Banders said when he found me with the body?"

"How should I know? I wasn't there," answered Ailsa.

"He asked me if Mars was a friend of my daughter's. How now, Ailsa; it's not true, is it?" Oban's voice searched for a negative answer.

"No," whispered Ailsa, "it's not true."

"You never saw the man except at work?"

"Just at work," she said.

"That's as I thought," said Oban, resuming his pacing. "I could have told him so, but I wanted to hear it from you first. I told him 'twas none of his business. Sometimes I wonder. You are often gone so long in the woods."

"I like it there," said Ailsa. "It's quiet among the trees."

"You have never met anyone there?"

"Never," she said, slowly twisting her hair.

"And I wonder what manner of thing was in our woods two nights ago to leave fresh scars on the madrone tree. Some trickery, for sure. Can you think of what it might be, Ailsa?"

"No," she said. "It has happened before."

"It's no mad beast, I tell you. 'Tis something done by the preacher to put the fear into his people."

"He believes in it himself," she said.

Oban paused and stared at her. "How can you say that? You have not spoken to him?"

"No," she said quickly.

"Then how do you know what he believes?"

"What I hear at the mill. He's said it for a long time."

"Aye, he's said it. He's said many things, but I care not for that. I'll watch from now on and see what takes place. It was for that reason I gave my cabin to the stranger. Two pairs of eyes are better than one, and the stranger is not taken in by tales learned by others. How is it that the schoolteacher is there as well?"

"I don't know. I think he had no other place to go."

"Give him a clear path, Ailsa. For all his schoolteaching, he's a man like others."

"You don't want me to see men, do you, Father?" Ailsa whispered.

He stopped before her. "I did not say that."

"But you warn me of them all."

"You are a young girl with time enough for men after you finish school. You have a duty here to your sick mother."

Ailsa said nothing. Oban paused in front of her finally and reached down to take her hand.

"You find it lonely, Ailsa?"

"No," she said. "In town they don't speak to me unless it is unnoticed."

"Ah, you see? Better you stay where your worth is known than bother with those who listen to evil tales." He pulled her gently to her feet and put his massive arms around her. "How was your mother when you left her?"

"She was sleeping. I think she's much better," said Ailsa, laying her dark head against his shoulder.

"Good. She will be up when the sun comes again." He pushed the hair back from her forehead and twisted his head to look down at her. "You will not be lonely while your father is here. Go now. It is time you were in bed." He kissed her cheek and released her. She stood a moment smiling at him before she turned and left the room.

Edward drew back from the window, his heart pounding. He had heard Ailsa deny any intimacy with Mars Venderstone, and she had made no mention of knowing him beyond the point of identification. He had seen her eyes lower when her father asked if she had ever spoken to Manley Foxx.

He retreated to the trees and circled the house. Two windows were now lighted in the rear. The second one must belong to Ailsa's room, but the blinds were drawn. He stood in the darkness for what seemed a long time, watching. Finally the light went out, leaving only the one in the invalid's room. He still waited until he heard the blind in the darkened room go up and then the scrape of wood as the window was raised a few inches. His lips felt dry as he crossed the back yard to the wall beside the open window. It was dark inside, but he could hear movements of someone settling herself in bed. He could see a thin line of light beneath the door which led into the hallway.

"Ailsa!" he whispered, and knew that the sound was only a breath against his moving lips. He waited and tried again. "Ailsa!" This time he was more successful. To Edward his voice seemed so loud that for a moment he was terrified. He hugged the wall, wondering at himself and hoping suddenly that nothing would happen and that he could escape undetected. But there was a movement in the room and he held his ground. A voice sounded so close to his ear that he jumped.

"Is that you, Edward?"

"Yes," he said, completely relieved now that he was discovered.

"What is it you want?"

"I want to see you. I told you I was coming back." His face was against the opening now and he caught the faint smell of her perfume.

"I can't see you now," she said. "I've gone to bed, and Father is in the living room."

"I know about that." His hand found the bottom of the window and he shoved it upward. "You can dress. I'll wait for you in the trees."

"Are you crazy, Edward? I can't come out tonight."

"Please!" he said. "Please, Ailsa!" With a remote corner of his mind he heard his own words repeated as blatantly and loudly as though he were a mendicant begging alms on a street corner. The corner of his mind laughed loudly and stretched out an empty palm.

"Of course not," she whispered, and her voice was faintly puzzled. "Why don't you come sometime tomorrow?"

"Your father," he said.

"He won't bite you." She laughed softly. "But he will if he catches you stealing about the house at night." He saw her hand reach up to close the window.

"Ailsa, you must listen to me! I'll wait for you."

"You'd better go, Edward," she said. "I think you must have had something to drink and you aren't used to it."

"I have not!" he replied and felt anger flooding him at the accusation. "You can come if you want to. You've done it with others!"

There was a sudden choking silence as she peered out at him.

"What do you mean?" she said, and her voice was tight.

"I mean you can come. I'm as good as any." He stopped. Something had gone all wrong. He was suddenly hating her. Then he heard a broken sob and the window went down. For a moment he stood in horror, expecting to see the light from the hall flood the room as she went for her father. But seconds passed and the room remained dark. He turned at last and fled, running for the safety of the trees, running from something in himself that had showed itself in all its ugliness beneath the window. Now, indeed, he could never speak to her again, never look at her, never think of her name without seeing himself crawling through a mire of ugly intentions. The feeling swept over him that he was at last truly mad, and he welcomed the idea as a refuge. If she should tell someone! But he had seen already that she didn't tell such things. He could pose in safety awhile longer, long enough to get out of Jonesville forever.

He stumbled on through the trees until he finally remembered the flashlight in his pocket. The narrow beam ahead brought him back to reality. He had to return to Bleeker Twist and tell him who Oban's guest was. That was all. That was easy. Then tomorrow he could go away.

The cabin loomed in front of him at last. He paused a few seconds before the door to regulate his breathing before he pushed it open and stepped in. The room was just as he had left it. The cat lay sleeping on the bunk and Bleeker Twist sat at the table writing with a stub pencil. He turned his head as Edward entered the room.

"Good! You are back." He laid the pencil down and shifted his chair so that he could cross his legs. "And did you accomplish your mission?"

"Yes," said Edward, and wondered if Twist would note the shaking of his voice. "It was Ivor Jones."

Twist stared at him a minute. "Ivor Jones! Well, now, that is worth knowing. You didn't by any chance learn why he had called?"

"No," said Edward. He went over to the stove and picked up the coffeepot. It was empty.

"I thought you might have overheard some of their conversation."

"No," said Edward, and somehow he knocked over the coffeepot while trying to set it back on the stove. He picked it up and replaced it successfully this time. "I didn't have a chance. I only got there in time to catch a glimpse of him as he left." Then he went cold all over. He wanted to sit down, but the only other chair was directly across from Twist. He walked stiffly across the room and sat down next to Andramalech. He could feel Bleeker Twist's eyes following him.

"Well," said Twist, "then what?"

"What do you mean, 'then what'?" Edward stroked the cat. Twist stood up and came over to rest his elbow against the upper bunk and look down at Edward.

"My dear fellow, you obviously have something to tell me."

"I don't want to tell you anything. I found out it was Ivor Jones and that's all there is to it."

Twist shook his head slowly. "If that's all you wanted to tell me, you wouldn't have been so concise in explaining that Jones left at the moment you arrived. In that case you would have returned at least thirty minutes ago."

Edward looked up at him. "Damn you," he said. "Damn you." Then he looked at the cat again because he thought he was going to start crying.

"I see," said Twist. "It was a slip. Slips are not accidents, Edward. There's something you want to tell me. What was it? Did you see Ailsa again?"

"Leave me alone!" shouted Edward, rising angrily to his feet. "It's none of your business!" He stared frantically around the room, but the hard lines of the cabin held no sanctuary. He dropped to the bunk again beside the cat and was unable to hold back his tears any longer. He sat sobbing with his head on his knees and drew a strange comfort from Bleeker Twist's hand slapping him gently on the shoulder and Bleeker Twist's voice saying, "Well, well, we shall look into this, Edward. You are really a decent fellow no matter what you think now. I suggest a good night's sleep to prepare us for the funeral tomorrow."

CHAPTER THIRTEEN

☙ ☙ ☙ EARLY TUESDAY MORNING THE REVEREND FOXX AROSE
and dressed in black. He took particular care with his grooming
and finished off with a pair of black silk gloves. Then he went
outside and got his car from his garage. He drove the short distance to the parking area near the church, where he left the car.
He walked the rest of the way stolidly, without haste. He unlocked the great front doors and fastened them back. Then he
walked up the silent aisle and mounted to his pulpit.

From his inside pocket he drew the notes for the funeral address and fastened them with a clip to the pulpit in front of him.
Then he stood for a few minutes contemplating the dark interior
and following the lines of the great redwood columns upward
to their vaulted convergence above the nave. He descended at
last and went back to his car, leaving the church doors wide for
any early worshiper who might desire to enter.

He drove back past his house and across to the opposite side
of town, where he stopped his car in front of Ivor Jones's house.
Only the twittering sparrows broke the morning stillness as he
walked up the flagstones and tried the latch on the door. It
failed to give under his hand and so he was obliged to use the
iron knocker, which he did with a firm and rapid insistence. He
used it twice more before he heard footsteps approaching. The
small grilled window in the center of the door opened, and Ivor
Jones looked out at him sleepily.

"Good morning," said Foxx crisply. "May I come in?"

"What do you want around here this time of day?" growled Jones.

"I'd rather tell it to you than to the town," replied Foxx, his face close to the opening.

Jones reluctantly unlocked the door and opened it wide enough for Foxx to enter. "I didn't send for you."

"No, you didn't." Foxx walked on into the living room and took a seat unbidden. "I have a full day before me and felt that if I saw you at all, it must be before the funeral."

"Oh, that," said Jones. He tightened the sash of his dressing robe and got a cigar from the box on the table. He put it back without lighting it. "Mind if I make myself some coffee? I haven't eaten yet."

"I'll be brief. You can make coffee after I go."

Jones had already started for the kitchen. Now he stopped and looked back. "I'll make coffee," he growled. "You can come with me and talk while I make it if you're in that big a hurry." He plodded on out of the room. Foxx didn't follow him. He sat in his chair, drumming its arms lightly with his fingers while he waited. He heard Jones turn on the tap and adjust the gas flame. Then the old man returned to the living room.

"It will be a few minutes," he said. "What's on your mind?"

"I am thinking of Mars Venderstone," said Foxx, "and the way he died."

Jones grunted. "I should think you would. You've preached about the evil bull so long you've got a man killed by it."

"Mr. Jones!" Foxx's voice was sharp. "That is not an attitude I can tolerate."

Ivor Jones grinned and sank into a chair. "Well, what do you want?"

"Whether your mind can embrace the possibility or not, the demon has materialized," said Foxx. "It is time the matter was put to rest."

130

"You're right there. And the best way to do that is to stop talking about it. You can find some other subject."

"If you wish to cast aside the evidence of your own senses, you may do so. I am none the less bound to do my duty as I see it. And my duty bids me tell you once more that the unbelievers who live in the Bull Woods must go. The Woods themselves must come down. If you choose to use the timber for your mill, there is no harm in it, but one way or another that spot of evil must be cleansed. That is what I came to see you about."

Jones found a handkerchief in his dressing-robe pocket and blew his nose. "And how," he said, "do you propose that we persuade the—ah—unbelievers to leave?"

"The simplest way, if they refuse to leave at your request, is to discharge the two Kildonans who are in your employ."

Jones shook his head. "That's no good. Oban Kildonan is a thrifty man. He must have considerable savings. He's also of an age where he can collect a pension if he wants it. That wouldn't make him leave."

"Then buy the Bull Woods from him," said Foxx.

"He won't sell," said Jones.

"You seem very certain."

"That's my opinion," said Jones. "Oban Kildonan is a very stubborn man."

Manley Foxx stroked the side of his thin face with long fingers. "We have seen what can happen in the Bull Woods," he said. "I cannot wish for such evil to befall any man or woman— even those who have set themselves apart from our community and have mocked my teachings. I cannot wish it."

"If you'll excuse me," said Jones, "I think my coffee is done." He arose and went back to the kitchen, reappearing a minute later with a steaming cup. "Sure you won't have some, Manley?"

"Thank you, no."

Jones stood in the middle of the room and sipped at his coffee loudly. "That's better," he said, then looked sharply at Foxx. "Now let's get this straight and let's leave the bulls out of it.

131

You want the Kildonans either to conform to your standards or to get out of the vicinity. That's nothing new; you've been wanting it a long time. You want me to do something about it and that's not new either. The only new thing I can see is your hint that something unpleasant will happen to them if they stay." Jones waggled a thick finger. "Now you listen to me. Oban Kildonan is no friend of mine. If he left town, I wouldn't shed any tears. He was putting ideas into young Venderstone's head. But there's going to be no more people dying or getting hurt in the Bull Woods, see? Too many people might think I had something to do with it. I'm the only one Oban Kildonan can hurt, and I've kept him isolated. You forget it."

The Reverend Foxx looked up at the old man and smiled grimly. "If you are suggesting that I can control the evil of the Woods, you are mistaken. You are likewise mistaken when you say that you have kept Oban Kildonan isolated. He has taken unto himself the schoolteacher and Bleeker Twist, the stranger. A stranger who practices the black arts. They are a danger to my flock and must go."

Jones snorted derisively. "The black arts! What do you know about Twist?"

"I have had a report on him. He has curious books," replied Foxx coolly. "His purposes are contrary to mine and those of my church."

Jones looked at him with narrowed eyes. "So you know what's in his cabin. You've done some spying, eh? Is that it? And it was you then, last night, who showed a light on me and refused to answer when I called. That's why you come to me this morning and try to force me to take action."

Foxx returned Jones's stare for a moment. Then a dry chuckle broke from his lips. "A light?" He stood up, leaning forward so that his face was no more than a foot from the old man's. "I see now what you have done. You have already gone to Oban Kildonan. That's why you are so sure he won't go. You've no doubt told him that he is in danger and that the danger comes from the church." He laughed again, quietly and mirthlessly. "You have tried to safeguard yourself should harm befall him. You have no doubt even tried to enlist his support. You've placed yourself against me, Ivor Jones!"

"I'll place myself against you when necessary!" snapped Jones with rising anger. "You've grown too big and I'll trim you down to size if I must!"

"There was a time," continued Foxx, giving no heed to Jones's words, "when your interests ran parallel to those of the church. Because of that you assumed that I was your servant. Don't say that I have ever given strength to that belief. It is only the church I serve. If you are against it, you are against me, and I shall oppose you as mercilessly as I have opposed others!"

Jones shook his head with contempt. "You're a fanatic, Manley. Cool down a little. I built your church and I paid for it. It stands on my property. I brought you here for my personal interests and when you stop serving them, I'll kick you out again and get someone who knows where his bread is buttered. You go back and have your funeral and tell the people what gibberish you please about evil demons, but leave my affairs alone or out you go!"

Foxx smiled bleakly. "I am not a man of wrath and I do not act from spite. But do not be deceived by your sense of temporal power. The spirit of the people belongs to the church. If the church wills that the mill stay idle, it shall be that way. If Mammon is your god, you may grovel all you please."

Jones stepped back, his jaw sagging. "By God! Are you threatening me with a strike?"

The smile stayed on Foxx's face. "Your material mind would no doubt construe it as such, though I would remind you that no call is made upon your wealth. You are asked to rid Jonesville of nonbelievers and to cease supporting them any longer."

"And after that," whispered Jones hoarsely, "you think you really will have the upper hand!"

"What you call the upper hand belongs to the church already.

It is too late for you to marshal support from the enemies of the church; they would not trust you. Your only choice is to see that they go!"

The old man trembled with rage but managed to control his voice. "And how do you propose that I accomplish such a thing? I ask you that again!"

"I have suggested several peaceful methods," replied Foxx evenly. "For reasons of your own you seem to think them impracticable. Perhaps the people will help you if you ask it of them. I only want to make it clear that from now on no dissenters will be tolerated. The church is to be supreme and is to be regarded as such."

"You're absolutely mad!"

"I may differ from others in my devotion to a higher duty, but it is not madness. In my calling it can be regarded as the only true sanity. Good morning, Mr. Jones. I shall expect to see you at the funeral." Foxx turned abruptly and walked out of the room. At the front door he paused and returned a few steps. "I realize," he said, "that you still may believe your money all-powerful, and that you may contemplate calling upon outside assistance. Let me advise you that I have not been so careless as to neglect the mundane affairs of the church. Its books are in order; its debts are paid. Those members who have served on committees have acted beyond reproach. You cannot say as much for yourself." He turned again and left the house.

Ivor Jones did not move until he heard the sound of Foxx's car starting outside. Then he stepped to the window to watch the car drive away. After that he went to the telephone and called Sheriff Banders at his home in Ludlow.

CHAPTER FOURTEEN.

❦ ❦ ❦ HE HAD BEEN THERE MANY TIMES—FIFTY-TWO TIMES a year for eight years except the year when he was sick one Sunday and the two summers when he had to go away to keep his teacher's certificate up to date. Hundreds of times he had sat on the rough seats with his feet on the heavy plank floor, looking up toward the shadowy figure of Reverend Foxx. Foxx was there now, high above the heads of the congregation in his raised pulpit which was carved entire from a giant redwood stump that still sank living roots into the earth beneath the sawdust. Each year saplings sprang anew from the roots, thrusting their slender stems inquiringly into the dusky interior in a vain search for sunlight.

Many hundreds of times and now the last time. You walked through the valley for many miles until you finally topped a ridge, and then you didn't see the valley any more. You lived in a house for years, going in and out, and finally you went out for the last time and never returned. Going out the last time was no different from the others: the same steps, the same things seen to right and left, the same slow absorption of space into the funnel of a hungry perspective. Only the knowledge was different—the awareness of pulling the circle shut behind you so that you were back at the beginning again, with things past hidden in a sack of time and no longer having meaning.

"Let those of you who have loved this man in life rise now

and view his body once again before it passes from your sight forever."

The voice of Manley Foxx was low and resonant, rippling across the surface of the eternal mystery. High behind him was the organ with Stella Graw mobile and black against the dim light of the keyboard. The music rose from the walls and fell from the vaulted ceiling.

Someone was plucking at his sleeve. It was Bleeker Twist, standing up, motioning him to rise also. The people were filing slowly past, moving in a dark line along the outer perimeter of the church toward the foot of the pulpit. There Mars Venderstone lay in his coffin. It was clear now. Even in death there are conventions.

Ula Westerly had the children in tow, school having been dismissed for the funeral. They filed by Edward along the pew ahead, staring at him openly and curiously because he was no longer their teacher. He had done something evil and wasn't quite the same man any more. Others stared at him too, surprised at seeing him present.

I'm sorry, he thought in response to their stares. I came only because Bleeker Twist insisted. I really don't care about funerals at all. I never enjoy them very much.

Along the outside wall he went, dwarfed by the giant redwood trunks, sprinkled by music, and up to the coffin. Peasley Muse had been more efficient as an undertaker than as a coroner. The skull was no longer crushed. The black hair was smooth over the white forehead and the face was handsome in waxen calm. Mars Venderstone was dead, and he was no more dead from having been killed in the Bull Woods than had he been killed elsewhere. There are no degrees of death. Dead, deader, deadest— no, the words were never used that way. Dead, dead, dead was better, much better. Who was it that walked by the coffin with bowed head and knew exactly how he died?

Mrs. Grumpley was crying. He had heard Mrs. Grumpley cry in church dozens of times when the mystery passed too close to her. It was a high, jerky, gasping cry which would pass for a laugh in the parlor. The noise was partly stifled by a wet handkerchief and kept changing in volume and quality as the handkerchief opened and closed on her nose. Everyone heard Mrs. Grumpley and tried hard to pay no attention.

The lines from either side met at the coffin and then turned side by side down the broad center aisle back toward the pews. He saw Ailsa Kildonan just before he turned. She was approaching the bier, her cheeks pale, but with bright spots up near the temples and her chin raised. The sight shocked him. In eight years he had never seen her in church before, but the shock was more than surprise at her presence. It was the final incongruity that a representative of the Bull Woods should appear at the coffin. He had shrugged at the stories, but for eight years he had been told that the Bull Woods were evil. She walked alone, for those ahead of her moved quickly, while those behind held back.

She was behind him when he turned and he could see her with his mind, standing by the coffin and looking down at Mars Venderstone. A pulse of jealousy ran through him. Even the dead. He had to turn around and look. Everyone else walked with steadfast eyes and somber tread, but he had to turn around.

She wasn't looking at the coffin at all. She stood in front of it, quite alone, but her face was turned upward to the pulpit where Manley Foxx dominated the moving people below. He saw the back of her head and the square set to her shoulders. Then he faced forward again and plodded through the dusk to his seat.

"He died in the days of his manhood. He died in the struggle against the forces of darkness."

How could things be so lucid and so muddled at the same time? He had never sat in church before with such a feeling of detachment. He was not a part of it any more. He was an onlooker, an outsider, a man among people whom he had never really known and whom he would never see again.

"He must not die in vain. Our brother's defeat must become our victory. The dark places must go; the altars of evil must be destroyed; those who worship there must be driven out."

But a disease does not belong exclusively to the place where it is contracted. When you leave the place behind, you take the disease along with you, and that's the only thing memory has left. Mr. Foxx did not make good logic. How could anyone die in vain? You could live in vain, but not die. Dying always achieved its end. Dead, deader, deadest.

Someone plucking at his sleeve. It was Bleeker Twist again, standing up. Everyone was standing up. The coffin was coming down the aisle and Stella Graw was playing a funeral march to keep it from coming too fast. The children in the pew ahead were craning their necks to see it as it passed, and three of them stood on the seat. Ula Westerly pushed them down again, saying "Sh-h-h" so loudly that everyone near by looked at her and one little girl sniggered.

The pallbearers walked on out of the church and the pews emptied in a double line behind the coffin. The people followed it under the Gothic gateway into the gray day.

"Can we leave now?" asked Edward.

"No," said Twist. "Let's see it out."

The procession moved slowly from north of town where the church stood to the south where the cemetery lay close to the mill. In front of the cemetery gates the Tree of the Dead towered upward into the low mist, and here the pallbearers stopped. A pair of boots was taken from the coffin and given silently to Cliff Jorgensen, the climber.

Jorgensen hung the boots at his side and then, while the people formed a great semicircle around the tree, he flung a rope around its base and hooked it on either side of his belt. He dug his long spikes into the soft bark, leaned back against the rope, and started up. The Tree of the Dead was twenty feet across the base and soared some two hundred and fifty feet into the air, where its top had been shorn off to make way for a small platform hardly larger than the tapered trunk which supported it.

Jorgensen clambered on, flipping the loop of his rope upward as he came horizontal with it. He slowly dwindled in size until at half the distance he looked like an elongated beetle. Higher yet, the mist swept around him so that at times he was hidden from view completely. He finally reached the top and kneeled, then stood, on the tiny cylindrical platform. He spread out his arms, a boot in either hand, and the call of his voice floated downward. He kneeled again and the people could hear the faint tap of his hammer as he nailed the boots down.

Then he was coming down again, leaping out from the tree and letting the rope pull him in again as it tightened around the increasing trunk. Finally he stood on the ground before them, smiling at the accomplishment of his task.

This was the note of festival. When the procession moved on, the faces were eager and the eyes hard.

Manley Foxx arrived to stand beside the grave, murmuring inaudibly as the coffin was lowered. Then he walked away and his steps kept time to the hollow thud of clods falling on the pine boards. The grave was filled quickly, a mound made, and the flowers put in place. The procession broke up into little knots of people who talked in low hurried voices and sent secret glances at Edward and Bleeker Twist. The voices stopped when Ailsa Kildonan left the grave. The women drew in their skirts and stared openly, while the men shuffled uneasily and averted their eyes. Ailsa walked slowly with a swing to her shoulders, never looking back as she left the cemetery and went down the deserted street toward town.

"Now can we get out of here?" demanded Edward.

"Yes," said Twist. "I think that is all."

They followed the same path Ailsa had taken, walking silently until they reached the town.

"I'm sorry you are determined to leave today," said Twist. "It is a mistake."

"It's no mistake. I've got to get out of here."

"You may regret it."

"There have been very few thing I haven't regretted."

"A weak rationalization."

"You're thinking about what people in Jonesville will say if I leave suddenly. They'll connect me with this thing forever. Well, to hell with it. I don't care what they think, and I won't be here to listen to them talk."

Twist didn't argue. "We still have several hours before the bus comes. Suppose we have a beer together and then go back to the cabin and get you packed."

"The packing won't take much time. I'll take the trunk and send for the other stuff when I find out where I'm going to be. If you move before then, you can dump it."

"All right," said Twist. "Did you remark a notable absence among the mourners?"

"Who besides Oban Kildonan?"

"Ivor Jones was not present."

"No, he wasn't."

They took a booth in Larry's Bar and ordered beer. Twist lifted his glass and offered his toast casually.

"Here's to Ailsa Kildonan who will haunt Edward Spence to all eternity."

Edward set down a full glass. "I don't find that very funny."

"True, none the less," mused Twist. "What else could have kept you in Jonesville? Not Miss Graw, the organist. You had opportunity to investigate that a long time ago."

"Can we talk about something besides myself?"

"But you hold some key information, Edward."

"I don't know a damned thing."

"I am not referring to what you know. I'm thinking of the feelings you must have about this town. How did you like Foxx's threats?"

"Did he threaten? I wasn't listening during the service."

"I didn't think you were. He was very confident."

"He is always that."

"But this has to be something new. The situation in Jonesville is changing."

"How do you know?"

"Because you can't leave a killer at large in a town of this size without some action being taken. I do not think I shall stay in the cabin after you are gone."

"Mr. Spence!" The broken call came from the front of the saloon. Edward craned his neck around the corner of the booth. It was Floyd Hooks. The dowser stood just inside the doorway, gaping foolishly at the empty room. His cry had been prompted by hope rather than discovery, because when he saw Edward's head, he grinned happily and trotted forward. He had a white envelope outstretched in one hand.

"What is it, Floyd?"

"For you." Floyd shoved the envelope across the table.

"For me? Who's it from?"

Hooks shook his head. "For you," he repeated.

"But who gave it to you?" Edward turned the blank envelope over in his hand.

"You might determine that by opening it," suggested Twist. "Unless you want me to open it."

Hooks looked alarmed at this idea. He backed away from the table until he reached the center of the room, then turned and fled.

Edward ripped open the seal and pulled out a note. Twist slid from his seat and came around to the other side of the table where he peered over Edward's shoulder and read:

DEAR MR. SPENCE:
　　I'd like to see you as soon as possible. You'll find me home any time during the afternoon.

IVOR JONES

Edward wadded the note in his hand and threw it to the floor. Twist immediately retrieved it.

"Even if you don't intend to report to him," he said, "I shouldn't discard this so casually. I sense that Mr. Jones has gotten himself into a situation, and it might be unwise to scatter evidence about which would connect you with him." He put the note in his pocket.

"I know what he wants," said Edward bitterly. "He expected me to leave Jonesville, and instead I went to live with you. Now he wants to tell me to get out of town. I'm leaving town anyway, so there's no reason for giving him another opportunity to bully me."

"Quite to the contrary, Edward," said Twist. "Since you are leaving town anyway, there is every reason why you should take advantage of the situation to bully him. You must go see him, Edward."

"Why?"

Twist laughed. "Have you no interest in anything outside of yourself? If your own curiosity is so lacking, go see him to satisfy mine."

"I don't see why I should bother. He has no further hold on me."

"Fah! Edward! You sound like a pouting boy. Your pride has been nothing but a burden to you of late anyway. Cast it off and go see what he wants." He took Edward by the arm and propelled him toward the door. "Don't you find it at all strange," he said, "that the only person in town he could trust to deliver his message was the village half-wit? Such a man is hard pressed. Go see him and then come back. I'll meet you here."

Having been pushed as far as the sidewalk, Edward felt disposed to go on under his own power rather than be pushed the rest of the way. Twist walked with him along Main Street until he came to the cross street which led to Ivor Jones's house, where he stopped to let Edward go on alone.

It was on his return to Larry's Bar that he met Stella Graw and Ula Westerly. They had been part of a group returning from the cemetery and which had split up on the street corner ahead of him. Now they approached, and he noticed the sudden cessation of talk between them when they saw him. They were giving him wide berth on the sidewalk, but he insisted upon stopping before them and bowing.

"Good afternoon," he said, and his eyes took in the close-fitting black crepe dress which sheathed Stella from beneath her round chin to just above the ankles. The two women said nothing but fell into single file to get past him. "I cannot let the opportunity pass, Miss Graw," he continued, "to tell you how much I appreciated your fine work at the organ this morning. It is the first time I've had the pleasure of hearing you play. Your talent is not being wasted."

They got by him, but a flush of pleasure tinged Stella's face and her gait slowed perceptibly as she stole a glance at him. He laughed invitingly.

"And I must likewise congratulate you, Miss Westerly, on the admirable manner in which you handled the children throughout the ceremony. A very difficult task."

Ula Westerly stopped and looked at him. "That's kind of you to say." She added suspiciously. "You're Mr. Twist, aren't you?"

"But how good of you to remember! I was so wet the first time we met. I have been meaning to drop around and find out whether or not my cat damaged your sofa." He laughed and stepped forward. "I hope you will forgive me for speaking without an introduction, Miss Graw. A stranger must sometimes put himself forward if he is to meet the people he wants to know."

"Well," said Ula Westerly, "I guess it won't hurt to introduce you now. Miss Graw, this is Mr. Twist. And I might say, Mr. Twist, that you can sometimes meet the wrong people by putting yourself forward."

His eyebrows shot upward. "Indeed? I trust I haven't committed a social error?"

"You seem to have a way of putting your foot in it," said Ula dryly.

Bleeker Twist looked worried. "You know, I have wondered

about that. It is so easy in a small town. Surely, however, I am being impeccable when I address myself to the educators of Jonesville?" And he smiled hopefully.

"I daresay we won't get you into any trouble," replied Ula. "That's more than can be said of some."

"That's not very kind of you, Ula," smiled Stella. "After all, Mr. Twist is a stranger. He may not understand."

"Hmm," said Twist, looking puzzled. "It is obvious that I need instruction. Would it be amiss of me to accompany you home? I am simply walking about town while I wait for Mr. Spence."

"And what is Mr. Spence doing?" asked Ula.

"He is making preparations for leaving town."

"Leaving?" said Stella.

"Yes, he plans to go in a few days. He wanted to see about a ticket, but at present he is calling upon Mr. Jones."

"We were going to my house for a cup of tea," said Ula quickly. "You might come along if you want."

"I should be delighted," he replied, falling into step beside them. "I shall need someone when Edward is gone, and he has told me so much about you two."

"He has?"

"Nothing not complimentary, I assure you. I particularly wanted to meet you, Miss Westerly. Edward has told me something of your ability to—well, I don't know just what you would call it—communicate with the spirits."

Ula Westerly sniffed. "He never seemed to think so much of it when he lived with me. I don't explain it myself, but it's happened often enough."

"I hope you will tell me about it. You see, it is somewhat in my line—these strange powers of the mind. In fact, I'm writing a book on the subject. I might be able to incorporate some of your experiences in it. Perhaps some evening you will permit me to come over and make notes?"

"I guess it wouldn't do any harm," said Ula, a slight relaxation

144 🐝

appearing at the corners of her taut mouth. "What kind of book is it?"

"Oh, quite scientific. Of course, I should keep your identity secret unless I had your permission to do otherwise. Wherever possible I like to make full acknowledgment of my sources."

"We'll see," said Ula. "Maybe I can tell you a few things over tea and you can see if you can use them."

"I'm certain I can," breathed Twist.

At Miss Westerly's house Bleeker Twist and Stella sat down in the parlor while Ula went on to the kitchen. Stella sat stiffly in one corner of the lounge with her hands folded in her lap. Her arm-length black gloves extended up under her sleeves and the collar of her dress was high about her throat. Her face was pale by contrast with her black dress. She was slightly cat-eyed, Twist noticed. The slant of the eyes gave the impression of vitality—suspended vitality, energy held in abeyance. She removed her hat and patted her golden hair. Bleeker Twist watched her with silent interest.

"So Mr. Spence is leaving?" she said at last.

"He says he is. I suppose there is nothing here for him now."

"No," she said slowly, "I suppose not." She brushed a wrinkle out of her skirt and looked at Twist with somber blue eyes.

"I'm afraid I was the unwitting cause of his trouble," said Twist.

Stella shook her head. "He knew what he was doing." She spoke slowly and the words were bitter. Her long black fingers ran lightly along the arm of the lounge. "He could have been in worse trouble but for you."

"How is that?"

"When Mars Venderstone died. It's a good thing for him you were there too."

"Oh," said Twist. "I hadn't thought of that. Although it works both ways. Of course, if it hadn't been for me, he would have been here at Miss Westerly's."

"Maybe," she said, and the fingers kept stroking the arm of

the lounge. Ula Westerly brought in a tray with cups and saucers.

"You said Mr. Spence was seeing Mr. Jones?" she asked.

"Yes," said Twist casually. "He had a message."

"What does Mr. Jones want to see him about?"

"That I don't know. Perhaps he wants some information about the school before Mr. Spence leaves."

"You're sure he's going?"

"He certainly says he is."

"It's funny Mr. Jones would want to see him if he's leaving. Stella knows all about the school." She returned to the kitchen for the teapot.

"I am surprised," said Twist gravely, "to find that anyone could have thought Edward Spence in any way connected with Mars Venderstone's death."

Stella flushed. "People try to think what's possible."

"Then I take it you don't accept the view taken by your church?"

"Yes, I accept it," she said quickly, "but it's an allegory. Evil is something apart from the people who practice it, but it still has a human source."

Twist nodded. "I see. Is that what the rest of the townsfolk think?"

"To some it is very literal." She looked in the direction of the kitchen. "Others think differently."

Twist didn't have time to ask her what she meant because Ula came in with the steaming teapot and filled their cups.

"So kind of you," he murmured. "Mr. Spence has told me, Miss Westerly, that you predicted Mars Venderstone's death. Perhaps one shouldn't speak of it at such a time, but I have come across so few authentic cases."

"Yes," she said in her flat voice. "It was Friday night. That was two nights before he died. I had a vision."

"A vision?"

"The figure of a man appeared before me."

"But how amazing! Where did this take place?"

"I'd just gone to bed. The light in my room was off, but there was enough light to see by from the arc light on the highway. It was dim, but my eyes were used to it by the time it happened. I was about to go to sleep and something made me open my eyes. There was the figure of a man standing by my bed."

"Good heavens! How frightening for you!"

She shook her lank locks. "It's happened before, so I knew what it was. Not that it doesn't make one a bit nervous." She laughed. "The figure seemed awfully dark."

Twist leaned forward. "But what was its quality? Could you see through it?"

She shook her head again. "It was solid like a man, only somehow darker and with indistinct features. It just stood there, looking down at me."

"And what did you do? Did you try to speak to it?"

"I think I tried, but it's hard to make the words come out. I just lay there waiting and watching to see what it would do next."

"And what did it do?"

"Nothing. After a few seconds it sort of backed off toward the door and then faded away. I turned on the light for a little while before I went to sleep."

"I should think you would! And you say this sort of thing has happened before?"

"Oh, yes. Several times."

"And always followed by a death?"

"Well, four years ago—no, I guess it's been five now—the vision of John Forbes came to me one night. He was the foreman of the millpond. And not more than six months later he was crushed when he slipped between two logs. He was a strong man, too."

"Could you tell last Friday night that it was Mars Venderstone you saw?"

"I think I must have known," she said, "although it didn't

occur to me who it was until later. It was such a big man, and dark. I think something kept me from being sure until it was too late to warn him."

"Ah!" Twist leaned back in his chair and sipped at his tea. "This is fascinating, to say the least. I find your mental block against recognition particularly telling in view of the manner of his death."

She nodded sagely. "I've thought of that. There was something dark across his face like a veil—an evil veil." She looked keenly at Twist. "You were there, weren't you?"

"You mean when the body was discovered? Indeed I was."

"You were right there after it happened?"

"Well, pretty close to the time. I had just returned from town. In fact, I had been here."

"Here?"

"I came looking for Mr. Spence, but he wasn't in."

"Oh, I see. For Mr. Spence."

"Yes. Very unfortunate for me not to see anyone. I don't think the sheriff quite believes me. If only you had been here, I would have had a witness."

"I didn't hear you," said Miss Westerly.

"No. You must have been out. I knocked at your door. I wanted to ask about Mr. Spence."

"Oh," said Ula. "That must have been after I left. I went to the movie."

"Hmm," said Twist. "I find it surprising that the motion picture runs on Sunday. I should think the church would be against it."

"It's because of the mill. Mr. Jones thinks it's best to have a movie week ends instead of just a bar. More people are at work on Monday."

"Yes, that explains it. I suppose most of the town goes to the movie?"

"A lot of them, anyway." She licked her lips and took a noisy

148

sip of tea. "Was there anything about the body—that is, anything that didn't come out at the inquest, that might show just what happened?"

Twist shook his head. "I think the coroner covered everything very carefully. Hmm, except one point. You see, I'm certain the death was witnessed."

"Witnessed?"

"Someone laughed. Gruesome to think of, isn't it? But I don't believe Mars Venderstone would laugh one second and cry out in terror the next. I may be mistaken."

"I know who could have laughed," said Ula.

"I don't think we should repeat that story," said Stella. Her gloves were off now. Her white hand played with her teaspoon. "Ailsa has a poor enough reputation, but there's no proof it was she."

"Ah?" said Twist. "What's this? I hadn't heard."

"Well, you wouldn't hear anything living where you do," said Ula.

"It's just a story," said Stella, "and no one has the right to repeat it, but stories are bound to arise when a father and daughter are alone so much of the time with the daughter's mother bedfast."

"Indeed, now. This is a little beyond me."

"You see?" said Stella. "We've shocked Mr. Twist. It's best not to say any more."

"But I don't see," said Twist. "That is, it seems to have nothing to do with the death of Mars Venderstone."

"Well, she doesn't mix much with men, and there's a reason," said Stella. "I wouldn't say this if it weren't that Mr. Spence—" She stopped, flushing.

"There's no harm in saying that, at any rate," Ula broke in. "Edward Spence better keep away from Ailsa. Oban Kildonan doesn't like other men around. I'm sure he doesn't know about some of her carryings-on."

Bleeker Twist set his cup on the tray and tugged at his collar, swallowing hard. "I believe I see what you mean," he said. "Dear me. And you think she would laugh while—" He left the question hanging.

"I won't say such a thing," said Stella. "Is there more tea, Ula?" Miss Westerly left the room with a backward glance. Stella leaned forward. "I was only thinking of Mr. Spence," she said.

"But then there were the curious marks on the madrone tree. I can't see—"

Stella shook her head. "The lash marks? That is something no one can explain. They have been there before."

"I see," breathed Twist. "Then there is not necessarily a connection." He swallowed hard again and laughed nervously as Ula returned. "I certainly must express my gratitude to you ladies. I have apparently been living in a fool's paradise with little realization of what goes on around me."

"It's nothing you should repeat," said Stella, "but I thought you might suggest to Mr. Spence that he be careful, although if he's leaving town anyway—"

"But perhaps not for several days," said Twist, rising. "In fact, I think it best that I find him right away. He might think I have gone on to the cabin and try to follow me. I've certainly enjoyed our discussion. Most informative! The tea, Miss Westerly, was delicious."

Ula Westerly followed him to the door. "It may be you'll be needing a place to stay if you're leaving the Bull Woods."

"I have thought of that."

"I haven't let Mr. Spence's room yet. It would be a quiet place to work."

"I'm sure of it. And you could help me so much with my book."

Miss Westerly colored unbecomingly. "Well, I'd be on hand if you needed me for anything."

"I'm sure of that, too," said Bleeker Twist, and with a doff

150

of his hat he went out to the front gate and started down the
street.

"My, my!" he muttered to himself. "To think of it! It is incredible, and yet it is the only explanation. How shocked poor
Edward would be!" And he laughed nervously as he hurried
back to the saloon.

CHAPTER FIFTEEN

❧ ❧ ❧ AILSA KILDONAN LEFT THE CEMETERY AND CONTINUED on into Jonesville. She walked with her face straight ahead, ignoring the new hostility she met in the attitudes of those who passed her. It came largely from women. The men she met, if they were alone, nodded even if they didn't speak.

She had to wait about fifteen minutes in front of the general store before Mr. Dodge got back from the funeral and opened for business. She checked for mail, bought some groceries, and started out again. Her father's car was parked in the church area. It was the lone vehicle when she arrived. Through the trees she could see the church doors still standing open, although no one was about. She set the bag of groceries in the back seat and was about to slide under the steering wheel when a man stepped to her side. It was the Reverend Foxx. As she hesitated with her hand on the open door, he closed it, so that she stood outside the car facing him.

"You will forgive me," he said softly. "I could not help but notice your presence here today, and I felt I owed you my deepest apologies for words in my funeral message which you may have misunderstood."

She stepped back from him suspiciously. "I came because of Mars Venderstone, not you."

"I understand that, of course," he said. "But I wanted you to know that your deference to the dead was not unnoticed."

"All right," she said. "If you mean it, it's nice of you to say it. I have to go now." She reached for the handle of the door but he kept his hand on it. She flushed. "I have to go."

"I do not intend to detain you, but I can tell by your voice that you do not believe me. Before you go, I want to convince you of my sincerity."

"It doesn't matter to you what I think."

"Not what you think of me personally," he replied, "but it matters a great deal what you think of me as a channel through which the truth is brought to the people. That is the only role which concerns me."

"I don't understand that kind of talk and I have to go home. Please let me in the car."

"Ailsa," he said, and his voice was so low it trembled, "let me explain to you that I never act out of personal malice. Your family has stood apart from the church in a community where you have been the only dissenters. It has been my solemn duty to warn others against such conduct and to point out your family as an example of wrong living. This does not mean that you must carry the burden of guilt yourself or that you are beyond redemption. I would rather welcome you into the fold than drive you far from its gates."

"If you're asking me to join the church, I won't do it. You asked me once before and I told you I didn't like it."

"You were a child then," he said, speaking more rapidly. "You have grown older—more mature. The loneliness of life without spiritual guidance must have made itself felt upon you by now."

"There's nothing wrong with my life. And if you haven't anything against us, then you should stop talking about us. You've made things so we haven't got any friends."

"I can give you back your friends along with many new ones. I long to give you my own friendship." He dropped his hand from the door handle, stepping forward at the same time so that he still blocked the way.

153

"Your friendship is one I'd just as soon do without. My father would laugh at you. Now let me in my car."

He shook his head sadly. "Indeed, I know your father might laugh. It would be up to you to bring him to a sense of understanding. You have it in your power to save both yourself and him."

"I'm not worried about being saved. We know why you're here and it isn't just because of being a preacher. Old Ivor Jones keeps you here to tell the millworkers how evil money is and how blessed it is to work for next to nothing. You can't tell us that. That's why my father gets the highest pay in the mill. So don't say any more to me about saving anybody."

The Reverend Foxx folded his hands in front of his chest to still their trembling. "You are woefully mistaken, child. Ivor Jones is nothing more than another member of my congregation, a wayward one at present, since he was not with us today. I shall reprimand him for it."

Ailsa laughed scornfully. "You're mighty big all of a sudden, Mr. Foxx!"

"Please do not speak of matters of which you know nothing. Ivor Jones has only the power of worldly possessions which are as nothing beside the power of the church. He has permitted you and your father to remain here and has given you the means of livelihood. He can do so no longer without my permission."

"So now you're going to try to get our jobs!" The spots of red in Ailsa's cheeks burned brightly.

"Ah, how foolish you are! Your work at the mill means nothing to me. My only concern is that all the people within the limits of Jonesville worship at my church. I have no choice in the matter. Death has resulted from one such failure and can easily occur again. I want to save you. I want to lead you from the path of sin you have chosen. You are too young and too beautiful to be destroyed!"

"Just what do you want, Mr. Foxx?"

"It is the one who returns after knowing the pleasures of evil

154 🐛

who receives the greatest honors. I want to place you high in the church, an example of devotion. I would make you my handmaiden."

"Handmaiden to God!" laughed Ailsa. She stepped forward, putting her hand on his shoulder. "You begin to sound like other men I've known, Mr. Foxx. Get out of the way!"

He stiffened under her touch, but his body didn't yield to the pressure. "Yes," he replied in a strained voice, "handmaiden to God! Honor for yourself, safety for your father and mother. Do not cast the opportunity aside!"

She brought her other hand against his chest and shoved. He dropped back a step to retain his balance and she caught the handle of the door, swinging it open. He leaned against it with his shoulder.

"But hear the rest!" he cried, anger showing in his voice at last. "The opportunity which comes from heaven cannot be scorned. The alternative is destruction! You and yours shall be smitten as was Mars Venderstone, whom you attempted to lead to your evil ways!"

She stared at him, sudden fear puncturing her anger. "Why you're insane!" she cried. "Insane! Insane!"

She wrenched at the door but he pulled her back from it, whirling her to face him while his fingers dug into her shoulders.

"God's will!" he gasped. "You will come to me!" And his breath was hot against her throat.

Ailsa lashed out at his face and brought her knee up hard into the pit of his stomach. He stumbled back, a trickle of blood starting from a deep scratch on his forehead. Ailsa leaped into the car and slammed the door, jamming the lock down as she did so. But Foxx made no attempt to follow. He stared at her with black hatred in his eyes as she wheeled the car around and started for the highway. Through the rear-view mirror she saw him take a handkerchief from his pocket and press it against his forehead. Then he turned and walked with stiff dignity toward the open doors of his church.

CHAPTER SIXTEEN

❧ ❧ ❧ "HE TOLD ME," SAID EDWARD, "THAT I COULD HAVE MY job back."

"Ah, now! That must have been worth hearing. And what did you tell him?"

"I told him I didn't want the damned job back. I told him I was spending my time very pleasantly and that I was going to get out of Jonesville and stay out."

"Did he like that?" Bleeker Twist pushed open the door of the cabin and went in. He immediately flopped on the bunk to rest after the walk from town.

"I gathered that he didn't like it a bit," said Edward. "At least he did the unprecedented thing of telling me my pay would be raised. It was a good raise he mentioned, too."

"That should indicate he was really worried. You still refused him, I trust?"

"Oh, I turned him down, all right. I told him he could go to church and pray for a schoolteacher. That's what he told me to do—go to church."

Twist laughed appreciatively. "You amaze me, Edward. How did he like that?"

Edward strode up and down the room. "He said, 'To hell with the church!' Those were his exact words. He said he didn't care whether I ever saw the inside of a church again, that he wanted me for a schoolteacher anyway."

156 ❧

"Ha! It appears a great rift has opened up between church and state. And throughout all this, you still refused him?"

"I did. I told him I was through with teaching in Jonesville. I told him that if ever I taught school again it would be in a place where the teacher was given the respect his training called for and where a teacher could lead the life he pleased outside the classroom."

"Bravo!"

"Then I told him, if he ever wanted to see me again, to come after me himself and not send for me by a half-wit." He paused. "Perhaps that was a mean thing to say, but I was quite worked up. After that I walked out on him and came back to the saloon to meet you. Where were you, by the way? I had to wait some time."

"I had gone for a stroll and met some friends of yours. Miss Graw and Miss Westerly. Very charming ladies. Edward, do you know that it is already five o'clock and that the bus comes through at six? Are you up to hiking back into town carrying a trunk?"

Edward stopped pacing the floor. "I suppose I'm in no hurry. I had no idea it was so late."

"And we have not eaten since breakfast."

"Well, we can at least do that. I can take the bus tomorrow. What did Ula Westerly have to say?"

"We talked chiefly about her visions. It seems she is subject to hallucinations of men calling at her bedside after she has tucked herself in. As far as I could gather, she has so far been unable to get one of the hallucinations into bed with her, but I think you were wise to get out of the place. She would have had you in bed with her either imaginatively or otherwise sooner or later."

"I assure you it would have been imagination."

"That would be terrible. The effect of her stories would be every bit as bad as though it had been the real thing, and you would have had nothing to show for it. Edward, I told you some

157

time ago that I had the feeling this town was evil. I heard something today which confirms that belief. Such confirmation I would not wish on the world's nosiest investigator. It is beyond rational thought, but there it is—as plain as a primary textbook. I have it and I don't know what to do with it." Twist got up and walked over to the window.

"If it's criminal, you should turn it over to the authorities."

"It has become criminal, although originally the motivation was exactly the opposite. But I cannot turn it over to anyone. What convinces me would make the authorities laugh in their beer. There is a vast difference between knowledge of the truth and proof of the truth. I know who killed Mars Venderstone. I know why he was killed and what weapon was used. I have pieced it together from things I have seen with my own eyes and from gestures and words which are like great signposts to one who has some knowledge of the mind. And yet, short of a confession, I have nothing which would classify as legal evidence."

"But if you know that much, you still have a duty to place your suspicions where they can be evaluated. In time evidence might be found."

Twist shook his head. "I have a duty to myself to complete certain studies I have begun. I cannot carry them out if my means are depleted through successful slander suits and my reputation ruined at the same time." He turned from the window with a sigh. "Edward, when you delve too deeply into the workings of the human mind, the world becomes a place of terror. The arbitrary line drawn between sanity and insanity fades out so completely that in every man you see the potential maniac ready to vent his rage against the world whenever conditions arrange themselves to permit it. Fear is our constant guardian, because it is only fear that keeps the delicate mechanism in place. Small fears, many of them: fear of being laughed at, fear of physical injury, fear of losing money, fear of being jailed or losing prestige, love or admiration. And over and above the little fears, we have the great all-abiding fear of each other. Fear is our bulwark. Against it beat a thousand desires and hatreds which become gnarled and twisted seeking an outlet." Bleeker Twist stalked up and down the room.

"Sometimes we break through the fear, and if we do it without injury to ourselves or others, it gives us great mental relief and exhilaration." He shot a finger at Edward.

"Such was your recent experience with Mr. Jones. You traded position and economic security for peace of mind. You gave hatred a natural outlet and let it expire harmlessly. At the same time you killed the fear which had held it in place. You are better for it. Your voice is more confident, your step firmer; there is a flush of health in your cheek." Bleeker Twist paused by the hook on the wall to dig his tobacco out of a coat pocket and fill his pipe. He walked back to the table where Edward sat, and aimed the pipestem at his breast.

"In Jonesville," he said, "you have a miniature of the world. It is the complete microcosm. Don't make the mistake of believing that only kings and princes are capable of great emotions. Their's are only the more obvious. Jonesville, too, has its royalty, and it is merely fate which keeps the ruler of Jonesville from being ruler of the world. The capabilities are there and the same methods would suffice. It is just as difficult—yes, it is more difficult—to achieve greatness in the microcosm as in the macrocosm. In the former one must overcome the barrier of personal flaws. It has been done here as it has been done elsewhere. And, as always, it has created emotional strains which someday must crack the structure apart." Twist took another turn about the room, tugging at his nose as though to collect his thoughts on its long tip before spreading them before his companion.

"What," he said, gouging space with the pipestem again, "is leadership? Does it spring from an ability on the part of the leader, or does it spring from a demand on the part of the people that they be led? An ancient question, but it must be answered. My answer is the second alternative—always the second. The greatest leader is helpless when the need for his presence is past.

Caesars always die! But when the need is present, a leader will be thrust forward, whatever his caliber. Witness the lamas who place the crown of their ancient tradition on the brows of an innocent child." Twist was silent again while he circled the room.

"Have I posed a contradiction? Seemingly so. On the one hand I have indicated that a tyrant has grown up in Jonesville, and on the other I have said it is the people who have placed him there." For a moment he held the two thoughts on the fingertips of either hand. Then with a gesture he dissipated them both. "No contradiction. The effect is simultaneous and the leader is but a reflection of the people's minds. He is their totem to ward off evil—their monument to fear. What evil is in Jonesville to create such a figure?" He dropped into a chair across the table from Edward. "Edward, you are silent."

"I don't know how you could expect me to be otherwise."

Twist smiled. "Do I bore you? But I must have my thoughts in order. Besides, I am always leading up to my last question. What evil is in Jonesville? Can you tell me that, Edward?"

"From your remarks of a few minutes ago, I thought you knew. I was waiting for you to tell me."

"Mine is the knowledge of a single incident. I want a composite. I want to know you, Edward. Irrational as some of your actions have been, you are basically rational, as are all introspective people."

"Thank you," said Edward, shifting uncomfortably in his chair.

"You have lived in Jonesville many years. You know the people. You have feelings about them in relation to yourself. Such feelings are never groundless, even though they may be false. I want to know about them."

"I'm afraid I don't know what you mean," replied Edward. He found himself beginning to perspire under this sudden attack. Twist stood up and turned his chair around so that its back was against the table. He put his foot on the seat and leaned on his knee, looking down at Edward.

"I can help you," he said. "I can tell you exactly what I mean. Have you been embarrassed recently? Tell me about it."

Edward laughed nervously. "You're embarrassing me now."

"Exactly. Because you have recalled at once just such an incident as I suggest. Tell me now; I want to know what sort of fungoid mental growth has sprung up in the shadows of Jonesville."

Edward shook his head. "It's not that I wouldn't tell you anything that seemed important. It's just that I don't believe I can. What I said would never give you the true picture. It would sound dirty, and it's not."

"I agree. Tell me about yourself, Edward."

Edward shook his head again. He wanted to get up and go outside for a breath of air and at the same time he took an egotistical delight in the attempts Twist was making to pry into his secret mind. It gave his thoughts a sense of importance they had never had before. He wanted the conversation to continue but knew of no way to continue it without doing what Twist asked. And he felt powerless to do that. Thoughts of Ailsa kept coming into his mind and just as rapidly he tried to brush them aside with some foolish notion that if he didn't they would come out in the form of words in spite of himself. He glanced up at Twist, wondering at the long silence.

"I can help you, Edward." Twist was looking at him.

"No," he said.

"Look at me, Edward."

Bleeker Twist's eyes seemed abnormally bright. They were fixed and unblinking. Twist lifted a finger and waved it slowly back and forth.

"No," said Edward. "None of that stuff."

Twist laughed. "Don't be alarmed. It's entirely up to you." He waved the finger slowly back and forth and Edward found his eyes following it.

"I wish you wouldn't do that," he said. "It makes me feel foolish."

"It needn't," said Twist. "It's very relaxing. Emotionally, you are a tired man."

"But it won't do you any good."

"Well, perhaps not." The finger kept moving. "As I said, it is entirely up to you. It requires a little effort of concentration which I cannot do for you."

"And besides, it wouldn't mean anything."

"That depends." Twist's voice was a low monotone. "I haven't had opportunity to tell you much about it. You see, in the beginning hypnosis was used in the psychoanalytic process. Sigmund Freud introduced the method and for some time used it almost exclusively. He departed from it later because he felt that under hypnotic influence the subject was prone to tell too much of what was suggested to him instead of freely recalling his own experiences. So he adopted the method of free association. You do not need to listen if you would rather not, but there is no harm in listening. Just follow my finger with your eyes. There is really no hocus-pocus. The purpose of watching my finger is simply to tire the eye muscles so that you begin to think you are getting sleepy. It brings about one of the symptoms of sleepiness."

"This is silly," said Edward.

"The method of free association is the psychological opposite of hypnosis, but like many opposites the two are fundamentally identical. Examination through free association is a long process. Under such a method the subject picks and chooses at seeming random from the thoughts and recollections which drift through his mind. These recollections in turn recall others associated with them, but it would be just as true to say they suggest others. In fact, what the subject really does is to induce in himself a state of high suggestibility—a form of self-hypnosis. The operator merely interprets the data given him by the subject. Under direct hypnosis—there now, if you shift a bit lower

162

you can rest your head on the back of the chair and be more comfortable. After awhile we shall move over to the bunk where you can stretch out. As I was saying, under direct hypnosis it is possible to let the subject do his own interpreting, a method of my own which I shall tell you about later. It is particularly effective when both the subject and operator know in advance what phase of mental activity they intend to explore. It is too bad that Freud failed to go further along his original path, although, of course, he was dealing much of the time with a type of mind which was unable to bring itself to the concentration necessary for sleep. I think it would be a good plan now to move over to the bunk; you are ready to relax. Do not mind Andramalech; I'll put him in the upper."

Edward stood up and walked over to the bunk. He felt a little ridiculous and faintly alarmed at the prospect of a new experience. He needn't do it, actually. He could sit down on the bunk and laugh and tell Twist to forget about it, that he had just been pretending to cooperate. But somehow that would seem silly too, now that he had gone this far. The fact was that he was doing just as Twist suggested; he was walking over to the bunk. He was lying down on it and watching Twist lift Andramalech to the bunk above. It was much more pleasant. His neck hurt where it had been cramped against the back of the chair. That was foolish too—to sit in an uncomfortable position for no reason at all except that it seemed to be expected of you. That was the reason for doing so many things—simply because it was expected of you: unpleasant things, things you would never do otherwise, things that bored you and wasted your time and gave you indigestion. That was also why you refrained from doing still other things, because to do them would be to shock someone or hurt someone's feelings. You couldn't stand up and scream at a tea party and you couldn't walk up to a pompous man and dig him in the stomach with your finger, saying "Cootchy, cootchy!" But it was easy to lie down on the bunk because that hurt no one's feelings, and it wasn't boring, even though you were doing it because Bleeker Twist told you to. It was his responsibility. All you had to do was lie there and not be responsible to anyone. It was a tremendous relief, really, that feeling of suddenly transferring responsibility for your actions to someone else. You could relax as you had never relaxed before. You had to hang on to the relaxation, though. The sense of responsibility kept coming back toward you and you had to keep throwing it off. You had to concentrate on something and close your mind to everything else. The finger moved back and forth; you could watch that. And you could listen to Bleeker Twist's voice talking about things that had no immediate relationship to your life.

The finger moving. And if you watched it long enough, the room in back of it became strangely dark. In the dark were two beads shining; those were Twist's eyes. Sometimes you were aware of the whole head and sometimes everything would disappear but the finger, making a white band with its circular movement over your head. It was hard holding your eyes open, hard to listen. Sometimes the whole picture would reverse itself. As though lightning had flashed, the room and everything in it back of the finger would be dazzling white and the finger would be jet black against it, moving slowly between you and the light. That was easy to explain. It was just the chemistry of the eyes, the little rods and cones surfeited by the same image playing against them and suddenly rebuilding to give you a negative picture of the whole scene. It was the eyes—the sense you most trusted—making white look like black and black, white. The ears, too, grew weary of the play of words and did tricks with them. "Sleepy you are. Sleepy you are," Twist was saying, only you knew he was really saying, "You are sleepy," and, indeed, he was quite right. You were sleepy. You were sleepy whether he told you so or not. He had nothing to do with it except that the responsibility was his. Or was he saying, "You are sleeping"? That was queer, because you didn't feel as though you were really asleep, although the darkness came for longer times now and sometimes the finger and the room would disappear as entirely as though a great black wave had rushed over them. Then they would emerge again, the waving finger, floating gradually upward. Those black waves had a regularity about them. They came on steadily, each one deeper than the last, each a little longer, washing out both sound and vision. They were even fearful, and you felt like fighting against them the way you would against torrents of water pouring over you. Except that after awhile you began to understand them. They didn't suffocate. They didn't even mean oblivion. Inside the blackness was a crystal clarity of thought where the mind sat back untouched and untouchable, as though in a locked room where all the keys were inside and nothing could ever move the door from without. It was safe there. You could forget Bleeker Twist, forget Ailsa Kildonan. They were things remote, things outside the locked doors. The finger was still there, waving slowly, but it meant nothing any more. It was Bleeker Twist making a foolish gesture, Bleeker Twist waving at you when you were no longer there. He was peering in at you through the senses that were your windows to the outside world, but he couldn't see you because you were locked up in a deeper room. All he could see was the clutter of doubts and superstitions and little bits of knowledge which had been picked up by the eyes and ears and nose and which you used to furnish the parlor of your mind. These he could see and these he could have. They were his responsibility. In the dark room there were no furnishings. There was only the steady, sure pounding of the heart, and the warm flow of blood shutting the locked room off like an island from the rest of the universe. There was the vast intelligence of the blood moving darkly and guided by a volition which belonged to you and the dark room.

For a long time now the black waves had ceased recurring. At some point, too long ago for memory, a wave had swept over you which failed to fall back again. Under a weight of darkness you lay in incredible silence, lulled by a gentle swaying motion. That was the breath, coming and going, but it need not be your breath. The sensation was poignantly familiar; it did not come as a memory but as a rediscovery of something ever present, something that had been covered up and now had been found again.

In the parlor of your mind something was stirring—voices, a sense of light. That was silly—a sense of light when you were locked up in darkness. But there it was—light, an awareness of the body, sound, Bleeker Twist's voice, movement, something touching your hand. It put you outside the locked room again. It put you outside and inside at the same time, with the locked door in between. That was nothing new, either. That's the way it had always been, except that you hadn't realized it before. You had lived so much in the parlor that you had forgotten about the warm room deep in the blood. Now you knew about both at once. You knew about both as though you sat on a mountaintop looking down into two valleys which started from a common spring and went their divergent ways thereafter.

Bleeker Twist's voice again telling you to open your eyes. They had been closed, then. It was an effort, but it could be done. Your eyes were open but you were still asleep. There was the bunk overhead and the dark face of Andramalech peering down at you. There was Bleeker Twist standing over you, smiling, and the finger wasn't waving any more. There was his quiet voice accepting all the responsibility, telling you what to do and say, removing all indecision. He kept recalling things to you and the recollections came like pictures in which you saw yourself moving and felt yourself thinking, but it was somehow not you any more.

"You can speak," he said. "Try it. Tell me your name."

That was very familiar. They were the same words he had said to Ailsa Kildonan when she lay in this same place. Ailsa had answered. You could answer.

"Edward Spence." You felt your lips move and heard the words.

166 ❧

"Good. It is simple, isn't it?" Indeed, it was simple. It was almost delightful. How odd to be delighted by being able to speak. It was something like a game.

"I want you to remember what we were talking about before you lay down on the bunk, Edward. Will you do that?"

That was easy, too. Twist had been talking. He had been explaining the process of hypnosis. And before that he had been talking about Jonesville and its people—about evil. You could remember it all.

"Do you remember I asked you to tell me about yourself? That is a big subject. I really didn't mean everything—just the things that seem most important to you. We might start with something very recent. What happened last evening after you watched Ivor Jones leave the Kildonans?"

This was part of the game too, but it wasn't delightful. You felt uneasy and there was a trembling along your arms. You didn't have to tell. Just because Bleeker Twist asked you wasn't enough of a reason. If you shook your head very hard and made your arms move, you could wake yourself up the same way you often did at night when a dream became too uncomfortable. Or you could let the dream continue after you had reminded yourself that it was only a dream. As long as you knew you could escape when necessary, it didn't hurt to let things go a little further. Besides, the responsibility was Bleeker Twist's. What had happened at the Kildonans was embarrassing and you could give the embarrassment to Twist.

"I saw Ailsa." You felt the lips move again.

"Did you speak to her?"

"Yes." No need to volunteer. Wait for the questions. Twist would gradually strip the covers away to leave you lying exposed and naked.

"I see. Tell me how you managed it. Did she come outside?"

"No. There was a window."

"A window? You mean you spoke to her through an open window?"

"Yes." It was easier now. The trembling in your arms had stopped and the sense of relaxation had returned. It was a relief to tell someone about it.

"Why did you speak to her?"

The part of you in the locked room heard the question, too, and knew the answer. That's where the answer should come from, but it was an answer compounded of blood and heartbeats and which had no verbal translation. "I don't know."

"Let's put it this way. You were feeling pretty low when you got back here, weren't you?"

"Yes." That was comprehensible. The meaning was clear to the part of you that lived by means of language.

"And that means that you did something you weren't very proud of. Now, what did you do?"

"I asked her to come outside."

"Would she come?"

"No."

"Ah, I see. No wonder you felt low. You were repulsed—you were unsuccessful. What did you intend to do had she come outside as you asked?"

There was no answer to that. You hadn't gone that far. You had merely been concerned with telling her you wanted her outside. "I don't know."

"That must have been a handicap to your approach. One generally performs the first act best when he knows what the second is going to be. Have you ever been with Ailsa alone?"

"Yes."

"When was that?"

"The night we came here."

"Of course, I remember. You and she went back to the house together. What happened?"

"I touched her." How idiotic that sounded. And yet the physical touch was the thing you remembered. It was the thing which had happened.

"And before that had you ever been alone with Ailsa?"

"No."

"You had spoken to her?"

"Yes."

"Did you see her often?"

"No."

"How often?"

"Sometimes on the street in town."

"And how long have you known her?"

"Since I came here. Eight years."

"Now, Edward," Bleeker Twist paused for a long time. You kept waiting for his voice because you wanted him to go on asking questions now. You wanted to get rid of this thing, explain why it was important. "Now," he repeated, "I just want you to talk. I want you to tell me about yourself and Ailsa. Not about anyone else. Tell me about the eight years."

Andramalech had his eyes closed. His head still protruded over the top of the upper bunk but the chin was raised and he wasn't paying attention any more. You didn't interest him. This was harder because it wasn't chronological in your mind. You couldn't start with the first day you came to Jonesville and go on from there. You couldn't even start with the first day you saw Ailsa, because you couldn't remember what day that was. It was something that had grown, but it hadn't grown from Ailsa. It had been a thing in yourself which needed an exterior object for gratification—a dream object. That's what you were telling Bleeker Twist. It wasn't the way you had thought of it yourself before, because you had never thought of Ailsa as a projection of yourself. She had been something real, not a symbol. And now she was nothing but a symbol.

"I didn't have any knowledge of women—no experience. I was a schoolteacher. The town was strict. Everywhere there was fear that some gesture might be misinterpreted. If I called on a mother regarding a child, it always had to be in the evening when the father was home. If he wasn't home, I couldn't stay.

It didn't matter who the woman was. The touch of a hand could contaminate. A man and woman together engaged in evil."

The lips kept moving. Things were coming out of dark corners. You saw the hips, the breasts, the limbs—always clothed, alway hidden, but bulging at you, never talked of but always present. You saw the straight lips and heard the whispered voices and saw the unnaturally bright eyes turned upward to catch a glimpse of sin.

"She was very young when I first came. Fifteen, I think. I wouldn't have noticed but that people talked about her. And being so young made her something completely lost. But she could walk through the town smiling, and that made her shameless, as though she were courting the evil that others hid beneath their skirts. She smiled at me once; perhaps I had been here two years then."

Wasn't there a way to tell it without making it sound sordid? Nothing had ever happened, really. Nothing but thoughts. She was young and lost already. She wouldn't object to advances. She would be able to tell you what to do, train you in lust in the dark shade of the forest. You would meet her there—these were dreams—and all the advances would be hers. The dreams had to arrange that. A tree had fallen and you lay beside it, stunned but otherwise unhurt. That's where she found you, helpless to repel while she laid slow kisses on your lips and stripped your body to look for wounds. Or it was down by the surf, dark in the night, and you had been thrown by the wild waves against the rocks of the Black Angels. She was beside you, pulling off her blouse to bind your head, throwing her coat about your shoulders and pressing her naked body against you to shield you from the cold.

"They became very real, those dreams. On week ends and of evenings when I knew I was unobserved, I would slip into the forest near her home. It seemed that any chance meeting would suffice. No message needed to pass between us. Her desire would drive her on, and all I had to do was find an excuse for accepting

170 🐟

her. Nothing happened, though. Sometimes I would see her walk outside the house to get a log for the fireplace or at other times of the year to cut a few flowers from the garden. It always shocked me to see her perform these common tasks. To me they were a pretense she put on to shield her true character from her family. Sometimes, too, I saw her in the trees when she went for walks alone. That is when I should have made myself known to her, but I never could. That is when I first discovered the madrone tree."

The madrone tree was naked and that's why it was evil. That's why the Reverend Foxx used it as a symbol. You stood by the graceful trunk with the fleshlike bark and looked at it with strange jealousy. Ailsa often passed near here. Perhaps her hand had stroked its skin. To her the legend of evil had no meaning. You, too, had touched the tree and then drawn back, filled with revulsion. The tree was masculine. It grew from the spot where the missionary had died and symbolized the victory of the evil forces. In the dark shade of the forest where the eyes of the town could not see, it thrust its pink stem upward. The people might revile the meaning it had for them, but still they worshiped.

"Years passed and our relationship became no closer. I don't know when it was that I finally realized it was no longer Ailsa I secretly courted but only my dreams of Ailsa. It shocked me when I found out. I found myself going to bed early in order to think about her undisturbed. Hope of actual conquest no longer played a part. It worried me because it seemed abnormal. It was abnormal. The character of the dreams changed, too. Because with belief in their final fulfillment gone, they no longer needed to pay lip service to reality. I no longer needed to create a natural setting and bring about our meetings through a logical sequence of events."

You found her in the dark caverns or floating on the waves of the sea. You found her in torment, burned and flogged by enemies. No longer must you wait to receive her advances. You were the aggressor now, courting directly the sensual lust she aroused in you. You took her by seduction, by deceit, by rape. She fought back and the blows were sweet to your flesh.

"I didn't like the change. There was no tenderness. There was only the bald fact of passion and a strange hatred which had no reason for its existence except that through it I could bring the dreams to a fiercer culmination. I had to do something about it. I tried putting more time in at my work; I sought company; I wrote scores of letters to old friends. But I knew finally that the only way to escape was to bring to the dreams some essence of reality. I had to court Ailsa with my physical presence. It was like a duty and it filled me with fear. She saw other men sometimes, any one of whom might take her beyond my reach. My need was urgent. Still, so long had the habit of inaction been established that I could do nothing. It had been that way for several months when you arrived."

Death came quickly to Mars Venderstone and it filled you with a horror that was akin to fascination. Death where the naked stem of the madrone tree licked upward toward the sky. Death near the house where Ailsa lived. You saw Ailsa and spoke with her. You had already told of these last meetings and it was easy to speak of them again. They were so trivial compared to the dreams, but their reality was so gigantic compared with illusion. You saw Ailsa in the arms of her father; you heard her deny being in the company of men. It was untrue, and the untruth was like a confirmation of all you had ever thought. She would accept your passion and shield it from the world. That's why you were finally so bold, so rash, so unbelievably clumsy and so wrong. Because at the moment of realization it was not the sensual embrace you wanted but only an understanding of your desire, a tenderness which died in your inept hands.

"I do not know that there is any more to tell. Nothing has ever happened, really, although it seems that a great deal has happened."

It was almost over. Whatever came next, the thing had to end. You were tired looking at the bunk above and at the sleeping

172

head of Andramalech. Your eyes were tired. You wanted to close them and go back inside the locked room. Only the room wasn't locked any more; it wasn't even there. That was surprising, even alarming. There was no place to hide. But then there was no reason to hide, either. The dark corners had been swept out. There was only one room in the mind and it had about it a sense of orderliness and cleanliness.

"Hmm," that was Bleeker Twist's voice. "Most interesting." How casually he took it all. "Is there anything else you want to tell me, Edward?"

"No." Rather nervy of him. You hadn't told all this because you wanted to. You told it because Bleeker Twist asked you to and that made it almost mandatory.

"Close your eyes, Edward." That was easy to do. "In a few minutes you are going to wake up. You have been asleep for nearly an hour, so that it has become dark outside. When you wake up, you will find that you remember all this just as though you hadn't been asleep at all. It will seem as though you have been lying in the bunk telling me about it."

Well, that's the way it did seem. Any time you really wanted to, you could have sat up in the bunk and told Bleeker Twist to go jump in the lake. You had simply told him a few things about yourself because it was a relief to get them off your mind. It had been easier to do it while pretending to be asleep. You were still pretending, lying with closed eyes and waiting for Twist to tell you to open them.

"I think you are awake," he said. "Are you?"

"Yes, I'm awake," said Edward. "This is all very interesting. You were telling me something about hypnosis."

"So I was. It's wholly a matter of theory—just what goes on in the mind. We may have time to go into it in some detail later. Right now it is more urgent to examine some of the facts you have given me."

"You mean there is something substantial in all that rubbish I poured out?"

"To be sure. I found particularly significant that bit about the madrone tree. What you must understand, Edward, is that no man is a unique creature. What has occurred to you has undoubtedly occurred to others. Regarding the madrone tree, I think your feeling is the general one. There has been an effort to make it so." Twist walked over to the table and retrieved his pipe.

"Evil," he said, "is a concept belonging only to the human species, and it almost invariably springs from some type of sexual repression. If the individual is so conditioned that normal sexual activities are felt to be evil, then in time that individual may come to court evil directly. Metaphorically and otherwise he will sell his soul to the devil because that is the only way any gratification can be achieved. The alternative is to to become an ascetic. In Jonesville repression has been heavy and constant. Not only that, but a symbol of evil has been erected outside its gates where those who find repression unbearable may worship. It has now resulted in a murder and that is the only overt act of evil so far committed." He lit a pipe and started to continue but his monologue was cut short by a knock on the door. Twist strode across the room and opened it.

Ailsa Kildonan stepped into the cabin. She was calm but her face was pale.

"Good evening," said Twist. "You look worried. Please sit down."

She glanced at him and then at Edward.

"I want to talk to you, Mr. Twist," she said.

"Of course. I'm delighted."

Edward stood up. "I'll go," he said quietly. He felt unusually calm as he got his jacket down from the hook on the wall. Ailsa was just another person in the room. True, she was someone he liked, someone to whom he owed an apology. He put on the jacket. If an apology was due, he ought to make it. He paused at her side.

"I'm very sorry about last night," he said.

She looked at him oddly. "I don't think it's a thing we need to mention." Then she glanced at Bleeker Twist.

"It's all right," said Edward, following her glance. "I've already told Mr. Twist all about it. I told him I had been rude to someone I liked very much. It worried me. I thought Mr. Twist could tell me what was wrong with me."

"Instead of which," said Twist, "I let him figure it out for himself."

Ailsa looked back at Edward. "But what you said—what you thought about me—it isn't true."

"I know it," he said. "It was just that I wanted it to be true at the time." He paused. "You see, I'm not a very bold person. Will you forgive me?"

Her eyes searched his face for several seconds and then she touched him lightly on the hand. "Why don't you stay too? I came to tell Mr. Twist about Reverend Foxx. I'm afraid of him. I can't tell Father, though. Father would kill him."

CHAPTER SEVENTEEN

✿ ✿ ✿ FOR THE SECOND EVENING IN SUCCESSION IVOR JONES watched from his window while night came, but tonight his body did not sag with dejection. As he moved slowly and ponderously back and forth across the long living room, his step was firm and his jaw was set with determination. He was liberal in his use of snuff and there w.~ contempt in the gesture of his head when he spat at the fireplace. He was shaggy, like an aged lion.

The mist rolled in from the sea and spread through the redwoods. From his window he watched the top branches fade from sight and then saw the mist itself become invisible in the greater darkness of night. He let the fire on the hearth die out.

At nine o'clock a rap on the door punctured the silence of the room. He opened it quietly to let Floyd Hooks slide into the room. The dowser stood in the darkness, grinning in expectation while Ivor Jones went to the bedroom for a coat. He came back and stood before Hooks while he buttoned it around him.

"We are going to the Bull Woods. Do you understand?"

Hooks kept on grinning. "Bull Woods."

"That's right. You know them pretty well, don't you?"

Hooks bobbed his head proudly.

"I want you to keep watch. Do you understand? You will stay by the edge of the timber nearest town, walking back and forth. If you see anyone, you will whistle. Do you understand that? You will whistle."

176 ✿

Floyd Hooks stuck two fingers in his mouth and blew. A high piercing whistle filled the room. Jones struck the hand down.

"Not here! Only if you see somebody in the woods."

"I was showing you," said Hooks, his head drooping.

"That's all right. I know you can whistle. Come on, now. I'll tell you what to do again on the way."

They got the car out of the garage and drove off slowly without headlights. Jones followed the route he had taken the previous night for part of the distance, but instead of cutting back toward the highway after he had passed the town, he continued ahead on a dirt road which grew fainter as they progressed. It ended finally in an expanse of giant stumps. Beyond the stumps the dark wall of the Bull Woods towered against the sky.

"Get out," said Jones.

They got out and walked until they came to the line of green timber.

"The highway is over there," said Jones, pointing. "I want you to walk there slowly. When you come to the highway, turn around and come back here. Keep walking back and forth and keep your ears open. If you hear anyone, find out who it is. If anybody enters the woods from the town, whistle. Can you tell me what you are supposed to do now?"

"Walk back and forth," said Hooks. "Listen. If anyone comes, I whistle." He made the gesture of whistling but was careful not to blow on his fingers.

"That's right. Keep going back and forth until I get back. Now be off with you."

Hooks grinned and started away along a path between the stumps and the high trees. Ivor Jones watched him until his figure was lost in the night. Then he turned and plunged into the Bull Woods. He slowed down after a short distance. In the darkness the roots caught at his feet and his strained breathing jarred the silence. He paused to let normal respiration return, then moved on with the unerring instinct of an old woodsman.

This was a damn boring business, having to make his own

investigation. The job couldn't be given to anyone else, though. No one could be thoroughly trusted. Foxx had them all scared stiff of the Bull Woods. If he asked someone to spend a few nights watching, the person would be likely as not to run to Foxx and tell him about it. Well, it was his own fault for not doing something about the preacher sooner. Foxx was all right except for these superstitions. They hadn't seemed so bad either, at first. But when it got to the point where they were going to be used against you—well, that was a different matter. All right to scare the employees, but they weren't going to scare Ivor Jones.

He stopped again. His heart was pounding rather hard. This wasn't like walking on level ground. The feet kept slipping on the damp vegetation and sometimes he had to catch at the rough bark of a tree to keep from falling. Just as well to take it easy. There might not be anything tonight. There might not be anything for a week, but sooner or later he'd find out what was going on. Then he could let it be known. What really happened could never be as bad as what people imagined happened. When they found out the truth, Foxx would be laughed out of Jonesville. They'd have to laugh at someone because they couldn't laugh at themselves. Ridicule was a good weapon. Only first he had to find out the truth for himself and make sure he had a reliable witness to help him out.

He went on. Damp in these woods. He hoped he wouldn't catch pneumonia. Cold, too, and he was perspiring. He'd feel it when he stopped moving. Some sort of monkey business going on. Monsters and spirits were all right until they started killing people, but that was going a little too far. Killed one of his best workers, too. Well, he'd find out who was behind it and have him in prison. He'd have to find something else to keep the employees quiet, but that could be attended to later. He had to take care of one thing at a time, and the first thing was to take care of Foxx. Why, the man had even threatened him with a strike! Next he might try to take over the mill in the name of his church.

Jones leaned against a tree and chuckled. The impudence of it! And Foxx had told him there was nothing he could do about it. He'd show him. Wait until he found out what the monkey business was and let the people know. Maybe right now he didn't have anyone he could trust but a half-wit, but pretty soon every-body would be on his side.

It was a long way to that clearing where the madrone tree stood, and his legs were getting tired. He ought to do more walk-ing. He wasn't that old yet. Maybe he couldn't do anything else that a man is supposed to do, but he ought to be able to take a little walk through the woods without getting all tired out. Get-ting old had some compensations though. You could have female companionship without worrying about it. That was something else he could do once he got Foxx out of the way. He wouldn't have to go to so much trouble hiding his relationships. There was nothing wrong with them except what people would think. After Foxx was gone, maybe they wouldn't be thinking those things all the time.

He had to find out about this monkey business, though. There wasn't anything tangible except those marks on the tree. The rest of it didn't matter. People might say they had seen some-thing strange in the Bull Woods, but that was imagination. Peo-ple were always saying such things. He wasn't bothered by imagination.

He stopped and peered through the trees. Surely he had seen a light? He didn't want anyone to find him walking around in the forest. That could make it look bad. Someone might get the idea that he was behind the monkey business and had taken a part in the killing of Mars Venderstone. There it was again. He saw it when he moved, rather dim. He walked toward it cau-tiously and wished he had thought to bring a weapon of some kind. He didn't expect to need one since all he intended to do was watch, but there was always the possibility that he might be dis-covered. What had killed Venderstone wouldn't hesitate where he was concerned.

It was a window, that's what it was. It was a window in a cabin with a light inside. Oban Kildonan's cabin, of course. That was where this fellow Twist lived and where the schoolteacher had gone. There was another man who was going to have to get out of town when this thing was over. He'd given Spence a chance to come around, and Spence had turned it down. Spence could have helped him. But Spence had enjoyed insulting him instead. Well, he wouldn't ask twice. He was going to take care of things himself the way he always had before when he wanted them handled without mistakes. After that he'd whip the town back into a shape to suit him.

He went away from the light again. At least the monkey business hadn't seemed to bother Twist or Spence. That was comforting. Though why should he think it comforting when he knew someone was behind the monkey business? Someone had to be behind it, and he thought he knew who it was. He didn't need comforting; all he needed was to know the truth.

The forest had some damn queer noises in it at night. Even after spending a lifetime in the timber, there were still some noises he couldn't understand. That twig snapping. What would snap a twig? There was no wind, no rain. Only the mist. And there was that scraping sound like a boot slipping across a rough root. That's what he would think of, naturally. He had come to the forest to find someone, and if he expected success, he had to find him. He hadn't expected anything so soon though. He intended to meet someone first. His witness.

He stopped to listen. Maybe he was mistaken. Or maybe that was his witness coming to meet him. If so, he was away off the course. Nothing happened when he listened. He heard noises only when he was making them himself. Maybe that explained it. After he had passed, the twigs he had bent into the ground would straighten out; branches he had pushed aside would swing back into place. He should have brought a gun. He hadn't imagined just how it would be. Sitting alone in the house, he had seemed so safe that he couldn't think of how it would be to feel

180

otherwise. That was lack of imagination. Well, it was a good thing. If he had imagination, he wouldn't be here at all. It was damned dark. He had a flashlight in his pocket but he couldn't use it. It wouldn't do any good to announce his presence to the whole forest.

There now, what was that noise? That was no twig snapping and no branch going back into place, either. It had a regularity about it. Twigs didn't snap that way, one after the other and about ten seconds apart. They didn't make quite that noise, either—like muffled pistol shots. And anyway, the noise was in front of him where he hadn't been yet. Someone else had to be making it. Someone or something.

He stopped again. Maybe this was it. If it was, he had to go easy. He was making a lot of noise himself the way he was wheezing, and his heart was throbbing until it was like a hammer in his ears. Just take it easy. Cool off first and then go on to the madrone tree. If there was something there—if there was someone there—he could sit back and wait for his witness, unless his witness was there already. Then they wouldn't need to wait. They could see what it was and then get out of here.

He moved on again. The cracking sound was louder, and he thought he heard something else now. Sounded like a woman crying. What the devil would that be? There shouldn't be anyone but himself out here in the Bull Woods—nothing, that is, except himself and whoever he was going to find. That funeral today. He should have gone just to look things over. It was to the left, much nearer now. Quite definitely it could be sobs—sort of a snorting like somebody out of breath. He almost sounded like that himself. He ought to wait a little longer but this was a good chance. If his witness was there, he would already know what it was. Damned queer. Good thing he had no imagination.

That was the clearing where the madrone tree grew. Must be. That pale thing in the center would be the tree. And that noise —the cracking, the snorting. He couldn't see a damned thing with the mist blotting out the stars. Something moving though.

Moving toward *him,* by God! And no gun—if a gun would do any good. His hand fell to his pocket. Whatever it was, he was going to see it. He wasn't going to run now. This is what he had come for. He was going to see it. He was going . . .

Andramalech threw back his head and wailed just once. After that he sat staring at the window for five minutes.

"You can't pay any attention to that cat," said Bleeker Twist. "If you do, he'll drive you crazy. I've seen Andramalech stare at a blank wall the same way he does at the window. Cats are dramatic animals."

"Makes one nervous all the same," said Edward, watching the cat.

"Oh, yes. They do things like that for a mouse or for the wind or for nothing at all. Andramalech, go lie down."

The cat looked at his master and yawned. Then he licked his paw and rubbed it against his eye. He cocked his head to one side, looking at the window, and then with a sudden rush and a long leap he made the sill. He sat there looking at his reflection in the glass.

"You see," said Twist. "That's all he had in mind. He's vain."

"Yes," said Edward, "he's—" He never finished his thought. His mouth sagged farther open and his gesture remained frozen in air. He stared at Twist.

"My God!" whispered Twist, springing to his feet.

Somewhere a man was yelling. Twist charged across the cabin to the door and flung it open. The cries continued, louder now, drawing closer. And then above the cries came the maniacal laughter. Twist grabbed the lantern.

"Come on! Let's get there this time!"

They ran full tilt into the forest with the lantern pushing back the shadows ahead of them. The cries stopped but they could hear the heavy footsteps of someone running.

"This way!" shouted Twist, making a sudden turn in his course. "We'll head it off!"

They were too late to head it off, but they weren't too late to see it. Twist stopped in his tracks, holding the lantern high. Hurtling past them in the uncertain light was Ivor Jones. He had a flashlight in his hand but its beam was an erratic plume of light spinning among the trees. His shaggy locks were wild; his mouth was open and gaped crazily as he strained for air; a blue flush darkened his face. His ponderous body sped down the dark corridor of the trees with an agility unknown for forty years. But not for long. Even as Twist and Edward watched, the stride broke into dizzy lurches. Jones's head turned as he fell, the distorted terrified face staring into the light.

They ran to his side and Twist dropped down beside the body. A dry rattle was coming from Jones's lips. The heavy legs moved aimlessly, kicking at the matted ground. Then they were still. Twist laid a hand on the old man's breast.

"Is there a doctor in Jonesville?"

"The company doctor, Archie Brill."

Twist stood up. "Let's get him! The old boy is done for unless someone gets a needle in him. Leave the lantern here. We'll send Kildonan back to stay with him and we'll borrow the car to go for the doctor."

Edward stared at his friend, then looked back into the forest from where Jones had come. "But he was running from something! We can't leave him!"

"We can't take him!" cried Twist. "Come on!" He seized Edward's arm and started running in the direction of the Kildonan house.

They had hardly left the circle of light when the sharp report of a pistol sounded somewhere behind them. A bullet cut the foliage above their heads. There was another shot and then silence.

"He'll be killed!" sobbed Edward.

"And if we stay, we'll all be killed," snapped Twist. "We're unarmed."

Safety for themselves and hope for Ivor Jones lay with Oban

183

Kildonan, and so they sped recklessly on through the darkness, sensing rather than seeing the huge trunks which turned their path into a maze. The house finally loomed in front of them.

"Stay and watch the road!" ordered Twist. He left Edward outside the house while he ran across the yard and burst into the living room. Oban Kildonan came to his feet from a chair by the fireplace, staring at him.

"Ivor Jones is in the woods about two hundred yards in back of the house," said Twist, his words falling swiftly and quietly. "We left a lantern burning. I think he's dead. Someone is there with a gun. We want your car to go for the doctor."

Oban's stare continued a second. Then, without a word, he took his car keys from his pocket and handed them to Twist. Twist ran outside again, seized Edward's arm and made for the car.

"See anything?" he asked, as he leaped into the front seat.

"Nothing," said Edward, sliding in on the opposite side.

Before Twist had the engine started, Oban Kildonan appeared against the light of the front doorway, shouting back to someone inside the house.

"Mind that the doors and windows are locked, Ailsa," they heard him call, "and see that no one enters until I get back." He carried a rifle in the crook of his arm.

CHAPTER EIGHTEEN

✿ ✿ ✿ WITH BLEEKER TWIST AT THE WHEEL, THE CAR LURCHED giddily along the dirt road toward the highway. Edward felt as though he'd been suddenly incorporated into a great senseless machine of some kind. Since the moment in the cabin when he'd heard Jones shouting, he'd acted without thought of any kind, almost without conscious volition. Events whirred, and he kept pace with them. He was being stampeded. But in the car his body was temporarily idle and he was able to think again. His first feeling was one of sharp annoyance.

"This is absurd," he said. "There's no need in our both going. One should have stayed at the house."

"I'm glad you didn't think of protecting Ailsa sooner," said Twist grimly. "We'd only have wasted time. The fact is, we're both needed in town. We have a chance to settle this thing."

"But the thing—whatever it is—is still in the forest."

"Exactly. We have a head start and I intend to keep it. Someone in the forest has a gun and did not hesitate to shoot at us. I have no gun and couldn't hit anything even if I did. Oban Kildonan strikes me as a marksman who won't get buck fever if he finds something strange between his sights." He swung the car sharply to avoid a tree, then bounced forward onto the highway and headed for town. Edward's annoyance increased and along with it came a queasy sensation in his stomach.

"I don't like running away," he said.

✿ 185

"We're not running away," snapped Twist. There was tension there too. "Whoever was chasing Ivor Jones lives in Jonesville and has to return there. We have to arrive first, that's all. It's pure mechanics."

"You'll have a devil of a time watching all Jonesville." Twist's persistent didacticism grated on Edward's nerves.

"We won't watch all Jonesville. I know who we're after. I told you that before."

Edward didn't ask for the name. He stifled the impulse the moment it arose. Or perhaps it was the hollow pit of his stomach that made him refrain from asking. He recognized the queasy feeling now. It was a sense of guilt. He was suddenly afraid to have Twist name the person in the Bull Woods. In some indefinable way he felt responsible for that person's behavior even without knowing who it was. He felt a sense of identity, and he didn't want that identity revealed. Twist glanced at him curiously.

"Are you still afraid? Even after this afternoon?"

"This afternoon?"

"You told me a great deal about yourself."

"I suppose I did." For a moment he resented Twist's knowledge. Then he said, "Perhaps that's why I'm afraid. You told me something I'd never thought of before—that I'm not necessarily unique."

"Well?" said Twist.

"I have the terrible feeling that the person in the forest is not so unlike myself."

"You know who we're after?"

"No," said Edward, but he knew what he thought. He forced his mind back to practical matters. "What are we going to do?"

"I'm not certain myself," said Twist. "But I'm quite sure our quarry will go either home or to the house of a friend. If we witness the arrival, it will be our first tangible bit of evidence."

"But you must know something already."

"I do," said Twist. "I know what makes the marks on the

madrone tree." He spoke quietly and his usual accent of wry humor was missing.

"I see," said Edward. Here was another thing he wasn't certain he wanted to know. He had an apprehension, a foreboding, about the nature of those queer welts.

"You mean you have guessed?" asked Twist. Again he refrained from telling what Edward obviously didn't want to know.

"I'm not sure."

"It was you, to an extent, who told me."

"Yes, I guess I did."

"You gave me a complete picture of the madrone tree—its physical appearance and the symbolic meaning it has come to have for the people of Jonesville. That's because you are a part of Jonesville yourself. The madrone tree is the symbol of license. It is naked; it is unrepressed. Against its smooth skin the mythical bull rubs its horns—the bull, symbol of virility and unbridled passion. And you have this symbol of license manifesting itself in a locality where the moral code of the entire community is based upon repression." He paused a moment. "That, of course, is natural. If there were no repression, there would be no need for such a symbol." He glanced at Edward again. "What did you think of Ailsa's story about Foxx?"

"You mean when he saw her after the funeral today?"

"Of course."

"At first I could think nothing except how unpleasant it must have been for Ailsa. And then—"

"Yes?"

"Then I saw it a little differently. Foxx said no more than I myself said on another occasion. It made me wonder."

"Made you wonder what?"

"Made me wonder just how many others besides myself have wandered in the Bull Woods to escape the influence of the town. Because that's all it amounts to in the final analysis. It means freedom. That's why the people always envied the Kildonans— even while they made them outcasts. The Kildonans were free."

"And if they're to remain free, we'd better settle this thing tonight," said Twist. "Where do I find Dr. Brill's house?"

"The first one on the left as we enter town."

"Good. We'll waste no time in driving at any rate."

"Those marks on the tree," said Edward. He was able to think about them more clearly now; the foreboding was lessened. Talking helped dispel the apprehension and sense of guilt. "You say you know how they were made."

"Yes, I do. I said that part of the information came from you. You gave me the background. But the actual fact was told me by an acquaintance of yours. By Miss Graw."

"Stella?"

Twist nodded. "When I had tea with her and Miss Westerly this afternoon. I doubt very much if Miss Graw knows she told me, but she did."

"Strange that she would know," said Edward, forgetting for a moment that he didn't yet know himself.

"I can't consider it strange," said Twist.

"Perhaps not," said Edward. "She sees as much of Foxx as anyone in town. And still I'm certain—"

"What are you certain of?"

"I was going to say that I'm sure there was never anything between Foxx and Stella Graw except an admiration on her part. The admiration of a disciple for the master."

"Is that the doctor's house I see ahead?"

"Yes. Swing in close to the fence and I'll run in for him."

"Good. I want to watch the highway to make sure no one passes us while we're stopped." He brought the car to a halt before the picket fence. Edward leaped out, swung open the gate and ran up the steps to the house.

"Ivor Jones!" Dr. Brill was properly horrified. He flung on his coat, checked the pocket for car keys and picked up his bag. Edward ran back to rejoin Twist.

"He'll be on his way at once."

"Fine," said Twist as the car shot forward again. "Now to our task. You were about to tell me why you were certain there was nothing between Foxx and Stella Graw."

Edward felt himself flush. "Because I believe it's been I in whom Stella has been interested. Not that she ever showed it. I just have that feeling."

"She never showed it at all?"

"No," said Edward. "She was always very circumspect—to my relief, I might add. Except—and I hadn't thought of it until now—the night I left Jonesville."

"And what happened then?"

"She came to my apartment. Rather odd, looking back. She wouldn't have done that ordinarily. I supposed she'd come about school work or perhaps to get material for gossip. I was upset at the time about losing my job and having to move, so I didn't pay much attention to her. I remember getting a little angry because of what she implied had gone on between me and Ailsa. She told me I didn't need to go to the Bull Woods."

"And what did she mean by that?" asked Twist softly.

"I don't know," Edward said. Then his flush suddenly deepened. "My God, I do too know! She was trying to tell me—I'm sure I'm not wrong about this—she was trying to say—"

Twist groaned. "She was trying to give you some encouragement. Is that it? And what an effort it must have cost her! To come out openly with such an invitation! What do you know about Stella Graw?"

"I thought I knew her well. Perhaps I didn't know her at all."

"I had an advantage over you when I met her. I had no previous prejudices one way or the other. She's a beautiful woman by purely physical standards. By mental standards I'm not so sure. She has absorbed the teachings of Jonesville completely. She fears evil, and yet it fascinates her. She was avid for details of events in the Bull Woods, drawn and repelled by them at the same time. Her concept of Ailsa is shocking, to say the least, and yet that concept is only a reflection of herself. By imputing vices to Ailsa, she gets vicarious enjoyment for herself."

"Stella Graw! I can't believe it." But as he spoke, he knew he did believe it. A person like himself; except that Stella's dreams had been about him!

"When she came to you that evening," continued Twist slowly, "it must have been with the realization that it was the last chance she'd have to save herself. She, too, wanted reality."

"And I didn't help her any," said Edward.

"Don't blame yourself. I'm not sure that you could have helped at all. With Stella the repression had already caused a rupture along other lines. A new habit had been formed. Those marks on the madrone tree—"

"Yes?" whispered Edward.

"Are made by a whip. They are lash marks. Stella told me so. It was a slip of the tongue."

"A whip?" He asked the question, but he needed no further confirmation. Remembering the appearance of the marks, it was plain enough. "But how would Stella know?"

"How would she know," replied Twist, "unless she used the whip herself?"

Edward sat stunned. "But I thought that Foxx—"

"I know that's what you thought. But Foxx has no need to vent his rage on the symbol of evil. Each Sunday in church he finds an outlet for his emotions. The church is his sublimation. Even with Ailsa—he wanted her for the church, not himself. Stella has no such outlet; her whole life is proscribed on every side. As the schoolteacher and church organist her behavior is under constant surveillance. She must court the most circumspect friends and adhere to every local convention. It was too much. Outside the limits of town the madrone tree beckoned to her. If she could not have love, then, at least, she could vent her hatred against the symbol of license. It was a satisfaction of sorts. It was a fantasy which harmed no one."

"But it's insane!"

Twist shook his head. "No more so than Jonesville. However, it was an aberration which might have been considered insane—

or worse yet, immoral. So she must have been in constant terror of discovery. And yet she couldn't resist the impulse. She tried to enlist your aid."

"Which I refused," said Edward.

"You could have done nothing else. But afterwards—stung by your rebuff, she went to the Bull Woods. I think we'll find she was driving Foxx's car which she uses on evenings when she practices the organ. Nothing would have happened if Venderstone hadn't followed her. He was watching Foxx, if Ailsa has given us the facts right, and no doubt followed because of the car. Instead of discovering Foxx, he discovered Stella and she turned on him. She struck him down and then struck him again and again to ensure his silence. Who can say that at the moment she didn't enjoy doing in reality what she had so far done only by representation?"

Edward grasped for a flaw in the argument. "But Venderstone is a strong man. What did she strike him with?"

"The butt end of a leather whip," said Twist, "is almost always loaded with shot. It is a superblackjack. One blow would stun an ox." They were both silent a moment.

"You turn off here for her house," said Edward.

Twist switched off the headlights and slowed the car to a crawl as he turned off the highway.

"The first one is the parsonage," said Edward. "Stella's is the small house on the other side."

"I'll be able to watch both," said Twist. "We aren't certain she'll go directly home. Meanwhile you drive on over to Miss Westerly's and keep watch there."

"Good Lord, what will I say if I see her?"

"That I can't tell you. At least note the time. We may have a long while to wait since she was still in the forest when we left. And even if she had a car, it must have been at the edge of the woods where she'd have to go on foot to get it." The car rolled slowly along the road in front of Foxx's house. Then abruptly Twist clamped on the brake. Both men stared through the uncurtained window into the lighted interior of the house. A wave of relief swept over Edward, and the images Twist's words had erected were suddenly dispelled. It was Edward who spoke.

"And if Stella Graw was behind us when we left the Bull Woods," he said, unable to keep the faint sarcasm from his voice, "tell me what she's doing drinking tea in Foxx's parlor?"

It was true. Stella Graw sat primly in a straight-backed chair with her skirt carefully smoothed over her knees. Foxx was entering a door at the far end of the room. He carried a tea tray in his hands.

Twist made no reply to Edward's remark. The car started moving again, very slowly. The headlights flashed on.

"Well," said Edward, "do we go on to Ula Westerly's?"

"Oh, no!" groaned Twist.

"Where then?"

"It occurs to me," and Twist's voice was small and dry, "that there were two people near Ivor Jones when he lost consciousness. They were you and I, Edward. To all appearances we have now run away. We had better get back. Oh, dear, yes, we had better get back!" And he whirled the car about in the roadway.

"But what was chasing Ivor Jones?"

"That," said Twist, "is what we'd better find out at once for the sake of our own health. Oh, dear!" The car gathered speed.

"The doctor will be there," said Edward. "What will you tell him?"

"I'll tell him nothing," said Twist. "I've talked far, far too much!" They left Jonesville behind them and roared once more toward the Bull Woods.

CHAPTER NINETEEN

❧ ❧ ❧ IVOR JONES'S BODY STILL LAY IN THE FOREST. THREE lanterns now repelled the darkness as Edward and Twist approached through the trees. Dr. Brill knelt beside the body. Oban Kildonan stood at the edge of the shadows, his rifle under his arm. A third man, William Banders, sat on a redwood log near by and waited while the doctor worked.

Brill looked up as Bleeker Twist and Edward came into the light, then returned his attention to Ivor Jones. Banders gave them a sharp glance but said nothing. Brill finally stood up.

"It's no use," he said. "All indications point to complete heart failure. His heart has been bothering him for several years and any unusual and prolonged strain would have been sufficient to bring about death. I couldn't have done anything even had I been here at the time he fell." Brill disjointed a hypodermic needle and put it back in his case. He stowed away several bottles and snapped the case shut. "I guess you can take over, Sheriff."

Banders got up slowly and walked over to Twist and Edward. "Don't wander off," he said caustically. "I'll want to talk to you." He went back to Dr. Brill.

"Have you been treating Jones in the past?"

"For many years. I'm the doctor at the mill."

"This heart condition—was it something dangerous?"

"For a man of his age it was. I sent him to a specialist about three years ago. The verdict was the same as mine. It couldn't be improved, but with moderate exercise and careful diet he had nothing to worry about. I understand, however, that tonight he was running."

"He was running, all right," said the sheriff. "Anybody know about his heart except you?"

Brill shrugged. "I haven't told anyone, but there's no reason why he mightn't have."

"Nothing else on him that would give any other reason for his death?"

"Well, there's no evidence of any kind of blow except on his forehead where he plowed into the earth as he fell. The skin is scraped but there's no bruise. The heart was sufficient to cause death under the circumstances. In fact, prolonged violent exercise for a man as old as Ivor Jones could result in death whether there was heart trouble or not. If anything else is suspected, there'll have to be an autopsy. I can't perform one out here in the woods."

" 'Course not," said Banders. He looked at the body at his feet. "Something's up, though. You see, that's how I happened to be here. Jones called me this morning. He said he wanted to meet me near that madrone tree about nine-thirty tonight. Wouldn't tell me why; just told me to be there. With a man like Ivor Jones you don't ask too many questions until you know what it's all about. So I told him I'd come. He gave me pretty specific directions, but I was never in these woods until last Sunday night, so I didn't get here quite on the dot. Maybe I was five minutes late. I heard shouts and came running. When I got here, he was lying just like he is now, with a lantern burning beside him. I heard someone running on ahead and let fly with a couple of shots, but I didn't see anyone. A little later Kildonan got here and told me you were coming."

"That was us you shot at," said Edward. The words popped out. It was a relief to find one thing which had a logical explanation. Banders stared at him.

"I already figured that out. Suppose you come over here, young man." He led Edward about twenty yards from the others and squatted against a tree.

"When anyone dies around here, you're always Johnny on the spot, aren't you?"

"I can't help that. I'm living in these woods."

"Yeh, that's right. You moving trunks again tonight?"

"No, I'm not," snapped Edward.

"Finally got moved in, eh? That's fine. I remember now. Last time I talked to you, you'd just quit teaching school. What'd you quit for? This isn't the end of the term."

Edward flushed. "I was let out."

"You mean you were canned? That's pretty. You didn't tell me that."

"You didn't ask me."

Banders picked up a twig from the ground and commenced chewing the end of it. "Why wasn't you in the cabin tonight?"

"We were until we heard the shouts."

"Who would *we* be?"

"Bleeker Twist. He lives there too."

"Oh, yes. There's always Mr. Twist. Well, I'll have a talk with him later. You got here before I did. What did you see?"

"We saw Jones. He was running when we first saw him, running with his mouth all twisted up. He didn't see us until he fell. I remember how he looked at us then, his eyes staring into the lantern light."

"Looked scared, did he?"

"He looked terror-stricken."

"So what did you do then?"

"We went to him, of course. He seemed to be dying. We thought the best course was to go for a doctor at once, so we did. We left a lantern so it would be easy to find the place again. That's when you shot at us. Naturally, we thought it must be the person Jones was running from, and not having any gun, we didn't stop."

195

Banders chuckled. "I bet you didn't! So you went for the doctor. Then what?"

"Then we came back."

Banders's eyes narrowed. "You sure took your time about it. Brill was here a good ten minutes before you were and he had to get his car out of the garage. Where have you been?"

"Well—" Edward hesitated. "We drove on a little way first. We had to find a place to turn around."

"It took you ten minutes to turn around, is that it?" The sheriff stood up. "Now look here. Nobody's trying to do anything right now except find out what happened, but pretty soon I'll have something else on my mind. There was that fishy death Sunday night right here in these same woods, and I'm not forgetting it. The way I've got it for the record, you were one of the fellows who found that body too. You and Twist and Kildonan, the same three that's here tonight. So don't start telling me anything crooked. You didn't spend ten minutes finding a place to turn the car around. It would turn on the highway. What were you doing?"

Edward's flush deepened. There was no reason for not telling the sheriff what they had been doing except that Twist's suspicions had been proved so utterly false that to voice them would sound like a hasty and ill conceived alibi.

"We checked to see if a certain person was home," he said finally.

"Yeh? Who?"

"I'd rather not say. If Mr. Twist wants to tell you, it's up to him."

"Maybe you want to be sure you tell the same story, is that it? What were you checking on people for?"

"Because Mr. Twist—well, because we thought it might throw some light on this thing. This person couldn't be here in the woods and at home at the same time."

"That's sure a fact. Who was it?"

196

"Well, as long as we found the person in Jonesville, it doesn't matter much, does it?"

"You can't tell," said the sheriff. "Then what did you do?"

"Then we came back here."

Banders tossed his twig on the ground and spat out the chewed wood he had in his mouth. "Seems to me from what I know of Jonesville, nothing much ever happened here that Ivor Jones didn't have a hand in."

"That may be true."

"You're damned right it's true. You can't be in politics in this county and not know about Ivor Jones. He's got his finger on schoolteachers too. If you were canned, Ivor Jones had something to do with it. That's right, isn't it?" Banders leaned forward to peer into Edward's face.

"Yes, that's true."

"Did he can you personally, or have somebody else do it?"

"He told me himself. I got formal notice by messenger."

"Uh-huh. When was that?"

"Last Sunday."

"Last Sunday. My, my. Several things happened last Sunday. You got canned and came to live in the woods. Then Venderstone got killed and you helped to find his body. Tonight Ivor Jones dies and you're right on hand to find his body too. And to think he just had you canned! Well, well. What were you canned for?"

"That's my personal business."

"Maybe that's what you think. When people start dying, nobody has any personal business. You might as well tell me because I'll find out for myself in Jonesville anyhow."

Edward's face felt hot. "There's no truth in the charge!"

"Then you shouldn't mind telling me what it was."

"Conduct unbecoming a schoolteacher." Edward spoke the words and snapped his lips together. This was getting pretty uncomfortable. Banders leered at him.

"That's good. Maybe you was taking the kids behind the school and teaching them to smoke, huh?"

"It was nothing, I tell you! It was pure imagination!"

"Well, don't get worked up about it. You aren't charged with anything so far. You aren't in jail yet. Did you see anything behind Ivor Jones that could have been after him?"

"No."

"Hear anything?"

"Nothing but your gun."

"Uh-huh. Well, let's go back and join the others. Don't try running off. I'll have lots more questions." They walked back to where Twist, Brill, and Kildonan stood in a group about the body.

"I suppose it isn't right to leave him laying there," said the sheriff. "But I don't want anybody thinking this party is over yet."

"I cannot stay longer," rumbled Oban's deep bass. "I have only a wife and daughter at home. I've stayed here this long because you asked me, but now I'm going. If you want to talk to me, you know where to find me." He started resolutely toward the house.

"Hold on," called Banders. "We'll all go with you. Give me a hand with the body."

Kildonan hesitated a moment, then came back. He handed his rifle to Brill, then bent over to hook his arms under Jones's shoulders. Banders lifted the legs and together they got the body off the ground and started forward. The group was silent until they reached the house. Oban released the body to knock on the door.

"It's me, Ailsa. You can open up now." There was the sound of a sliding bolt and the door opened. "It's a bad business," continued Oban. "Go back with your mother and stay till you're called."

They carried Ivor Jones into the living room and laid him on the couch. Oban brought a quilt from the hall closet and spread it over the body. "There," he said. "Now that I'm here, you can take all night if you so please."

"It may not be so much longer," said Banders. "Doctor, I'm through with you if you want to go."

"Then I shall," said Brill. "I'll be home if you want me."

"One thing." Banders lifted a finger. "Don't talk about this now. Not until morning in any case."

"Very well," said the doctor. He picked up his bag and departed. They heard his car drive away toward town.

"Now," said the sheriff, "if there's a room where we could have a little privacy, I'd like to talk to you and Mr. Twist."

"There is a kitchen," said Oban. "No one will be using it if that would suit you."

"That'll be fine." Banders stood up and with a jerk of his thumb gestured to Twist. The kitchen led directly off the living room. They stepped into it and closed the door. The sheriff found a stool to sit on and Twist hoisted himself up on the drain by the sink.

"Well, Mr. Twist, we meet again."

"Eh? Oh, yes, yes, of course."

"And how is your cat this evening?"

"Andramalech? Quite fine, thank you."

"Any strange behavior?"

"No—well, he was staring at things again."

"What things?"

"The window."

"Uh-huh. Now," Banders put a beefy hand on either knee and leaned forward, "just what do you know about this?"

"Very little, I think."

"Then it shouldn't take you long telling it."

"Surely, Mr. Spence has told you."

"Never mind what Mr. Spence may or may not have told me. I want you to tell me."

"Certainly," sighed Twist, "if you insist. We were sitting in the cabin when we heard the loud cries of a man's voice."

"What kind of cries?"

"Loud, I said."

"I know. But were they scared cries or what?"

"Hmm, well, it is more difficult than people think to tell what emotion prompts a cry. Surprise, certainly, and some horror I should think. I must confess that I am somewhat conditioned by the events of last Sunday night, so that any cry at all would have impressed me as being motivated by terror."

"Let's not worry about your condition. Your heard these yells, these cries. Then what?"

"Then I threw open the cabin door to hear them better. That was when we heard the laughter."

"Laughter? Someone heard laughter last time. Was it the same?"

"I didn't hear it last time."

"How did it sound?"

"Well, there again previous conditioning prevents a truly objective analysis. When one hears a laugh in the dark forest under such conditions, one cannot help but believe the sound to have madness in it."

"You thought it was mad laughter, then?"

"Excited laughter, I should say. The type of laughter which springs from nervousness rather than amusement."

"How long did it last?"

"For a very brief duration. Of course, we didn't give it much attention since the cries were much stronger and seemed to be approaching. We ran in their direction."

"And met Jones?"

"We didn't meet him. He ran past us at right angles. We got a fairly good look at him."

"Uh-huh. Now, Mr. Twist, who was it you went to look for in town?"

Twist glanced at him sharply. "Well, now. How considerate of Edward that he didn't tell you."

"I told you not to bother about what Mr. Spence maybe said. I asked you a question."

"I heard you quite clearly and I suppose I must answer it. In my slow-witted way I believed I had discovered who killed Mars Venderstone last Sunday evening. I believe the same person must have struck terror into Ivor Jones. And so I planned to park in front of that person's home and wait for him to emerge from the forest. Unfortunately, the person was already in Jonesville and could hardly have been pursuing Ivor Jones."

"But I want to know who you were after."

"Dear me. But how embarrassing to tell you."

"It can be more embarrassing if you don't tell me."

"Hardly. Nothing is so embarrassing as being forced to exhibit one's stupidity. In fact, I won't do it."

"You refuse to answer the question?"

"Quite so."

"Remember, now. Ivor Jones has been murdered."

"Murdered?"

"Well, you saw it for yourself." Banders glared at Twist.

"So I did. So I did. But it just now occurs to me that you will have the very devil of a time proving Ivor Jones was murdered."

"I will, eh? Well, let me tell you that when the second man dies mysteriously in the Bull Woods, something is fishy. They'll have a hard time saying Jones's death resulted from misadventure."

"Indeed they will," said Twist. "In fact, the verdict will hit the case dead center. Jones died from heart failure, one of the most common causes of death in the world. That will be the verdict."

"Sure. And someone who knew he had a weak heart gave him a scare. That's murder."

Twist stared at Banders until the latter began to feel uncomfortable. "Hah!" he exclaimed finally. "That is it!"

"What is? You mean he was scared to death?"

"No, no!" said Twist. "I mean he wasn't murdered at all!"

Banders heaved himself to his feet. "Now I suppose you're going to say Jones isn't lying there in the other room dead?"

"Nothing of the sort. I'm saying that Jones wasn't murdered. He died of heart failure."

"It's the same in either case."

"But Jones will be murdered yet!" Twist waggled a finger at him. "Tell me this, Mr. Banders. Why haven't you continued your investigation into the death of Mars Venderstone?"

The sheriff flushed darkly, "Who says I haven't?"

"I say it. He was killed Sunday and today is Tuesday. Since Sunday night I've seen no visible effort on your part to do anything at all. You let the coroner's verdict stand. Who told you to?"

"You're taking a lot for granted."

"I'm taking nothing for granted which isn't as obvious as the nose on my face."

"You're absolutely wrong!" said the sheriff hotly. "We've been quiet, that's all."

"Someone told you to be quiet."

"Maybe someone did, and maybe I just decided it was best that way. There's no use yelling murder until you can bring in the murderer."

"Is that what Jones told you at the inquest?"

"He said that a murder verdict could lead to the wrong people getting hurt."

"And you paid attention?"

Banders put his fists on his hips, glaring at Twist. "Sure. I paid attention. Ivor Jones is a big man in this county."

"Was," corrected Twist.

"But don't get the idea I haven't done my duty. I've sure checked on you, for example."

"Indeed? And what did you learn?"

Banders sat down again. "I learned that you're a professor on leave."

"I told you that much myself."

"All right. But it doesn't mean anything to me where this case is concerned. And let me tell you this—nobody is going to say I'm keeping quiet from now on!"

"You are certainly expending no end of breath and getting nowhere." Banders was momentarily speechless. Twist hopped down from the drainboard and commenced pacing the short confines of the kitchen vigorously.

"I am stupid! I have overlooked a simple fundamental!"

"All right," said Banders. "Suppose you let me in on the secret."

"Quite so. After all, it is your responsibility." Twist paused in front of him. "We must return to the scene of death and retrace Jones's path."

"I'm the one that says what we're going to do. Now stop hopping around and answer some questions."

Twist waved the order aside. "My dear fellow, I know that to give the appearance of having done your duty, you must talk to everyone within miles of the death scene. You must ask endless questions about where each person was and why each person was there. If you write it all down, you will have a large volume when you are finished, and you can present the volume as material evidence of your industry. It would be a handy thing to wave in front of the voters in the next election. In the meanwhile you accomplish nothing. Now don't swell up; it does no good to get excited; I will not be impressed. You may have your eye on me as a potential killer, but even if you proved I was the murderer, you would still be wrong. I have no reason for doing such a thing. I never spoke a word to Ivor Jones in my life. That is unfortunate, because had I done so, his death might have been prevented. But we still have opportunity to stop this thing before it goes any further. Let us get back to the forest."

Banders eyed him critically. "I intend going back to the forest, but first I want all the information you've got."

"Nonsense! Until you have observed the evidence of the forest itself, you cannot know what information you want. You will reap a tub of rubbish and leave the valuable material untouched."

"And what do you think we're going to find there?"

Twist tugged at his nose. "Mars Venderstone had his skull crushed."

"I know that. And I know how the people in Jonesville look at it. Your preacher has an explanation."

"Exactly. And if the people of Jonesville can believe Venderstone was killed by some supernatural force, how much easier to believe that Jones was killed the same way. Jones hasn't a mark on his body; he was fleeing in terror. Now tell me; what frightened him?"

"That's just what I'm trying to find out."

"You knew Ivor Jones?"

"I did. He backed me in the last election."

"Was he a man who would run from any human agent?"

"He was a hard man. He wouldn't run from anybody."

"And yet, he ran. He ran so hard it killed him. You see how foolish it is questioning people when none of them could have frightened him to death? I tell you we need to know what lies in the forest."

Banders looked at Twist curiously. "None of us saw anything in the forest."

"The forest is a big place. Don't forget that Mr. Foxx believes absolutely that it contains an evil spirit which can manifest itself in physical form. It would take something like that to frighten Jones."

The sheriff dug his hands into his pockets. "I'm not going out there to look for spirits. They'd laugh me out of the county."

"They'll laugh harder if you let two men die and never uncover the cause of death. And let me add this," Twist thumped him on the breast bone to emphasize his words. "Unless you uncover the cause of death tonight, you may never uncover it."

Banders shuffled his feet uneasily. "There are other people

besides those who were at the body. Kildonan has a daughter and a wife."

Twist's eyes took on a sudden gleam. "Indeed he has. They are in the house at present where you can talk to them whenever you please. Why not arm yourself with a few facts before you do any more questioning?"

"You seem mighty sure we're going to find something."

"I made a horrible error tonight," said Twist. "I must rectify it as soon as possible. Shall we go?"

Banders opened the door and walked back into the living room with Twist at his heels. Oban Kildonan and Edward sat silently waiting.

"We're going to look around a little more," said the sheriff. "Twist here seems to think he has an idea."

Edward raised his head. "Another idea? Splendid," he said caustically.

"Come, Edward, do not be so harsh with me." He glanced around the room. "I will need your daughter's help, Mr. Kildonan."

"My daughter does not leave the house tonight," replied Oban evenly.

"But a guide is essential. She knows the forest."

"No," he said.

"There will be three of us with her—four, if you wish to come yourself. She will be safe."

"Nothing is safe in the Bull Woods tonight."

Banders looked at Twist curiously, then stepped forward. "I guess I'll have to insist," he said.

Oban shook his head, but at that moment Ailsa herself stepped into the room from the hallway. Her face was pale.

"I'll go, Father," she said. "I heard what was said."

"You'll stay with me, Ailsa."

She walked over to his chair. "I've got to help them. I've heard about Ivor Jones. You know what they'll say in town."

"I care not what they say in town."

"But this time they won't stop with words. They'll come for us. I'm going." She left the room quickly before he could reply and returned, wearing a leather jacket. The old man rose to his feet.

"I do not like it."

"I'm going, Father."

Edward stepped forward. "I won't leave her side, Mr. Kildonan."

Oban glanced at Edward contemptuously, then his gaze softened. "It may be you'll be as safe in the woods as at home." He sank back in his chair.

"Have you examined the contents of Ivor Jones's pockets?" asked Twist. "Was he armed by any chance?"

Banders walked over to the lounge and lifted the blanket. Quickly he ran his hands through the dead man's pockets.

"Very little here," he said. "His wallet, some change, car keys, a handkerchief. No gun. He had a flashlight when he fell."

"You might take the keys. If the car is near the woods, we will want to examine it." The sheriff dropped the key case into his pocket.

"I guess we're ready," he said. Equipped with lanterns and flashlights, the four of them trooped out into the night.

CHAPTER TWENTY

❦ ❦ ❦ THEY MOVED FOUR ABREAST THROUGH THE FOREST, WITH the great shadows circling around the core of light as they progressed. At the spot where Ivor Jones had fallen, they stopped.

"I think you told me," Twist whispered to Banders, "that he asked you to meet him at the madrone tree?"

"That's right," Banders replied.

Twist turned to Ailsa. "Will you lead the way?"

The girl looked at him with frightened eyes but nodded and started forward. Edward kept pace with her, the beam of his torch boring into the forest ahead. Twist came behind them, his eyes exploring the lateral confines of their course. He suddenly exclaimed sharply.

"We're on the right track, anyway." He ran a few yards to the left and bent over. "This should be his hat." He picked up a wide-brimmed felt and brought it back to the others.

"That's his hat, all right," said the sheriff.

Twist gave it to Banders. "See if it fits."

The sheriff eyed it suspiciously. "What for?"

Twist chuckled. "You might be mistaken for Ivor Jones. That should surprise the monster no end to see Jones walking around in the forest."

"Don't be silly," growled Banders. "It's no time for jokes."

"I'm quite serious," said Twist. "Try it on."

Self-consciously, Banders took off his own hat and put on the one Twist had found.

"It's too big."

"Ah, perhaps we can correct that." Twist took the hat again and found some scraps of paper in his pocket which he wadded up and stuffed under the headband. "Now try it."

Banders put the hat back on his head. "It will stay on but I'm damned if I want to wear it."

"My dear fellow, how delightful if you should become the object of an attack yourself. You would have solved everything."

"My duty doesn't go that far," returned Banders, but he left the hat on his head. They moved on until they came to the edge of the clearing where the madrone tree stood. Here they stopped again and looked at the scene silently. The pale stem of the tree glowed ghostlike in the lantern light. It looked incredibly lonely in the midst of the big trees. A seaward breeze had sprung up and swelled through the branches above them.

"We shall have to examine it," said Twist.

They moved into the clearing, the deep layer of humus underfoot deadening the sound of their footsteps. There was no body lying near the tree now, but otherwise the scene was much the same. Edward kept the beam of his light focused on the trunk itself. At fifteen-foot distance he could see the fresh marks. In spite of himself he recalled Twist's earlier version of the crime and saw the marks as long welts cut into the bark by a whiplash. He shuddered as they drew closer. Beads of sap glistened in the light. Twist stepped forward and touched the trunk with his finger.

"Ah," he said, "something has been here tonight." He turned back to the others and spoke in a low voice. "Earlier I had a theory. I do not think anything is wrong with the theory itself except that I applied it backward." He cleared his throat nervously. "You will forgive me, but I find it necessary to attempt a duplication of what happened tonight. We must witness this thing. Come with me." He led them back to the shadows of the redwoods, where he searched until he found a young sapling with a stem somewhat larger than a man's thumb. He bent it to the ground in an effort to tear it loose.

"Does anybody have a knife?" he whispered.

The sheriff produced a jackknife from his pocket and handed it to Twist silently. Twist cut the sapling free and trimmed all the twigs. When he had finished, he had a limber pole tapering to a lashlike tip.

"Perhaps we can call up the spirit of evil, eh? With some cooperation, we shall try. Tell me, Mr. Banders. You searched the forest thoroughly before the inquest, did you not?"

"All we had time for."

"Did you find any indication that Mars Venderstone was equipped with a light of any kind?"

"We didn't find anything."

"Yes, as I thought, this scene is generally played in darkness. So if you will put out your lantern and skirt around the clearing to the trees on the other side. Remain hidden."

"What's all this about?" growled Banders.

"Well, we shall have to see. You've gone along this far."

"It's damn' foolish."

"If nothing comes of it—and mind you, I don't say anything will—it is I who will look foolish. Now go along and let me have my fun."

"It's no fun," said Banders. He blew out his lantern and walked away into the night.

"Now, Edward," continued Twist, "if you will go some twenty or thirty yards to the right and secrete yourself."

"I'll do no such thing," returned Edward. "I told Oban Kildonan I'd stay by Ailsa."

"I heard you tell him that. And I thought at the time how rash you were, because you are not going to stay by Ailsa."

"And why not? Where do you think Ailsa is going to be?"

"Ailsa is going to take this long switch I have prepared. She is going up to the madrone tree and she is going to lay it on with all the strength she has."

"You're crazy!" hissed Edward angrily.

Twist spoke softly. "Let me point out that the clearing is empty and that you and I and the sheriff will have it surrounded. The center of the clearing should be a safe place."

Edward turned his light once more on the madrone tree. Its beam searched the dark mass of foliage that hovered over the sensuous trunk.

"I'm not sure of anything."

"Nor am I. Ailsa, are you going to do as I ask?"

"Yes," she replied faintly. Her dark eyes were large and her breast rose and fell rapidly.

"You see," said Twist to Edward. "Now go. You have your flashlight and can use it if anything appears."

Edward reluctantly withdrew into the trees. When he was gone, Twist placed the redwood sapling in Ailsa's hands.

"Now walk out to the madrone tree and start beating it with this. I may let you continue for about fifteen minutes. If you grow tired, stop and rest, but don't come out of the clearing until I tell you to."

Ailsa took the long switch in trembling hands and walked away from him. She hesitated once and then went on. Twist blew out his light. Among the redwoods was darkness, and in the center of the clearing the madrone tree was a pale shadow.

Her first blow broke loudly on the silence. It wasn't repeated for several seconds until Twist cupped his hands and hissed "Go on!" across the intervening space. Then the blows began to fall steadily and with gradually rising fierceness.

Listening among the trees, Edward felt suddenly weak. His eyes had accustomed themselves to the darkness and he could faintly distinguish the movements of Ailsa's body as she swung the sapling against the tree. There was an eagerness in the blows. He arose and groped his way back through the trees until he

210

found Bleeker Twist. Twist jumped at the touch of Edward's hand on his shoulder.

"You can't do this," said Edward. "It's absolutely mad!"

"Sh-h-h!" said Twist.

"Make her stop!"

Twist's hand closed down hard on Edward's wrist. "Be quiet!"

"But I can't stand it!" Edward dropped to the ground beside Twist and bent his head against his knees. He was dizzy. The horrid reality of the pantomime made him sick. Twist's grip on his wrist tightened.

"I think it's coming!"

The blows on the tree kept falling. And then from somewhere close at hand came the laugh. Edward jumped at the sound, his scalp prickling. Twist, too, was on his feet, his hand still clutching Edward's wrist. The blows on the tree had stopped.

"Damn!" breathed Twist so softly that Edward scarcely heard. "Why doesn't she go on?"

Seconds passed. Then Ailsa began again. The blows were slower, weaker. But the laugh was repeated. Edward lifted his flashlight but Twist seized it away from him with his free hand. Then he pulled Edward forward around the edge of the clearing. They crouched and waited. Again the laugh. And now it was Twist who raised the flashlight. Not twenty feet away among the trees was a dark blur of movement. Twist aimed and pushed the switch. The beam of light punctured the shadows. In its center, his mouth gaping with excitement, stood Floyd Hooks.

With a cry, Edward and Twist were upon him, seizing him as he started to run and bringing him down on the ground. The flashlight tumbled from Twist's hand and rolled away, but its light still gave their location. Banders arrived on the run and sat down heavily on Hooks's shoulders.

"Got him!" he gasped.

They got the lanterns on again and hauled Floyd Hooks to his feet. He stared at them wildly, his eyes filled with terror. Then

211

they were aware that Ailsa was still beating the tree, her blows almost a frenzy.

"That's all, Ailsa!" called Twist. "That's all!"

The blows stopped and Ailsa walked toward them uncertainly out of the darkness, still bearing the sapling in her hands. Hooks stared at her and struggled to escape. He raised a shaking finger in her direction.

"The white thing!" he gibbered. "The white thing!"

"And now we have seen it!" a new voice cut in coldly.

The men whirled in the direction of the sound. Walking toward them out of the night was Manley Foxx. But he was not alone. A group of men surrounded him. The gaunt frame of Mr. Goss was at his elbow. Foxx raised an arm and extended a finger.

"We have seen it!" he repeated. He pointed at Ailsa.

CHAPTER TWENTY-ONE

❧ ❧ ❧ BANDERS DREW A GUN.

"Stand back," he cried. "Damn you, stand back! What is this?"

The group of men paused while Foxx stepped forward alone. His face was set with harsh lines but his eyes danced with a strange fire. His voice was cold.

"Put your gun away," he said. "We are armed only with resolution. We have seen the evil with our eyes and will do our duty." He paused and with a flip of his hand waved his followers forward. They came on with slow sure steps. Banders dropped back a stride, his gun still in front of him.

"What do you want?" he demanded.

Foxx pointed again. His voice echoed the dignity of his dark figure. "We want the girl! She must answer to the people of Jonesville."

Ailsa shrank against the base of a tree, her eyes fixed on Foxx in terror. Edward placed himself between her and the approaching men, his fists clenched.

"Get back!" His voice was deadly. "Get back!"

Foxx looked at Edward contemptuously and strode forward again, paying no attention to Banders' gun. "Stand aside! We intend to see only that justice is done."

"Then leave this to the law!" cried Banders. "Now get back!"

Foxx glanced at him with glittering eyes. "I find the law participating in the evil ceremony. You are corrupt. The people of Jonesville are now the law!"

❧ 213

Banders exploded with a roar of rage and stepped forward, but he was intercepted by Twist who leaped between him and Foxx, shoving a finger a few inches from the latter's face.

"This man," he cried, "killed Mars Venderstone!"

At the vehemence of Twist's words, Foxx fell back a step but his expression never changed.

"What wickedness is this?" he said incredulously.

"It is true!" cried Twist, and then he swung with all his power against the tall man in front of him. The blow was unexpected and landed with full impact on Foxx's jaw. Foxx tottered a moment and then dropped silently to the ground.

"For God's sake get cuffs on him!" Twist whispered, and stepping over the fallen body, he faced the group of men.

"It's a trap," he said evenly. "Foxx has led you into it!"

For a few seconds the group hesitated, waiting for one of its members to take the lead. The few seconds spelled their defeat. Banders lost no time in whipping handcuffs from his pocket and snapping them on the wrists of the helpless Foxx. Then he stood up and advanced with his gun before him.

"Now get out of this, all of you!" He pointed his revolver upward and pulled the trigger. The report echoed through the forest and the shock of the sound sent the dark-faced men a step backwards. Banders walked on. "Start moving!"

They sagged back slowly at first, their eyes fixed on Foxx. Then, finding no rallying point, they turned and walked away, maintaining the dignity of their retreat until they had disappeared completely. Banders returned to the others.

"Now let's get out of here," said Twist. "See if you can wake him up."

Banders dropped down on his knee beside Foxx and shook the body roughly. Foxx responded with a deep breath. Banders stood up.

"He's coming around." He looked at Twist. "All right. You got us out of that one for the moment. What do you mean about this guy being the murderer?"

"That was for his mob," said Twist. "I had to shake them with something before I hit him. If you'd hit him first, we'd be in trouble."

"That's what I thought," growled Banders, scowling at the prostrate clergyman, "because we've got the killer right there." He pointed at the trembling Hooks. "It's enough for me. And maybe the preacher isn't so far off about other things." He looked curiously at Ailsa.

"Not so hasty," said Twist.

"I'm not hasty. You trapped him pretty cleverly, but there's no use wasting more time. The Kildonans didn't get their reputation for nothing."

"They got their reputation because they refused to believe in a lot of nonsense!" said Edward hotly.

"All right," said Banders, "say what you will. I've seen those marks on the tree, and I've see a woman beating it. Once you see the two things together, there's no doubting what's been going on. I won't try explaining it because I don't go for such stuff, but there it is. It's plain as can be. This lunatic we've caught comes and watches and takes care of any intruders. That's what happened to Vender one, and that's what happened to Jones."

"Please," said Twist, "don't refer to Floyd Hooks as a lunatic. I'm not at all certain he is one."

"He sounds like one."

"And so would you if you had three men leap on you out of the darkness. Let me talk to him."

"Go ahead if you think you'll get anywhere."

"Floyd," said Twist, addressing his captive, "calm down now. No one is going to hurt you." Hooks looked at him with frightened eyes. "No one is going to hurt you," Twist repeated. "But we want you to tell us a few things. Do you think you can do that?"

"Tell you?" mumbled Hooks.

"Yes. We want to know what you are doing in the forest."

215

"Sometimes I come for wood," said Hooks.

"I know. But what were you doing in the forest tonight?"

"Mr. Jones," said Hooks. "Mr. Jones."

"I see. You mean Mr. Jones brought you?" Hooks nodded vigorously. "Did he bring you to this place here?" Hooks looked scared and hung his head. "Where did he leave you?"

The dowser pointed through the trees. "His car."

"Hmm," said Twist. "You both came in his car?" Hooks nodded again. "Then why did you come here?"

"I heard it," said Hooks. "Like before. The white thing."

"You mean you heard something in the forest?"

"In the forest," said Hooks.

"Had you ever heard it before?"

"Oh, yes," Hooks replied with a trace of pride.

"Were you in the forest last Sunday—the evening Mars Venderstone died?"

"I was here," said Hooks.

"And what were you doing in the forest last Sunday?"

Hooks looked at Edward. "He brought me," he said. "My wagon."

Twist nodded. "So he did. You hauled Mr. Spence's trunk for him. Well, well. And then you ran away. Where did you go?"

"Hid the wagon," said Hooks.

"You hid it?"

"In the trees."

"And then you walked back. Is that right?"

"I walked back."

"And what did you see?"

"The white thing," said Hooks, casting a frightened glance in Ailsa's direction.

"Did you see it up close?"

Hooks shook his head. "In the dark. I ran."

"Had you ever seen it before then?"

"In the dark," said Hooks. He peered across the clearing toward the madrone tree.

216

"Then you don't know what the white thing is?"

Again Hooks stole a glance at Ailsa. "Like tonight," he said.

"Well, well. Can you show us where Mr. Jones left his car?"

Hooks bobbed his head eagerly and pointed.

"Good," said Twist. He stepped back to Banders and looked down at Foxx. "Let's get him on his feet. He can't be hurt much. I haven't much weight."

"Well, you used what you've got, I'll say that." They each took one of Foxx's arms and hauled him to his feet. For a few seconds he staggered between them and then slowly opened his eyes. He took in the scene silently, noting that his followers were gone. He looked at the steel menacles on his wrists.

"My hat," he said softly.

Banders got it from the ground and put it on Foxx's head. "You think you can be quiet now?"

Foxx spoke in the same low tones. "It is perhaps useless to point out that the only violence so far used has been used against me."

"You threatened to take the law into your own hands," snapped Banders. "I'm not forgetting it. But if you'll promise to come along without any trouble, I'll take off these bracelets."

"I can make no such promise," said Foxx with dignity. "I cannot remain in this company of my own volition."

"Then I'll have to leave them on," said Banders brusquely.

"Let's go then," said Twist. He took the dowser by the arm and started off in the direction Hooks had pointed out as leading to Ivor Jones's car.

"Here now," said Banders. "We don't need the car tonight. I've got my own car on the other side of the strip."

"Ivor Jones's car is closer to town," replied Twist. "Come on. We're not through with this thing."

After a moment's hesitation the sheriff took Foxx's arm and fell into step behind Twist and Hooks. Edward turned to Ailsa.

"Can you make it?" he asked.

She nodded. Her face was still white. Edward's hand found hers. "We'd better stay with them." They walked on after the others.

217

Floyd Hooks had no difficulty in walking directly to the car. It stood as it had been left, dwarfed by the stumps around it. The doors were not locked. Twist played the flashlight around the interior. Then he got in the back seat and sat down, pulling Hooks in beside him.

"There are six of us," he said. "I think we can manage all right."

"I guess it's better than walking at that," said Banders. "Only you have to drive about two miles to get around to the Kildonans from here."

"Very true," said Twist, "but we are not going to the Kildonans."

"And where do you think we're going?"

"I shall instruct you as we proceed. Please do not argue any more. I think I've demonstrated that I know what I'm talking about. You have the keys in your pocket, have you not?"

"Yes, I do," said Banders stubbornly.

"Fine. Then you can drive. You are still wearing Ivor Jones's hat, I see. Keep it on. Edward, you and Ailsa get in the front seat. And Mr. Foxx can sit beside me. It would be advisable if we all kept our heads down—except the sheriff, of course."

They followed his instructions. Foxx said nothing as he settled into the back seat. His attitude was one of resignation and forbearance. His eyes took no note of his captors, and once he was seated, he bowed his head on his breast and kept it that way.

"I'm going to look all alone," said the sheriff.

"Exactly. All alone driving Ivor Jones's car and wearing Ivor Jones's hat. If one didn't know Ivor Jones was dead, one might think you were he, particularly in the dark. Now if you will start the car and turn around, being careful not to run into one of those stumps, we shall start for Jonesville."

Banders started the car without further speech and got it turned around. He drove slowly. Twist pulled Hooks to a reclining position on the seat and then lay down across his body.

"Use your parking lights. Do you know where Ivor Jones lived?"

"I know the house," replied Banders.

"Good. Approach it slowly and drive into the garage. Is there by any chance a house key in that key case?"

"Yes," said the sheriff.

"That will save us the trouble of housebreaking, then. Listen carefully now. When we get there, you will let yourself into the house through the front door, if that is the proper key. I'm not familiar with the house, but it undoubtedly contains a living room with some chairs in it. You can sit down in one of the chairs near the window and turn on a table lamp so that you can be observed from outside. You had better leave the hat on and don't get too close to the lamp."

"You certainly don't mind what you do with me," observed Banders sourly.

"Not at all," said Twist. "After all, this is your duty. All you have to do is sit there."

"That's easy. And who do you think I'm going to fool? I've got the murderer in the back seat."

"If that belief adds to your peace of mind, by all means hang on to it."

"And even if I haven't got the murderer," continued the sheriff, "the murderer knows Jones is dead and won't be fooled."

"Quite so," remarked Twist; "so your mind is at rest. For my part, I am uneasy. As I explained to you earlier, Ivor Jones was not murdered; he died of heart failure. We have Dr. Brill's word for it."

"He was scared to death by that lunatic laughing."

"That could well be except that my recollection is that he started yelling before Hooks gave vent to his mirth. So it could not have been the laugh which prompted his stampede through the trees. However, do not let me upset you. I also told you, I think, that although Ivor Jones had not been murdered, there was the possibility that he would be. Since the man is dead, you will have to stand proxy for him in this final role."

"You think this is damned funny, don't you?"

"Not at all. I'm all nerves."

"I don't know why I should go through with it."

"Are we near the place yet? All I can see are the tops of trees going by."

"We're nearly there. Look now, I'll have a gun in my hand and it might go off unexpectedly, so if you've got any more plans in mind, you'd better tell me about them. I don't want to shoot any of you except on purpose."

"Don't worry about it. The rest of us will hide in a safe place until it's over. You understand, of course, that you may sit there the rest of the night with nothing happening? I can't guarantee the appearance of the killer. However, you will at least have the opportunity to search Jones's house to find out, if you can, why he wanted you in the forest tonight and what he expected to discover there."

"We'll look into it," said Banders. He turned into the driveway with the parking lights still burning. The big car rolled noiselessly into the garage. For a moment he remained sitting in the front seat, then carefully opened the car door and stepped down to the concrete floor of the garage.

"Here goes," he whispered.

"One moment," said Twist softly. "My last instruction is important. After you get in the house, come on through and make sure the back door is unlocked. You may have a chance to escape if you aren't too badly wounded."

"Damn you!" snarled the sheriff as he moved off silently into the darkness. He walked along the lawn at the side of the house until he came to the flagstone walk. Avoiding the stones themselves, he followed the walk to the front door. He restrained his impulse to knock before trying the key. The key went in easily. It was not a standard lock. He heard the bolt slip on the inside as he turned. He took the doorknob firmly in his hand and gently twisted. There was no sound at all as he felt the door give under his pressure and swing inward. He stepped through and closed the door carefully.

For several minutes he stood without moving. The interior of the house was blacker than the night outside and he was not familiar with the layout of the rooms. He extended a hand and found the wall of the hallway, then felt his way along until he came to the living-room entrance. At the far end a faint glow showed him where the windows were. He walked slowly forward, pushing his feet well out in front of him before putting any weight on them. Several times he came up against a piece of furniture and felt his way around it. He found the lounge and groped behind it for a table. Running his fingers slowly along its surface, he came to a lamp and let his fingers climb up its porcelain base in search of a switch. He hesitated several seconds, listening, before he turned it on.

For a moment the room seemed to swim with light. He turned completely around, surveying its dusky corners. It was empty. He went quietly back to the hallway and into the kitchen. The reflected light from the living room was enough to make out the back door. He stood beside it, peering through the window toward the garage. No one moved out there. The door had a bolt on it. He held it firm with his knee while he worked the bolt from its socket and slid it back. He tried the door to make sure it would open. Then he went back to the living room.

There was a chair by the window and the heavy draperies were pulled back at the sides. He sat down. The room seemed darker than when he had first turned on the light. It needed twenty lamps to make it cheerful. He eased his gun from its inside holster and laid it across his knees. Then he shifted his chair slightly so that he could face the hallway. There was no other entrance to the room.

The branches of a tree scraping at the window startled him and he twisted his head to look out. All he could see with the lamp burning in the room was his own reflection in the glass. He worked himself lower in the chair so that only the hat protruded over its back. Five minutes passed. He looked at his watch and could barely make out its hands in the feeble light. Five more minutes. Then he heard a knock at the door. It was faint, but he was sure of it. It could be Twist or one of the others.

He arose softly and stole back to the hallway. There was a little window in the center of the door. He opened it and peered out through the grill. The flagstone walk was empty. He closed the window again and walked slowly back toward his chair in the living room.

He didn't hear the front door open behind his back or see the cloaked figure peer from the hallway at his retreating form. He didn't hear the footsteps on the soft carpet, footsteps faster than his own overtaking him as he traversed the long room. The chair was right there in front of him, but behind him the dark cloak dropped back as a white hand came from under its folds. The hand held a heavy leather whip, but the whip was backwards. Its pliant butt swung down from the hand. The leash trailed silently on the floor. Then the hand swung upward and the butt arched through the air. The body bent as the forward stroke started.

Banders heard something then and whirled, his gun clutched in his hand. He didn't need it. The cloak had been stripped from the shadowy figure and the whip was in the hands of Bleeker Twist. There was not even a struggle. The three of them stared silently at each other.

It was Edward Spence who broke the silence as he stepped from the hallway.

"My God!" he breathed. "You were right! It's Stella Graw!"

And then there was another sound as for the second time that night Mr. Foxx lost consciousness. He sprawled at length on the hallway floor. He had fainted.

CHAPTER TWENTY-TWO

☙ ☙ ☙ BLEEKER TWIST AND EDWARD TOOK FOXX HOME AND PUT him to bed. Foxx's thin face was pale against the pillows and his eyes were somber. Twist found tea in the kitchen and brought him a cup, but Foxx waved it away.

"I require nothing. I have made a mistake in judgment but no error in principle. The evil shall go."

Twist pulled a chair up beside the bed and sat down.

"I'm not altogether sure of that."

Foxx looked at him briefly, then glanced away again. "How can you say anything else?"

Twist slowly loaded his pipe. He made no direct reply to the question. "When I was a child, we lived on the edge of town and near us was a dense thicket of wild plums and willows. It covered several acres. I played in it all the time, had secret paths and little openings where I'd cleared away the undergrowth." He smoked meditatively. "I firmly believed my thicket was inhabited by fairies—good fairies."

Foxx turned his head slightly to look at him again. "You are apparently trying to draw some comparison between your childhood thicket and the Bull Woods. There is none. We are grown up now."

"So we believe," said Twist, "but it is an interesting story none the less. I was not afraid of my fairies, you see. I decided to find them out. So I got some books on fairies and witchcraft and spent many hours studying. I found that there was a certain symbol—a sign—which could be drawn on the ground or formed on the ground with small twigs. This was supposed to lure the fairies who would manifest their existence by destroying it. The symbol was repugnant to them." He paused and smoked awhile. Foxx stared ahead with dark eyes, giving no indication that he was listening.

"I learned how to make the sign and went out to the thicket one day. I smoothed off a small patch of ground in one of my clearings and laid out the twigs. As I recall it, I made a square with several crossed twigs inside it. Then I went away to let the fairies do their work.

"I stayed away as long as I could contain myself—maybe five minutes. Then I came back. There were the twigs just as they had been left, but while I looked at them, disappointed, a beautiful swallowtail butterfly glided down and alighted in the center of the symbol. It stayed just a moment before flying up again, but as it arose, its weight dislodged the top twig so that it rolled across the others and completely out of the square."

"It is not impossible," said Foxx.

"I'm telling you exactly what happened. But the interesting revelation came later. I ran home, of course, to tell my parents that I had proved the existence of fairies. I also told my friends. They were naturally skeptical and so I told them exactly what I have just told you. And they laughed at me. They said, in effect: 'You haven't proved the existence of a fairy; all you have proved is the existence of a butterfly.' It did no good to explain that the butterfly could very easily have been a disguise. I had seen a butterfly, hadn't I? Then why try to call it something else?"

A spark of life flickered in Foxx's eyes. "You have my sympathy," he said.

"Yes," said Twist. "And you are going to need mine. For a number of years you have had your evil spirit in the Bull Woods.

The people would accept it as long as it was invisible, but now you are going to have a hard time convincing them."

"I shall not," said Foxx. "Haven't we had the greatest proof of all?"

"No," said Twist. "They will say: 'You have not proved the existence of an evil spirit; you have proved the existence of Stella Graw.' And they will laugh at you just at they laughed at me and my butterfly."

Foxx stared at him steadily. "But it proves the existence of evil."

Bleeker Twist shook his head. "But not in the abstract. You don't need to prove that human beings are evil. Most of us demonstrate it daily. And the day will come, Mr. Foxx, when all of us realize that we can't blame any force outside ourselves for the evil which comes upon us." He stood up and looked down at the reclining figure. "I'm not trying to convince you of anything. You are quite safe as far as any aspect of the law is concerned. But I, at least, cannot hold you guiltless for the actions of Stella Graw. They sprang from a harsh repression, a repression which you zealously preserved. That, too, is evil. Your people will tell you so if you ever face them again." Twist walked out of the room. Foxx's eyes followed him as he departed. The face on the pillows did not change; the stern mouth did not relent.

Edward met Twist in the next room.

"Banders is out front. His deputies have arrived and taken over. He's ready to take us home."

They went out and got in the car.

"How is he?" asked Banders.

"The same," said Twist. "Nothing can be done in an hour."

"We've done plenty in an hour," said the sheriff. "The schoolmarm is on her way to Ludlow. So is Ivor Jones's body. And we took the Kildonan girl home." He shoved his hat—his own hat—to the back of his head and slowed the car before turning onto the highway. "Was Stella Graw the one you went back to check on? The one you wouldn't tell me about?"

"Yes," said Twist.

"Then you'd better keep on telling. What the devil was Jones running from?"

"Nothing."

"Nothing? And shouting like that? You said yourself he looked terrified."

"And so would you," returned Twist, "had you just felt a violent pain tear through your chest and knew you were done for."

"Look now," said Edward, "there's no mystery any more as to who killed him. It was Stella Graw. You were right all the time. But a few hours ago you proved quite conclusively, I thought, that she couldn't have had a thing to do with it."

"Didn't I though!" exclaimed Twist.

"So how did she do it? We saw Jones running through the forest."

"We certainly did."

"We were ahead of her then and she didn't have a chance to pass us. We took the fastest route to town and, if you remember, I waited outside the Kildonan house when you went in after the car keys."

"I could hardly forget it."

"And I saw no one. You were in the car on the highway when I went in after Dr. Brill. Stella didn't get past us then either."

"I'll swear to it," said Twist.

"So then we drove directly to Foxx's house and saw her drinking tea."

"Not quite," said Twist. "We saw Mr. Foxx bringing in the tea. She hadn't drunk any yet."

"That doesn't change things any. The fact is that she must have been there five minutes ahead of us despite the fact that she started behind us and never passed us on the way. It's impossible."

Twist sighed. "The evening we first met, Edward, I told you that the solution to a mystery is always prosaic and never as enjoyable as the mystery itself. That is true in this case as well."

"I assure you a simple solution won't disappoint me. We know Ivor Jones ran so hard he died of heart failure, and we know Stella Graw was the cause of it. Yet you sit there and blandly suggest that no one was after him."

"Exactly."

"Then why in God's name was he running?" thundered Banders impatiently.

"Where women are concerned," said Twist, "men run for two reasons. They either run away from them or they run after them. In the case of Ivor Jones, it was not he who was pursued by Stella; it was just the reverse. Stella was ahead of us from the start." He chuckled dryly. "Jones must have been raging. We know there was a rift between him and Foxx. Foxx was apparently trying to take over the reins of power. To dethrone him, all Jones had to do was show that some kind of fraud was being perpetrated on the townsfolk by the legend of the Bull Woods. In fact, by tomorrow his intentions will have been fulfilled, although he won't be here to enjoy it. I find a certain poetic justice in his death as a result of the superstition he originally put upon the people. Nevertheless, he was a practical man and was probably looking for something more complicated than a woman lashing a tree. Imagine how he must have felt when he recognized the schoolteacher of Jonesville—a woman!

"She may have attacked him with the whip as she did Venderstone, but we know that Jones had a flashlight, whereas Venderstone did not. At any rate he became enraged enough to pursue her, thinking, no doubt, that he would grab her while he had the chance and relying upon your arrival, Sheriff, to help him out. So he bawled out in rage and set after her. But she was faster than he thought. We know the rest."

"We know part of it," said Banders. "She sure got to town in a hurry."

"We know that she was in the habit of borrowing Foxx's car. She ran back to it and drove the rest of the way to town. She started ahead of us and drove directly to Mr. Foxx's house, whereas we made two stops on the way."

"Then what the devil was Foxx doing in the woods?" asked Banders.

"According to Foxx, Stella told him she had seen something in the woods from the church. That's what made him gather up his committee and come out to put an end to the evil. But what struck me was that she should go to Foxx's house at all except to return the car before running home. The only reason I could think of was that she needed some story of her own as to where she had been. But tell me this: why would she need such a story?"

"Because Jones was dead, of course."

"You surprise me, Sheriff. Why would she need a story if he was dead? Who was going to accuse her?"

"You were yourself."

"Not when we found her in Jonesville peacefully drinking tea."

"Oh, I see what you mean. She needed a story because she thought Jones would be along any minute to accuse her of all this stuff in the forest."

"Exactly. To reverse the usual order of things, she needed an alibi because she thought Jones was alive. She was far safer with him dead. And when that realization came to me, I decided that she must have another chance to kill him. Which you gave her, Sheriff."

"My God, yes," groaned Banders. "Ugh, that whip!"

"The only weapon she knew," said Twist.

"If she hadn't come after me, she might have got off," said Banders. "She could always say that Venderstone jumped her in the woods, and after all, she didn't kill Ivor Jones."

"She will get off anyway."

"Insanity?"

Twist nodded. "And yet, she is as normal as most of us. She had an obsession which was not criminal in itself. Indeed, in her mind her actions were less reprehensible than the common habits of mankind. But she also had a constant and overpowering fear that her aberration would be discovered. There is no other horror like it."

"It's out of my line," said Banders. He drove the car down the Kildonan lane past the house and let Edward and Twist out. Then he turned around and drove away. The two men walked on to the cabin and went in. They sat down and looked at each other.

"Well, Edward, have you recovered from the evening?"

Edward shook his head slowly and reflectively. "How close one comes," he said. "What haunts me is the knowledge that in so many ways Stella is a lot like me."

"Was," corrected Twist.

"If only I had understood her Sunday evening when she came to my room at Miss Westerly's, this all might have been prevented."

"You couldn't have understood her then. You didn't even understand yourself."

"That's the first prerequisite, isn't it?"

"In my opinion it is. So do not blame yourself for the past."

Edward shuddered. "No, but I can try in the future to understand people before I judge them." He paused. "It's not easy. When you put that stick in Ailsa's hands—"

"I know," said Twist. "It frightened you."

"I hate to confess what I thought."

"You don't need to. I know what you thought. And I must say I admired the way you acted in spite of it. But you see, it couldn't be that way because Ailsa has not let repressive influences curb her natural instincts. True, she has had to tell her father a falsehood upon occasion in order to pursue them." He paused.

Edward smiled. "I'm going to the Kildonans for dinner tomorrow. Ailsa wants to talk to me about going away to school. I may even go back myself for awhile. I'd like a Ph.D."

"The same school?" asked Twist.

"Why not?"

"I love that expression," said Twist. "Why not, indeed?" The two men smiled at each other.

"I wonder what will happen to Jonesville now that both of its leaders are gone?" said Edward.

"Curious," said Twist. "I once mentioned to you, I believe, that I hoped to bring about an end to leaders. It appears from this example that they may bring about their own ends without assistance." He tugged his nose. "Still, your question is an interesting one. We may be fairly certain that whether Ivor Jones develops an heir or not, the sawmill will continue operation. And we may be fairly certain that Oban Kildonan will be able to speak openly from now on. Churches do not long remain empty because a particular minister is deposed. The people of Jonesville have been freed from the material tyranny of their patriarch and from the spiritual tyranny of Foxx's monster. Whether they can endure such freedom remains to be seen. And just because Andramalech is arching his back and hissing and staring at the door, do not open it. I have work to do!"